Ring of Fire

George Keithley

Plain View Press
1101 W 34th Street, Suite 404

www.plainviewpress.net
Austin, TX 78705

ISBN: 978-1-63210-009-2
Library of Congress Control Number: 2014953409

Cover art *Mount Lassen from Mount Brokeoff*
permission of Lenn Goldman, Artist
Cover design by Pam Knight

Acknowledgements

Thanks to all those who in various ways helped me with this book; especially Clark Brown, Tom Jenks, Craig Lesley, Dr. Philip Lydon, Kathleen McPartland, John Nelson, Gary Thompson, and my wife Carol Gardner. And to several members (anonymous here) of the Abbey of New Clairvaux, the Cistercian-Trappist monastery in Vina, California; and to the staff of the U. S. Geological Survey, Western Region Headquarters, Menlo Park, California. Thanks also to the late Oakley Hall, Hortense Calisher, George P. Elliott, and Dr. William Blackburn.

Several chapters from *Ring of Fire* originally appeared, in slightly different form, in *Colorado Review, Nexus, The South Dakota Review,* and in the anthology *This Little Bit of Earth.*

In memory of

Wallace Stegner

Contents

1 Hazard Zones 9
2 Two Families 27
3 Her Father's Daughter 35
4 Late Spring 51
5 At the Gate of Heaven 59
6 Why Do We Punish Desire? 69
7 False Color 81
8 Making Plans 89
9 The Ring of Fire 97
10 Swimming with Doctor Pell 113
11 Day and Night 117
12 Saturday Afternoon in the Arena 133
13 In the Chute 147
14 The Blind 155
15 Sunday Night 165
16 Necessary Questions 181
17 A Tourist's View of Hell 197
18 The Fire Watch 203
19 October in the Park 209

About the Author 221

First the elk felt something underfoot. Their legs shivered and that was all. Feeding, with their heads bowed, the sunlight blanketing their backs, they'd climbed slowly through the early morning, and each time the herd spread itself over fresh ground the females formed a wide cluster, keeping to themselves. Young males fed nearby while the full-grown bulls, their antlers lifting, dipping, foraged on their own.

Now the herd stood still.

Out on the north slope they stopped browsing the crisp green patches among the pines. They looked up toward a meadow purpled by Indian paintbrush where mountain goats grazed as quiet and white as the glacier overhead. Nothing stirred in the meadow and the elk turned away.

They stared at the lake below, their faces dark, their pale ears erect, alert. Sunlight on the water wrinkled once and stretched smooth. It wrinkled and smoothed again, a rippling movement like the one that had made their legs shiver. They shivered again. Their bodies were tan and they were beginning to fill out now that they'd had a month of good forage. Their legs were lean and brown, and they were brown in the neck and head with a long grey-brown muzzle of hair beneath their watchful eyes.

The dark-eyed elk watched the water below. The water rippled again. The sunlight wrinkled on the water, it rocked slightly, grew still, and their legs shivered. This time the whole herd turned. Now, suddenly, they bolted. By the hundreds the elk hurtled down the mountain.

All day they crashed through scrub growth and pockets of rockfall, dislodging rocks, spewing stones that tumbled behind them. They clambered down from the high slopes, trampling their forage, outrunning their cover, until they came at twilight into a clearing broken by bald outcrop.

The next day the sparse foliage and sunny rubble of the clearing gave way to green shade. Old growth pines provided cover as the elk thundered on, leaping over rotting logs, their hooves chopping clods from the floor, heaving silt and needles into the dim light. Finally at nightfall they broke free of the pines.

Daybreak found the herd far down the mountain in a meadow bright with lupine. They fed while the sun warmed the meadow but before it had climbed overhead at midday they were gone. They plunged through the shade of a hardwood forest where the finger-long leaves of hemlocks stroked their faces. On the moist floor their hooves hammered the maidenhair ferns into instant fossils, driving their slim spines into the earth.

Across the bottom slopes the elk charged through thin timber, the females running three or four together and the sunlight falling through the trees to strike the slender antlers on the young males and the high wide crowns worn by the bulls.

It was three days since the trembling in the mountain and under the lake had stampeded the elk down the slopes. At dawn on the fourth day they no longer paused to feed. They fled through a lush meadow that opened in the forest.

Now in their peril they were all thrown together, male and female, in a headlong fury that was vital, desperate, enduring. Often one of the herd, fatigued, struggling, its pink tongue hanging from its mouth, lurched, slumped, and was trampled in the rush. Still with their hearts slamming behind their ribs the elk charged, staggered, and ran on, their hooves pounding the earth and their ribs shaking.

1

Hazard Zones

Some people affect our lives profoundly no matter how brief the time we've known them. Though I met Doctor Pell eight years ago at Mount St. Helens, Washington, and our acquaintance lasted less than fifteen months, still he's always with me, on that green lawn of memory where our most vivid loves and errors wait for us. It's true, from those first days I had to deal with him not only as a public figure, quick-tempered and solitary, but also as a man with a family, because I fell in love with his daughter. But that isn't the whole story—

Today when I think of Robert Pell I see him in the deep twilight of an evening in the mountains; a trim man bristling with carefully directed energy, at the center of a gathering of people: his wife Annette and daughter Linda, his brother, his colleagues, those of us who struggled to work with him and those who crossed him. If this is his story it's ours, too; an account of the ways in which a man's love—or a woman's—binds us to one another or shatters us. He was, after all, a scientist renowned for his research, respected for his teaching; he might also have been a man much loved and admired, had his concern for his family not been so unswerving, and righteous, and fatal.

But that wouldn't be Bob Pell.

In the seven years since his death I haven't met another man more fiercely devoted to his family, and I don't hope to.

The infant who would have been my younger sister died at birth; the next day my mother went into coronary arrest and followed her. I was seven. From that day on I was raised by my father, a kind, genial, laconic man. I loved him, and though he died more than fifteen years ago, I miss him still. But I miss even more the family we never had: mother and father; brothers and sisters. I look at a couple with their children and wonder about their life together. Is it love alone that keeps them close? Then what is it that slowly, inexorably, separates them? What drew me to Mount St. Helens was the threat of an eruption in that picturesque volcano. Doctor Pell was the expert on volcanic hazards, with his office in the observatory only twenty miles from the mountain, when I arrived from San Francisco.

Early one morning a man and woman packing their belongings, closing their cabin, found themselves surrounded by a herd of elk. The elk had raced out from the forest at the base of the mountain and ran smack into the fence that flanked the couple's property. Later that morning the man reported this strange behavior to Linda Pell, assisting her father at the observatory. The man told her hundreds of elk suddenly had emerged from the woods and pushed over a wire fence. They forced it down, he said, then they tramped through the green brush and the little flowerbed that had been his wife's particular pleasure, and fled past the cabin. There were so many elk, his wife said, that even when they felt it was safe to leave their cabin, they could hardly drive their pickup out to the road without running them down.

All of us at the observatory should have been grateful: for their information about the elk, and because the couple was leaving. Most people weren't moving out. Two months ago the mountain had tossed billions of tons of ash into the atmosphere—an enormous cloud that filled television screens across the country. Now newspapers reported new tremors, and a crowd waited to see if it was going to blow again. Warned to evacuate the region, many merely retreated to their vans and station wagons on the shoulders of the approach roads. Families slept there at night, then passed the rainy days playing cards. Every morning I met people pacing the damp road from the observatory, listening to tiny radios for reports of more tremors, or an all-clear.

From the road you could see the high slopes of the classic pyramid volcano. The same view of Mount St. Helens you found on calendars in the offices of transportation executives, health officials, water control analysts, from Seattle to Portland. Glaciers gleaming above the meadow where mountain goats grazed. Below the timber line the thin pines where the elk had been frightened off. Farther down grew giant Douglas firs. These stood so close they made a dense blue shade, giving way to the dark green hardwoods where the road had cut through, before a steel barricade was placed across the pavement. Between two blinking lights on the barricade was a red-lettered sign.

NO ENTRANCE

-STOP -

RESTRICTED AREA

A trooper leaned beside the sign, watching people pacing impatiently in the road. Nobody wanted this duty, and it always was given to somebody very young, who would take care to be exact about it and not let people talk their way around him. A boy of nineteen who kept his helmet on so you couldn't see how young he looked. He wore his automatic rifle slung behind him on a leather strap so it rested between his shoulder blades, the way a young woman hiking here in the woods would carry her baby on her back.

In the middle of May it was still cold in the morning and after breakfast I brought over a thermos and talked for a while with the trooper. The steam rising from our cups left a warm film on our faces when we drank the dark coffee.

A stout man squeezed out of his van and trudged toward us. A woman and two children climbed out after him but they remained in the road beside the van. He must have been a fisherman who liked to work the mountain streams; he wore wide denims tucked into rubber waders just below his knees. You could see his anger as he lifted his feet and slapped them down flat on the pavement, making each step count. He'd had a long time to sit in his van thinking what he would tell the trooper. Now he was ready but he held back to see whose side I might take.

"You're with him?"

"I'm a civilian," I said.

"Geological Survey?"

"No."

His eyes measured me from the ground up: boots, slacks, jacket. He spied the notepad in my pocket and looked hopeful; if his argument failed to move the trooper, he might at least find himself in one of the papers tomorrow. "You a reporter?"

"Richard Darwin," I said and reached out to shake his hand. "From NEPA—the National Emergency Planning Agency."

"How can you plan an emergency?"

"We can't," I said.

He snorted with satisfaction. "That doesn't stop you from feeding at the public trough," he said. "Does it?"

"Before a disaster happens we need to learn how to survive it." For weeks I'd been meeting with state and local agencies about evacuation plans, flood control, medical facilities. There was little money for planning; only for relief afterwards. What I learned here could be put to use when I returned to San Francisco and reported to Noah Geyer, our director. Now, with his boots planted on the pavement, the man squared to face the young trooper.

"You can't close a national forest. It belongs to everyone."

The trooper knew better than to argue. He glanced around at the ranks of trees, their dark boughs spreading behind the barricade. "Forest isn't closed," he said, "just the roads."

Rubber waders stamped the pavement. "Christ! You can't close a state highway either. Don't you shitheads understand? People pay taxes for these roads!" He turned to me for an argument. "I own this road as much as anyone."

"Yes, you do," I said.

He tried the trooper one last time. "I have the right to drive my vehicle on it, as far as I like!"

The trooper had heard enough. "Turn your vehicle around," he suggested, "and you can drive as far as you like."

The man stomped back into his van and slammed the door. Opening it, the woman climbed in with their two children.

I emptied the thermos into our cups. "I'm leaving too," I said. "Briefing's in half an hour. I want to hear Doctor Pell."

"He's the only one who comes to see us," the trooper said. "The others think we're a bunch of goons."

"He knows better," I said. "He was a naval officer. His father was a sailor." In the navy Doctor Pell studied marine biology, leading to his fascination with volcanoes. "He built a house for his family in California; he wanted to settle down. He resigned his commission and put himself through school."

The young trooper looked into the forest as if to glimpse his own future in the shadows. "I'll never do that."

"You don't want a family?"

He laughed. "I don't want to go to school." The van made an angry turn, tires screeching, and we watched as it rolled away. Round rear windows stared back at us, glass eyes growing smaller as they receded down the road. "What about you, Dick? Are you ready to settle down?"

I was twenty-six that spring. If I ever wanted to live a settled life there'd be time later. "No—not for a while," I said.

"Not until you get back to the city."

"Especially not in the city."

"Where all the sweet ladies are," he said softly. "All those sweet ladies who won't let you sleep. I wish I was home."

"We all do," I said.

"Tomorrow," he said.

I walked back to the observatory, a cement building surrounded by a parking lot fenced on three sides by the forest. Cars filled the lot, and to avoid the crowd I went around the back and across a patch of lawn to Doctor Pell's office.

The door was open, and his daughter Linda sat at her father's desk with a notebook in front of her. With her master's degree from Stanford she'd been a lab technician in the Geological Survey station near San Francisco when her father phoned her to join us. "In your whole career," he told her, "you may never see anything like this again." He arranged her clearance into the restricted area, she arrived two days ago—one day ahead of the elk—and this was the first time I'd seen her.

I introduced myself and asked for her father. "He's already in the briefing room," she replied, looking up—just a glance from her large blue eyes—then she went on examining her notes. Harsh overhead light made the room look as ordinary as it was, but also brought out the red glow in her hair. Her shirtsleeves were rolled up, her elbows propped on the desk.

Tongue-tied, I admired the light in her hair and the curve of her neck, while I tried to think of something to say—anything—to prolong this moment. To lift her eyes from those pages of notes.

"Do you suppose tremors started that stampede?" (Oh, brilliant!)

"Yes—don't you?"

I did. And said so. Though I was only repeating what she surely knew. Still, this was progress, wasn't it? We'd just met, and I'd already demonstrated I had almost as much wit as a wooden post. But Linda did look up, perhaps puzzled that a man stood there babbling about an elk herd as if no one had work to do. Her upright posture—with shoulders squared—was her father's, but her narrow chin and fine mouth suggested a frankness, and firmness, that was her own. But it was her stare that stopped me from rambling on. Her deep-set blue eyes enlarged as she concentrated, as if her thought came swimming to the surface of a mountain lake, emerging suddenly cool and clear.

"That stampede *is* strange," she said helpfully. "Especially since the goat herd hasn't moved."

"It must mean trouble," I said.

Linda nodded, then lowered her head over her notes.

"Shall we walk over?"

"I'm not going." She turned a page.

I waited, unwilling to leave without her.

Her father did field work around Lassen Peak at the center of a volcanic park in the northeast corner of California. His mapping of volcanic hazards was vital to our agency, and he'd been my contact since the day I arrived. By now I knew his office as well as my own.

On the walls were a dozen pictures of various size and age, of Doctor Pell and his family. A sentimental man far from home, he'd surrounded himself with snapshots of the people he loved and the past they'd shared. On the wall behind Linda was a photo of his brother Ted, a youthful-looking priest, his face fleshy, his eyes too warm and happy for his abrupt white collar and black tunic. There was also a picture of his parents on a windy dock in Hawaii, a huge warship behind them, flags unfurled, gun turrets casting shadows: his father Jack, beaming in his seaman's uniform, and his mother Nancy, in a tropical blouse and skirt, clutching her straw hat in the wind.

The photos gave me an excuse to linger while I hoped Linda might change her mind. And these were family pictures; I wanted to learn whatever they could tell me about her.

On a corner of her father's desk Linda's likeness was joined in a twin frame with a photo of her mother. When Doctor Pell first showed me these pictures, I thought his wife Annette was singularly attractive without being pretty. Because she wore her hair drawn back you noticed at once her eyes, nose, mouth. Distinct and delicate lines. An unsmiling face that was being tested, tempered. She might once have been pretty as well, but what survived was more appealing than that.

In the other panel Linda was seated on a pony and smiling bravely. The sun was in her blue eyes and striking sparks in her rich red hair. Wearing jeans and a plaid shirt, she looked about eleven years old. Even allowing for the difference in age the freckled girl barely resembled the woman. Her face was softer, her color lighter, more like her father's.

"I know a little girl who loves horses," I said.

Linda's eyes flashed. "I'm not a little girl," she snapped. A small woman, she was younger than anyone else among the scientists or media. With two degrees and eighteen months of field work, she was not yet twenty-two. But I was beginning to learn how precarious her independence was, and fumbling to find some common ground to keep her interest.

"Dorothy is the daughter of the man I work for," I said. "In San Francisco. She's ten—and she's horse crazy."

Linda's laugh surprised me. It was full-throated, loud with delight. "I know what *that's* like."

"Her parents let her ride when they can manage it "

"Are there horses in the city?"

"In the park," I said. "And there are pony rides."

"How nice!" Her smile was gentle, and genuine, but brief. When she returned to her notes I tried again to persuade her.

"Sure you won't come along? To hear your father?"

"I'd go anywhere in the world if Daddy wanted me to." Linda's gaze was frank, friendly. "But the media unnerve him. It hurts to see that. And it's impossible to intervene. So—why watch his discomfort if I can't help him?"

"I see." I waited.

"A hundred people will be there. I won't be missed."

"Yes, you will."

She gave me a small warm smile.

I walked over the sunny lawn to the observatory alone.

Late-arriving reporters slipped into the briefing room already crowded with county supervisors. And Chamber of Commerce reps who'd come to speak for the people managing gas stations, grocery stores, bait shops. It wasn't only fishermen or cabin owners in vans and pickups; others were impatient to see the roadblocks removed. Eager too for the geologists and reporters to clear out. The geologists because at each day's briefing they'd explain the risks that required closing the roads. And reporters because they made these explanations public. Made it difficult to downplay the danger.

With Karla Meeske, a heavy brown-haired woman, one of the Geological Survey team who'd flown in from Denver, I watched Doctor Pell finish loading his slide projector. "Dick, do me a favor?" He looked up. "Introduce me today?"

I glanced at Doctor Meeske; surely she was a better choice. "No, no." She smiled shyly. "I don't want this mob asking me a million questions."

"Quite right, Karla," said Doctor Pell. He'd known she wouldn't want the duty and he meant to spare her. She beamed with relief and withdrew to the back of the room.

Most geologists avoided these briefings. They lunched in the commissary and ducked past the TV cameras, intent on studying the volcano. No one knew how much time remained to monitor the heartbeat of earthquake swarms. To examine gases escaping from the vent. To learn if magma was rising from its hot chamber. But none of us left them alone—we all wanted something.

Doctor Pell marched up to join me at the podium. He'd been a geologist for more years than he'd spent in the navy but his military bearing persisted. Facing his audience, with his trim build and unwavering posture he looked lean and tense. At his jaw, cheekbone, and forehead were pale patches like that color on the knuckles when your hand makes a fist.

I introduced him briefly: Professor of Geology at the University of California in Mingus. Our expert in the dangers to public safety. He bowed curtly, acknowledging in their faint applause this crowd's grudging respect for his qualifications; their misgivings about any conclusions he might reach.

"Here we are—" He turned to his huge map of hazard zones, which hung from the wall behind the podium. At its center stood the volcano within a red circle. A small white square marked the observatory at the edge of the red zone, the area of highest danger. Cooler colors expanded across the map like ripples over a pond. A proud and private man, Doctor Pell appeared uneasy, yet he spoke distinctly. Touching each zone with a pointer, he explained its dangers should the volcano explode: Hazards from the blast. Lava flows. Hot gas scorching the ground. Mountain streams blocked by lava, mud, trees. The flooding of lowland rivers. Ashfall settling over orchards, suffocating fields and towns. "At best we're guessing," he said, pointing to the border of the red zone. "You're no safer, really, on one side of this line than on the other. Wouldn't you say, Dick?"

"It's a question of how near you are to the blast."

"My point precisely," he said. "If you're close, you're going to get burned. Or smothered. Or drowned."

He told his audience, now, what his daughter had told us: Five hundred elk had fled down the volcano and forced those fences.

A voice called out: "Do they know something we don't?"

"Very likely," Doctor Pell replied. Laughter started up. He smiled and the room fell silent; what stifled us was his smile. With his eyes almost closed, his lips were stretched into deep lines at the corners of his mouth. He looked like a man trying not to cry, and I wondered if he'd developed this grimace in his childhood to disguise some loss or grief. I opened the projection screen and Karla Meeske flicked out the lights.

The first slide showed the Ring of Fire—the chain of volcanoes encircling the Pacific Ocean.

"Earth," said Doctor Pell, "might have been born from the fire within it. A volcano pumps out essential gases; pours life-giving minerals into our soil and water. Where does it begin?" Cartoon slides showed the growth of a Pacific Rim volcano, the ocean plate pushing against continental plates, thrusting up mountain ranges, causing earthquakes. We saw the vent forming; the cone rising; finally, the eruption—a cloud spewed from the volcano while red lava oozed down the slopes.

"In contrast," said Doctor Pell, "here's our sleeping beauty." On the screen the alabaster slopes of Mount St. Helens glimmered against a deep blue sky.

"Just here she seems to be filling out—"

Beneath the peak a bulge appeared. "The growth of this lobe is alarming," Doctor Pell admitted. "It's the most unstable sign on the mountain. I'll fly up tomorrow for another look."

Then a close-up of the mountain goats grazing on a high slope. Their heads were bowed, fleecy beards brushing the forage underfoot. "Whatever message from this mountain frightened the elk," said Doctor Pell, "it went unnoticed by the goat population. It takes more than a tremor to make a goat miss a meal. Especially old goats like these—" Laughter as the final slide showed his colleagues seated at lunch in the commissary.

Lights flickered on while Doctor Pell walked up to the map.

"Think of the earth's crust as its skull, with a membrane of flesh and foliage stretched over it. That membrane of life includes us. Tremendous activity within the skull—a shift of those plates sends its message to the surface like a shift in thought rising into action. Now the world is changing its mind." His pointer tapped the map. "And we have reason to tremble."

Feet shuffled nervously under chairs.

"Questions?"

Midge Wallace, a reporter from a Portland television station, began: "Last week you said scientists shouldn't make policy decisions. Whether to close roads. Or when to evacuate."

"I still say so, Midge."

"Why shouldn't the people who are most informed about the dangers be responsible for these decisions?"

"Because we're not accountable for our mistakes. We're not elected to our jobs; we can't be voted out if our judgment fails us. And it often does."

"So you don't *want* to be accountable?"

"Look to your elected officials," he snapped. "They're used to making mistakes and catching holy hell—"

Midge Wallace sat down as a murmur rippled through the room. Doctor Pell met it with his military formality. A brief bow, and he extended his hand toward the back of the room.

"What's the condition of the cone?" a man called.

"Unstable."

"Is gas escaping?"

"Certainly." His blunt reply was unsettling. Chairs scraped.

"Is that a dangerous sign?"

"If it's *burning,* yes, that's dangerous." His patience was as thin as his smile. "We can't see the cone at all times. Sometimes it's covered in cloud. And sometimes we have to sleep. We're only human."

The voice persisted: "You saying this mountain will blow?"

Doctor Pell glared from the podium. The little humor that lightened his lecture was drained out of him. "I'm not God," he remarked. "Karla Meeske over there is not God. Dick Darwin is not God, either. None of us can provide the certainty you ask for." Lifting his chin, he directed his voice to the back row. "It's my guess the mountain will blow. That's its function, that's what it's built to do. Are you astonished when your body performs its functions?"

A tense silence. Then another voice.

"Will it blow this week?"

Doctor Pell raised both hands high. When they fell to the podium a loud *thwaaack!* shocked the crowd into silence. "For this earth a thousand years is like one second in our life." He glanced at Doctor Meeske who gave a confirming nod. "A thousand years—the *least* amount of time that might tell us anything about our planet. Yet you wish to know what will happen this afternoon, in time to meet your deadline. Or close your cabin. Ladies and gentlemen, that's impossible. Good day."

With a wave—it was, actually, an ill-tempered salute—he dismissed everyone, striding from the room. The crowd pushed into the sunlight. I was closing the projection screen when Doctor Pell returned with glasses, ice, and a bottle of whiskey.

We sat in the front row facing the map. "Thanks for telling them I'm not God," I said.

"Well, you're not." Doctor Pell stretched comfortably. "But you pour a good drink."

"Much obliged." I brought the bottle and glasses into the kitchen, then we went back to his office. I was hoping to see Linda but she'd left. While her father sorted his slides into narrow boxes in an old wooden cabinet I looked again at those pictures on his desk. The fine-wrought lines marking her mother's face. And Linda, more proud of her pony than scared by it, squinting into the sun. "How long ago was this?"

He held the hinged frame like an open book. "Ten years ago?" he said. "She'd just learned to ride."

What could he tell me about her? "Is she good?"

"She was very good." He set down the double frame. I was disappointed; I wanted to hear more.

"And her mother. You'll be glad to see Annette again."

"Yes," he said, his face showing the strain. "I write her every day but that's not enough. Which reminds me—" He addressed a letter to his wife. "Will you pass the mailbox?"

I told him I would and he gave me the letter.

"That lobe on the north face—"

"Yes?"

"It worries you."

"It isn't pretty, Dick," he said. "It ought to worry us."

"When you fly the mountain tomorrow I'd like to go up. I haven't seen the lobe."

"My clearance is for early morning. Before the press planes arrive. By noon it's a dogfight up there."

We agreed to meet.

"Six-thirty. Don't be late." By way of apology for that tone of command in his voice, he shook my hand. "See you then, young man," he added warmly, and he offered that aching smile.

Al Chesney, a helicopter pilot in the Forest Service, took us up in a swift climb. Above the trees the mountain loomed, a mammoth iceberg in the blue ocean of the sky. Chesney revved the engine and we approached the cream-white volcano. A beautiful sight from ground-level, it looked ominous when we flew into the restricted airspace around its peak, hovering near the plume of yellow smoke. Ash had smeared the snowfield and the glaciers were fractured by stress cracks as wide as city streets. Chesney waited for the plume to blow off, then he banked across the steaming vent. Below lay that strange lobe, already longer than a football field and still growing.

Doctor Pell said it was formed by magma rising in the chamber of the volcano, forcing that deformity on the surface: "If the pressure grows too great and the slope fails you can see where the avalanche will fall—"

The blades whickered as we looked down at the mountain goats, their white hair flowing as they browsed among the wildflowers brightening a meadow. Rocks tumbling down to the lake would smash anything in their path: campsites, goats, boathouses.

Chesney began a wide arc for our last pass over the peak. Crossing the dark vent, Doctor Pell gripped my arm. "Look!"

Blue lights swam up, fish-like, glowing in the mouth of the mountain.

"Burning gases," he said.

We turned back.

At eight that morning Linda was in her father's office. We walked to the observatory for coffee. Half an hour later we were sitting in the kitchen when we felt the blast; then we heard the roar. Glass crackled around us, shattering on the sink counter and the floor. Coffee urns toppled, clattering across linoleum. In the briefing room the projection screen had fallen. Fold-up chairs were strewn from wall to wall. Her father's huge hazards map, ripped from the wall, lay in a heap like a collapsed tent. We ducked out, hurrying down the hall. But as we ran to the monitor room the roar rolled on and on.

The monitors showed us a jolting earthquake had triggered the eruption. It shook the mountain while magma was rising inside it; as Doctor Pell had feared, pressure broke the bulge, launching an avalanche that pummeled the mountain goats down the slope. Gases and magma blasted away the north wall of the cone, an explosion that rocked our building, twenty miles away.

The blast flattened the Douglas firs that had shaded the elk. It stripped branches and snapped the trunks at ground level. All the trees were flung down in the same direction, pointing the way for what followed. Down the mountain flowed scorching gas and ash overtaking every truck or animal in its path. It seared the ground, the fallen trees. Slowly the ashes settled, smoldering. By mid-morning it was dusk. We smelled sulfur in the air constantly but never saw the sun.

Karla Meeske, in radio contact with the Forest Service, was the first to report how quickly heat from the blast had melted the glaciers; the water sloshed down, mixing pumice, dead goats, and deer into brown sludge that swamped streams and sent floodwaters pouring into the valleys.

All day the mountain heaved up hot boulders, many as big as pickup trucks, while it pumped its column of ash into the atmosphere. Ash, fine as sleet, fell everywhere until the air and the earth around us were the same color.

Television crews joined us in the observatory. Removing their cotton masks, they gulped coffee in the commissary then rushed back to film the boiling column and its turbulent cloud.

"This will change forever how we look at volcanoes," Doctor Pell told a newswoman that night in the briefing room. He was exhausted but on camera he stood erect with his shoulders drawn back. "Twenty-five hundred times the power of the atom bomb that burned out Hiroshima. That's what our monitors tell us about the blast." He spoke with a troubling note of pride. And I failed to understand why he chose that comparison; the American military bombing a Japanese city. I'd forgotten the photo of his parents standing on that dock in Hawaii.

The newswoman responded: "You never expected this?"

Anger colored his face, the pale patches flushed; I heard the strain in his voice, the effort it cost him not to defend himself. "We *knew* the mountain would erupt," he replied. "Nobody expected an explosion of this magnitude."

The next day he arranged a pass for Linda to fly up with us. Wearing cotton masks, we climbed aboard in silence. Once we lifted off I could rarely find the horizon; the haze was grey-yellow or grey-brown. Lightning slashed the shadows. Then the haze parted and we crossed where the peak was blown away. Instead of a white cone I saw brown smoke and pale steam rising from a horseshoe crater two miles long and a mile wide. Farther down a mudflow filled in the valley, paved with falling ash. Steam fluttered across the surface. Blue flames leaped up and vanished. No sign of a stream, a road, or cabin. We passed over logging trucks upended in mud, among the blasted trees shoved down the riverbed. For two months I'd lived with the sense that this whole region was alive. Now only the crater lived on; the rest was a corpse. Ash began to clog our engine filter and we flew back as the darkness thickened.

The next morning helicopters combed the slopes and valleys as the National Guard and Search and Rescue teams began lifting out the living or marked the locations of the dead. Each day they found fewer survivors and brought in more victims. Loggers who'd continued working regardless of our warnings. Young couples who slipped through the checkpoints around the red zone on trail bikes. Campers who drove up a back road where there was no barrier. When we lifted them out of the helicopters we fit them into long green sacks, and the trooper at the barricade kept watch over these body bags, laid out beside the road, until the dead were brought to an aid station for autopsy and identification. All the ones I saw were clothed in grey ash. A few had been burned but most died of suffocation. Burn victims were dry and shrunken as if they'd been baked in an oven. The others were wrinkled and their mouths and nostrils stopped with ash. They died quickly, the doctors told us; ash had fused to the mucus in their air passages and plugged them shut.

When one man on a search party fell ill I took his place. Often our descent whirled up a rotor wash of ash which was slow to settle. But everyone aboard wore a mask, and once we touched down we went quickly to work. That morning we dug a jeep from a drift; its tires were melted and the plastic tail lights looked like globs of dried jelly. No sign of the driver.

In the afternoon we found the fisherman's van; it was nosed into a drift blocking a back road, the round rear windows glaring at us like the eyes of a trapped animal. Inside the mother lay with her arms around her daughter. The father had placed his sweatshirt over their faces to keep the ashes off. Then he'd wedged open a door to go for help. One leg was thrust out the door; boot and pants leg were scorched onto his wrinkled skin. The hair on these bodies was turned orange by the hot blast. I remembered I'd disliked the man when he stood at the barricade arguing with the trooper. He'd been belligerent and stubborn, and maybe he wasn't very smart—turned back by the trooper, he found an unpaved route partway around the mountain and it led him to this. But I looked at him lying among his family before we began to move them, I saw how he'd tried to save them, and I felt sorry and ashamed.

When the man I'd replaced returned to duty I was left behind to help unload the helicopters. In those first days whenever a search party returned a TV crew appeared with its cameras. The crew had heard the rumor that President Carter was coming. But only the search parties came and went. After a few days the camera crew, too often disappointed, gave up on the rumor, and they no longer met the arriving flights.

The air was cloudy and turbulent on the day the President was flown in. We were hoping for rain to wet the ash so search parties could identify landmarks buried under the drifts. His helicopter landed and we saw the presidential seal below the window where he peered out, a lined, worried face. Surrounded by security men, he waved, then moved quickly through the crowd. He wore a pin-striped suit, silk tie, hiking boots, and a look of troubled intelligence. I searched for Linda and found her walking a few steps behind me, her posture upright as her father's, her small shoulders squared in a brisk pink blouse she'd saved for a special occasion. I reached for her in the crush of press and onlookers pushing ahead to the observatory.

"Here, give me your hand—"

"I'm here, yes, let's stay close."

It was the first time I'd held Linda's hand, the first time we'd touched each other in any deliberate way, and I'd like to have seen if it meant anything in her eyes. But she stayed almost a step behind me until we were indoors.

I thought because he was a politician the President would be cheerful with the public, brusque with the press, and guarded about money. But he was soft-spoken, watching and listening throughout his briefing. It was local politicians who yelled at each other and argued about money, while he quietly asked them how he might help. We couldn't fly him up to see the smoking crater because of dense overcast, but he received a briefing from Doctor Pell, Doctor Meeske, and others, and he promised the government would give assistance. He brought us this promise in the midst of so much destruction. What else could he have done?

The next day it began to rain. President Carter sat at a long table with the governor and other politicians for a final exchange. He seemed embarrassed by the quarreling that went on around him; then he was gone. It rained for two days, a drenching rain, and when it stopped the search flights resumed.

After the rain the air was like wet wool with a foul sulfurous smell but the land was better defined. Helicopters hummed over riverbeds buried under steaming ash, then slipped around the bare slopes, looking for crumpled logging trucks, the roofs of vans, cars. The search parties worked quickly. That day and the next day they lifted out all the corpses they could find.

I was appalled and frustrated, and I was amazed that Doctor Pell's temper had abandoned him for a tender melancholy. Working with him that spring, I learned something about idealists. They're different; there's no denying it. You and I work at our jobs and dream when we can. But they live their dreams. Focused on a single goal, relentless, maybe ruthless—Linda's father was no exception—they surprise us when we catch them in a wistful moment. Day-dreaming and suddenly soft-hearted. I suppose it's what we should expect. Without their dreams they wouldn't be so driven. But we aren't often privileged to see those dreams—only the devastation they produce.

What I'd begun to see in her father was this sad calm—well, it wasn't calm, but it was quiet—which was at the core of the man. The object of his study, that pristine volcano, had let loose a violent force beyond anyone's control. Still he struggled to control himself and Linda; his defeat would not be total. But the struggle had exhausted him and I saw, in these moments of resignation, that the bedrock of his nature was patience. What he possessed beyond most men was his capacity to prepare himself, and the patience to wait for his opportunity. If his time had not come now it would come later. He would be ready. But he had not been ready for this.

Seventy people were dead or missing. We no longer waited at the roadside to receive the victims; search parties still went up but few returned with anyone but their crew. "Those who died—they were warned to stay away," I complained to Doctor Pell in the commissary kitchen. "Why wouldn't they listen?"

"It's tempting to play with fire, you know that." His eyes looked weary. Handing me a Scotch, he sighed, sat down. With a gentle sympathy he added: "Even the ones who are brought out alive. Do you think they wouldn't run that risk again?"

"But you teach what the hazards are."

"Dick, in time we'll learn how most things work. Even that mountain. I'm optimistic about our intelligence." Doctor Pell flexed his wrist and the ice clinked in his glass. "But not about our nature. We do pretty damn much what we want to, don't we?"

Already in the newspapers we'd read about survivors who swore they'd rebuild their boathouses, their bait shops, their lives. But nothing was more disheartening in my work than these days after a disaster. I had no authority to release funds for relief. So I packed my notes on preparedness and tried each day to book a flight to San Francisco. All I could do was help the Red Cross set up a prefab Emergency Center. When a delay developed over hooking up the switchboards I decided to search the area for school gyms or assembly halls where beds could be brought in, for the injured. I asked Linda if she'd come along.

"I wish I could." She rolled an oak swivel chair back from her father's cluttered desk. Spiral-bound notebooks; memos in his meticulous handwriting. Reports spilling from manila folders . An intercom box with a persistently blinking light.

Though she was resolute, vivid, Linda was one of those women who look refreshingly attractive in casual clothes and without makeup. She wore an amber blouse, tan twill pants, tennis shoes. Tilting back in the chair, she drew her knees up to her chest and wrapped her arms around her legs.

I picked up the blinking box to clear a corner of the desk, and sat down. "This would drive me crazy."

"Me too," she said, "if I answered it."

"You don't?"

"It's a direct line from the media center. They don't want me, they want Daddy. And he refuses to talk to them."

"Come with me," I urged her. "Leave a note for your father. Tell him we'll be back this afternoon."

"Dear Daddy." Linda pretended to write a note in the air above her knees. "I've gone to see the country with a beguiling bureaucrat. Don't wait up. Your darling daughter—"

"That should calm his fears," I said. "Let's go."

Linda rocked forward, drawing herself back to that morass of data yet to be logged. "Dick, what's wrong with this picture?" Her eyes were smiling. "I work for a geologist but I'm stuck behind his desk. You work for NEPA—you should be swamped with paperwork—and you're trotting around the country."

"You won't have to trot. A trooper gave me his jeep."

"I *am* sorry—but I have all this to finish." Her eyes asked if I understood. "Everybody knows I'm here because Doctor Pell sent for me. Without my father I'm another lab rat. My clearance came from him. I work from his office." Her hands flew over the clutter; then she planted her fists on the desk. "He's given me so much support. I can't let him down."

"Of course not. But take credit for your own achievements." Linda's father had boasted of her before she arrived—she was one of his prize accomplishments, wasn't she?—how, at Stanford, she'd completed a four-year program in three, and earned her master's degree the next year. Then her job in the lab. But Linda was as shy as she was proud, and she turned back my argument: "There's nothing remarkable about me."

She was bright. And pretty in an unstudied way. Now, because we'd been talking about her, a nervous blush colored her cheeks. "I think you're remarkable," I said. "Though it's nice that you don't."

A smile played at the corners of her mouth. "Dick, do you think I'm being *nice?*"

I laughed. "No."

Linda laughed too—and I realized how much I enjoyed her happiness, and that throaty laughter which surprised me when we first met. "I'll look in when I get back," I said. Time to leave; but I was reluctant to go. I asked if she'd come with me to the commissary later.

"I'll be joining my father for supper." She looked suddenly solemn. "Dick, if you're beginning to make love to me I wish you'd stop. We have so much work to do."

"I'll stop talking about it then."

"Thank you."

"But I won't necessarily stop."

"We'll see."

Ash had covered all the fields and small towns in a dense silence. Men and women in masks swept their rooftops, then shoveled the sidewalks clear. Children with brooms brushed out the apple orchards and asparagus fields. Handkerchiefs hid their faces except for their eyes. On the road back to the observatory I stopped while a crew cleared an iron bridge. Peering over their masks, they pushed wheelbarrows up to a railing. From the bridge an ashfall slanted down and settled over the riverbed. It was dusk when I reached the barricade and returned the jeep to the young trooper.

The next day I found space on a small plane out of Portland. Then I found Doctor Pell alone at his desk. He'd rolled up his shirtsleeves and he leaned on his elbows the way his daughter had done. "Linda should leave too," he insisted. "I want her to go back to California. At once."

"Have you asked her?"

"I see no need to ask." His temper flashed; he wouldn't concede any authority. But he cooled quickly. He was more upset with himself than annoyed with me. He could accept Linda's leaving if, like her coming here, it was done at his command. "No question, Dick, I shouldn't have brought her into this."

"I don't see why."

"I can't allow her to work near the crater. Until it cools she's wasting her time." He sat back stiffly; clearly he was concerned for his daughter. He'd phoned the Geological Survey headquarters about Linda's former job. "They'll be delighted to see her. They have work waiting for her in the lab right now."

I phoned to book the last seat on the flight for her, and the following day Doctor Pell drove us down to the city.

The silence of Portland wasn't surprising—the heavy ashfall had closed many streets; businesses were shut down. The airport lay muffled in a pall that clung to the landing strip as well.

A small prop-engine plane. Linda pretended to be anxious about the take-off, so we held hands. *Here, give me your hand. I'm here, yes, let's stay close.* We sat still, her hand was warm and calm, and I liked thinking I could comfort her. When our clearance came from the tower the plane crept down the runway. Trembling, it gathered speed, then it lifted above the ashen air that was like a shroud draped over the country.

2

Two Families

Leaving the plane with Linda, I was thinking how I wanted her to stay with me but she had to return to the GS lab. And I needed to develop a preparedness program for Noah Geyer and NEPA; to avoid that row of corpses at the side of the road. But then, as we entered the San Francisco airport, a frail woman in a flowery dress was waiting for us. Linda rushed over: "Mother!"

They embraced, they kissed, then I was introduced to Annette. Doctor Pell had told her what flight to meet, though it was a six hour drive from their home at Lake Elaine. She sent me a sly look. "He must not trust you with our daughter."

"With good reason," I admitted, and I was rewarded with Annette's quick smile. She was nervous, delicate; meeting her, even for the first time, you wanted to put her at ease. Remembering her picture on Doctor Pell's desk—long brown hair held back by combs; those anxious eyes—I felt we'd already met.

"Your father," she told Linda, "leaves nothing to chance."

"He wanted to fly back with us," I said. "He'll be home—"

"When he can—I know." Annette placed her hand on mine.

"Do you young people have plans for dinner?"

She'd taken a hotel room for the night and I invited them to a restaurant in North Beach. "Fine pasta," I promised, "and the best bread in the city." Today I remember little of that meal except that we talked about Linda's family—that's what I was hungry for. To be with Linda; to hear about the people close to her.

From Annette I learned Doctor Pell's father had been killed when the Japanese attacked Pearl Harbor. I asked about his brother, Father Ted. Two priests had been seated near us, but once they left Annette spoke frankly: "I love him. But he's no saint!"

His parish in Crags Landing was far upriver from Sacramento but still within the diocese of the capital. "So the bishop can keep an eye on him. His hobby is raising hell!" she said.

Just out of the seminary Ted joined in civil rights marches. Soon he was counseling anti-war draft resisters. He welcomed them to mass indiscriminately. "They haven't been home overnight—they're looking for a place to crash on Sunday morning."

"Mother, is that fair?" Linda objected.

"You defend him, dear, because he's fond of you. Bishop Moore is less enchanted. It's only a question of time before Father Ted is suspended."

He'd renovated a Victorian mansion, converting its ornate parlor and satin-walled bedrooms into a waiting room and offices, while he recruited volunteers to assist runaways, battered wives, abused children. Inevitably this patchwork but decorous dwelling was called Mercy House. "Bishop Moore knows donations don't cover expenses," said Linda. "He suspects some creative bookkeeping."

"He shouldn't have sent Father Ted to Crags Landing. In a small town it's easy to cause scandal." Annette turned her troubled eyes to me. "Are you from the city?"

"I grew up in Mingus."

"In the valley—"

"Yes."

"Are your parents still there?"

"My parents aren't living," I said.

"I'm terribly sorry."

My turn to speak of my family; I found I was selecting among a handful of facts and memories. No point in dwelling on the death of my mother or sister; people don't like to hear how something as natural as birth can go wrong. And talking about those years, even among friends, I've always felt this struggle between regret for what I lacked and pride in what I had.

"I was raised by my father," I said. Darwin's Dock was the boat landing on the Sacramento River where we sold bait, lures, and beer. Lunch for visitors from town. But much of my father's business was renting boats, repairing motors. A boat went dead in the water, the props caught in a snag—I'd learned to swim before I started school; I was more help to him in the water than in the shop. A high school coach recommended me for a scholarship to Berkeley. I made the all-conference swim team my second year. But that summer my father died and I left school to run the shop. Two years convinced me I didn't have his knack for it. I sold the shop and house, using the money to return to the university. But not to swim. The discipline—the attention to technique, morning and evening practices—all that effort had lost its purpose. "It felt like someone else's life," I said.

"You must miss the river," Linda added thoughtfully.

"Often," I said, though I've never longed for those 6:00 A. M. workouts. Six days a week. But any boy who grows up on a river knows that his later life, as a man making his way in the city, is a sham. He must make the best of it—the oversized buildings, the improbable lights and traffic—but his heart has been formed for the lean life of a marshland and his dreams walk on water.

"Bob keeps a boat on the lake," said Annette. "And he loves to swim."

"I still swim but not in competition. After my father died it didn't feel like a sport any longer."

"I'm sorry."

"Yes," I said. Did she often apologize for what she said? She'd been without her family so long that she flared up at the chance for conversation, then wavered, and quieted, like the candle flickering on our table. I looked at Linda, her chin propped in her hand, as vital as her mother but more composed.

At the observatory Linda dressed in jeans and a cotton shirt or a crisp blouse, pale blue or pink. Now she wore a skirt and vest. A little lipstick. A maroon hat with a round brim over her red curls. Wherever we were, around the observatory or walking through the airport, men noticed her. They turned away then they looked back. That cool stare and her slim mouth made her seem absorbed in thought; often she was. Some men who glanced twice must have asked themselves why. But attractive, yes, she was. Men saw Linda's red hair, her assertive walk, then they'd meet that remote blue gaze and catch themselves staring. I looked away when our waitress arrived with plates of steaming pasta.

I poured more wine and the candle wagged busily. "Please don't think I'm a dolt—" Annette lifted a forkful of spaghetti—"but I don't know one of those federal bunches from another. Which bunch is yours?"

When I told her she sighed. "We're known as NEPA," I said. "I wish we could be as brief about everything else."

"The work you've done with Bob—will that help people who live near Lassen Park? At Lake Elaine?"

"Your whole area is a volcanic field," I said. "It's one of our highest priorities."

"He actually talks like that," Linda teased: "I'm afraid it's in his blood."

"He sounds more than a little like your father." Annette turned to me. "We'll have the pleasure of seeing you again?"

"If I'm sent in—" I stopped; Linda was grinning.

"Tell your director if he sends anyone else we'll riot," Annette threatened. "Tell him we'll dunk him in the lake."

"With my help," I said. Linda laughed and we drank our coffee.

When we walked to the car the fog hadn't rolled in, the night was mild, shining. We drove to my flat on Stockton Street. Annette opened the trunk; I brought out my luggage while Linda waited in the car to say goodbye.

"I'll call you at the hotel," I said.

"No—we're going shopping in the morning." The brim of her hat bobbed in the window. "I'll phone when I get to my place."

"Tomorrow night?"

"Yes."

Taking her hand, I said goodbye to Annette. "Thank you for bringing Linda home," she said. "I trust you were a gentleman."

"My options were severely limited."

"What did I tell you?" Linda laughed.

Their laughter lifted into the night—Linda's full and throaty, Annette's lilting, musical. But with her father at the volcano and the priest at Crags Landing, I wondered about Linda's family. Were they always straining, parting, reuniting? Just then rising on tiptoe Annette kissed my cheek, a friendly peck that surprised me, and she slipped into the car.

In the morning my office was quiet as I began to write my report on what had happened at Mount St. Helens. I was forming a proposal Noah could submit to Washington, recommending a network of aid and communication, involving police, fire departments, paramedic units, gas and water companies, libraries (Linda suggested equipping bookmobiles with phones and first aid supplies in rural areas). Just before nine the staff gathered in the lobby, chatting as they moved down the corridor to their offices.

Later when I glanced up at the clock I saw Noah Geyer—his wide plain face, his gleeful green eyes—in the doorway. Noah's face was formed of generous curves, a rounded nose, a knob of a jaw. A face open to whatever it was turned to. "I like to watch a young man hard at work," he said. "I seldom have that opportunity."

"Except when I'm around."

He held out a cup of coffee. "Time for a break?"

"Always."

Noah shuffled over, careful not to jostle the coffee. A plump man, he moved comfortably, as if his body expected to bear up under whatever burden it was asked to carry. I took the cup and he pulled up a chair. "When did you arrive?"

"Last night. I flew in from Portland with Linda Pell."

"Doctor Pell's daughter?" Noah's face widened in a paternal smile. "You'll see her again?"

"I hope to," I said. "Frankly, I didn't expect to see *you*."

Noah laughed, embarrassed because he was prying for information, or even gossip, but he was so open he couldn't conceal it. He'd been a one-man agency for years. Given a staff for field work, he still took many assignments himself. But no longer. Now he met with us each morning; the rest of the day he worked at home where he could be with Edna and their daughter.

Dorothy Geyer was nine years old when I came to work for the San Francisco office of NEPA. I met her at a party in her parents' home; she told me she spent every day of winter vacation riding a pony in the park. She wanted a horse for Christmas, she said, but she wouldn't teach it tricks or ride it for show; she'd ride just for the friendship between them. Unless the horse *liked* to run. Then they'd try the track at Bay Meadows or Golden Gate Fields, she said; go south to Santa Anita. If they did *very* well they'd race in the Kentucky Derby and her parents might come along, or stay home and watch on television. She was full of promises meant for her parents which she practiced on me: She'd feed the pony herself, she promised. Groom it. Get a paper route to pay for hay, shoes. "How often does a horse need shoes? Does it hurt to put them on? Daddy says all they feel is the hammer tapping the hoof—it's not even a secret pain. It's not like when you bang your toe or an earache makes you yell your head off. The horse just gets antsy about somebody holding its foot so long." Teetering on one leg, she held her other foot in both hands. "I wouldn't like that either," she concluded. "Would you?"

I asked where the horse would sleep and she giggled as Edna's arm enclosed her. "The question is: when will this little girl sleep?" Her mother tugged her off to bed.

That was Dorothy at nine. The next year, after headaches and a chronic sore throat she suddenly weakened; doctors found she was fighting a leukemia that resisted therapy. She began bleeding; her spleen swelled up. During remission she rode in the park on a gentle horse. But no treatment helped for long. When she pleaded to be left at home, Noah moved his office into their house, with an extra phone for emergency calls.

"Dick, you should've phoned last night. I'd have told you not to work today."

"I want to finish this. I need to get it out of my head."

"You feel everything and nothing."

"I'm all right." But I wasn't. I'd come back from Mount St. Helens simmering with resentment. "We didn't have to lose so many, Noah. Not if they'd listened to someone who had their respect. Who could tell them to clear out, and they'd go."

His brow wrinkled. "One voice to speak for everyone? For the police. The scientists. The doctors. Dick, I'm not sure that can be done."

"We've seen what happens when it isn't."

Noah nodded; he'd been through it often. An earthquake near Los Angeles. Towns flooded in the Sacramento delta. Mudslides in the foothills, houses slipping away. The long days while the dead were identified. He already knew what I was just learning: we're haunted by hindsight.

"We learn from our losses," he sighed. "Our training comes at the cost of other people's lives."

"Never again," I swore.

"That's why we're here, isn't it?" said Noah." To make sure our mistakes happen only once."

I must have looked dissatisfied.

"Come over for a drink this afternoon?"

"I'd like to see Edna. And Dorothy. How is she?"

"Better. She has more energy. Edna thinks so, anyway. And I want to believe she's right." At the door he said, "Dorothy was quite concerned about you. We watched horror stories on the news every night, those cars pulled from the ashes and the bodies buried inside. She won't believe you're home until she sees you."

The Geyers' narrow house was reached by wooden stairs, each worn step showing weathered wood. Edna met me at the door; Noah stood at the kitchen stove with his back to us, tasting a simmering stew. He hadn't heard us come in and he went on taking nips from a wooden spoon. I saw the gleam in Edna's eye.

Older and taller than her husband, she had a dry humor and a serious oval face pale as the inside of a biscuit. She wore glasses perched low on her nose, and because of her height she seemed to be peeping over them as she slipped up to Noah and leaned over his shoulder. "Just what are you doing to my stew?"

He stiffened with the spoon in his hand. Then he turned, beaming. "This is delicious, dear."

"Only reason he married me," Edna remarked.

"Not the only reason." Noah's arm went around her.

"Get your buns out of my kitchen," she said.

We brought glasses and whiskey into the front room. File cabinets flanked Noah's desk. A sofa faced the fireplace and television. Noah poured our drinks and sank into a green easy chair. "I'm eager to read your reports, of course," he began. "But what's your opinion of Doctor Pell?"

"He has a hair-trigger temper," I said. "He wasn't the most popular man on the mountain. But nobody knows the hazards better."

"Dick, I'm pleased you could work with him." Noah had been the heart and mind of the agency for so long it pained him to let go. He felt guilty because he'd stayed home; now that I was back he wanted to give me more credit than I deserved.

"I relied on him because I needed him," I said.

"Difficult, isn't he?" The room was cool and Noah laid kindling for a fire while I filled our drinks. The little fire blazed up and I was glad to be with the Geyers in the close comfort of their home. Still the house had remained strangely quiet.

"Is Dorothy asleep?"

"Edna took her to the hospital."

"But she's improving—"

"Yes, she's using the swimming pool. A therapist helps her." Noah inspected his watch. "It's almost time to bring her back."

"It is time." Edna marched in and opened the closet.

"I'll pick her up," said Noah. "Put your coat away."

We went down the damp stairs to the car.

"How can this happen to Dorothy?" he asked. "Every time I go to that hospital I want to hear she'll recover, she'll be perfectly healthy, it's no more serious than we first thought it was."

Slumped behind the wheel, his large hands on his legs, he stared down the street. Pale house fronts followed one another down the hill. "Dorothy's awfully brave. When it's in remission, when she's home with us, she takes her medication without complaining. But, damn it, Dick, so much of her treatment is chemical."

Sorrow thickened my throat. "How much can she do?"

"Twice a week her mother takes her to the pool." Noah started the engine. "On weekends we rent a horse for her in the park. She can ride if she's careful."

Children's Hospital was a brick building ribbed with colonnades; a flight of cement steps at the entrance. I waited by the car. Before Noah reached the doors they opened and out came Dorothy with a blond attendant in a snug jumpsuit. Dorothy, green-eyed, grinning, hugged her father. She was a pretty girl, tall for her age—she had her mother's height—with straight brown hair falling below her shoulders.

I came up and said hello but Dorothy only stared at me.

"Who's your friend?" I asked.

"Joan. She swims with me."

Joan waved goodbye, trotted up the steps, and was gone.

Still Dorothy held back. "We worried about you," she confided.

"I missed you too."

"We saw everything on television," she said, taking my hand as we walked to the car. "The cloud. And the cleanup."

"Did you see me?"

"No—but we saw everything else."

Her father laughed. "Everything important."

Riding home she fell asleep, her hair over her shoulders like a shawl. She popped awake as we pulled up to the house.

At the wooden stairs Dorothy stopped, her hand on the rail. "What's up?" I said.

She stood silent.

"Go ahead," Noah urged. "Dick won't mind if you ask."

"When I'm better will you go to the park with me?"

"As soon as we can." I pressed her hand.

"Will you take me riding? Promise?"

"It will be a pleasure," I said.

"Not if you get beat." She broke out smiling.

"*Whoa*," said her father. "No racing for you. Remember that. See if supper's ready—" Dorothy nodded, spun on one foot, then went carefully up the steps.

Noah waited until the door closed behind her. "What do you think?"

"Her color's very good."

"Is it?"

Was it? It was two months since I'd seen her. Was her skin tone brighter? I couldn't tell. She'd been swimming; it might have been the exercise. "She looks perfectly healthy."

"She *does*, doesn't she?" Noah insisted. "We watch her every move. I look so hard for any sign of improvement. So I might be fooling myself, but I think she seems stronger."

I didn't have the heart to disagree.

3

Her Father's Daughter

A pot of green beans kept warm on the burner while I checked the flame in the broiler. I answered the phone, watching the stove as if it might explode. "Hello?" Linda's voice had a low, thrilling timbre; I could think of nothing to say, I just wanted to keep her talking. "What are you doing?" she asked.

"Poisoning myself."

"What?"

"Cooking dinner."

Linda laughed. "If it's so bad why don't you eat out?"

"I don't like to eat in a restaurant alone."

"Dick, is that an invitation?"

"It certainly is," I said. "Can you come to the city?"

"What night?"

If I asked her for Friday she might stay over for Saturday. "Friday? Meet at my place?"

Linda laughed again. "Now you have to clean your flat. I saw you with my mother; you like to make a good impression."

"You make a good impression too," I said.

Her voice fell suddenly flat. "Not for long, I'm afraid."

I set the timer on the stove.

"Dick?"

"Yes—"

"Don't expect too much," she said.

"What time will you be here?"

"Is seven too soon?"

"It can't be too soon," I said.

Linda arrived wearing a wide hat and a shimmering blue dress; the top was a middy blouse and the skirt was pleated. She turned on her heel and her skirt swirled. "I heard this was a good city for sailors."

"You're your father's daughter, aren't you?"

"Do you think so?"

She wanted to see my flat. I opened a bottle of wine and we walked from the tiny kitchen into the sitting room. Linda admired a china red lamp on a bookcase by the stereo. "Such a pretty glaze," she said. "I love how it glows in the lamplight."

"Yes." I looked at her red hair. The window was open; we heard the traffic in the street below.

Linda's heels clacked across the floor; a picture hung on the wall, a reproduction of Picasso's *The Embrace.* A former girlfriend had brought it to the flat; when she left, she left the picture too. Two nude figures stand together with their heads bowed so their faces are obscure. The woman is pregnant—the mound of her womb swells toward the man while his penis hangs slack. Her painfully thin arms embrace him. His arm seems to rest on her but he doesn't hold her. His other hand touches her but can't be seen. Both torsos are substantial; their legs so weighty they could be marble pillars. Her right heel is raised, thrusting her knee toward his knees. Your eye passes over their monumental thickness and her bending leg becomes an entrance to the temple of their intimacy. Or she might be genuflecting to the god of procreation. Maybe not; maybe she doesn't feel blessed. Still a mystery is at work in both of them. Though they look almost like sculpted stone, their bowed heads and his hidden hand and the swelling of her womb suffuse the picture with warmth. But because their faces are lowered, you can't tell if what they share is grief or joy. Linda liked the picture immediately. That had been my response too; and whether or not those lovers felt blessed, I did. Because she was holding my arm while she took in the painting; and because we had the whole evening ahead of us.

"It's quietly passionate," she enthused, and I realized I'd stopped thinking about the picture.

My flat was small, barely furnished, overpriced. Linda was pleased with it anyway, though her upright bearing as she toured the rooms suggested a military inspection. I had to remind myself it was her father's manner; she wasn't aware of it. She nibbled from a plate of cheese and celery.

"You swept the floor?"

"I was away," I reminded her. "Things were a mess."

"Bet you made your bed."

"In there."

Linda returned from the doorway of the bedroom, smiling. "Left your laundry out."

"I've been busy," I said.

"Let's go eat."

I remembered her warning: *Don't expect too much.* It helped to get away from the flat with its suggestion of a domestic arrangement, and go out for dinner. We chose a Russian restaurant on Clement, thrived on the slow service, candlelight, tea, dessert, drawing out the evening. After dinner we walked down the street in the cool night before driving back. At the stairs to my flat we faced each other, holding hands. "I should get my car from the garage," Linda offered. "It's late."

"It is late," I said. "You don't have to drive home. "

"I should."

"You can stay here," I said. "Will you?"

Her cool blue eyes made a matter-of-fact statement: "Dick, this isn't necessary."

"We have something in common," I said.

"What?"

"We've both kissed your mother."

"Mother?" Linda grinned. "You have not."

I remembered the peck on the cheek Annette had given me; I'd been too surprised to return it. "Yes, I did," I lied.

"Doesn't matter—we don't have the same taste in men."

"What's yours?"

"Oh, stop this." We kissed but her hat slipped back. She took it off, we laughed, and I stroked her warm red hair. We went upstairs to the kitchen and I asked if she'd like coffee.

"Do you have tea?"

"I don't. Sorry."

She made coffee and I poured two glasses of brandy. We turned off the lights except the lamp on the bookcase. Linda sat on the floor by the stereo, looking through record albums and tapes. "What do you want to hear?" she asked. When I put my hand behind her neck she turned and we kissed. My tongue touched hers and she drew back. "Dick, I can't be casual about this."

"All right," I said. "We have plenty of time."

"Do we, dear?" When I heard her say *dear,* that simple word, I was too moved to speak. We leaned into the lamplight to find an album; Linda chose one that blended a classical flute with a jazz piano. The flute soared, the piano swung along, we let it play over and over. We danced a little; when we kissed, her mouth opened and she didn't draw back. Soon we turned off the music and went to bed. The room was cool and we held each other and were quiet. When we were making love Linda cried out once. She sobbed briefly and made a gulping sound like someone eager to swallow her own grief. She smiled, but there were tears, and we were silent for a long time.

A dim light swept the room. Pale moonlight, it rose from the street traffic. It climbed the window, washed over the ceiling, and spilled down the wall where the mirror sent it floating across the room. Linda lay staring at the ceiling. Suddenly she sat up.

"There'll be blood on your sheets."

I reached for her hand.

As she looked down a few curls fell near her cheek. "Sorry about the noise. It's embarrassing."

"You couldn't help that."

"You were surprised."

How can you say this tactfully? To someone you love? "I thought you had been with other men," I said.

Linda bent forward as if in pain and the light from the street slid down her back. "Is that what you meant? When you said I made a good impression?"

"No, it isn't." I put my arm around her. She felt warm in the cool room, and she seemed shaken, uncertain. "But you've been living on your own. I thought you'd have met someone."

"I've had offers."

"Of course you would."

"Dick, do you understand?" Linda brought my hand to her mouth, pretending to bite it; she licked the soft flesh below my thumb.

"I've spent so much time *not* doing this. All my attention went to studying. To my training. To whatever my parents planned for me. Daddy especially. They've had their dreams. I always thought I should be their dream." She sat upright, squaring her shoulders. "I know what other girls were doing. But something else was expected of me. To justify their efforts. Their hopes. Father Ted says something's expected of all of us." She shivered. "What will he think of me? Now?"

"You're going to catch cold." I held her close.

Linda's laugh was muffled against my chest.

"I don't like to go on about myself," she said. "May I have a towel?"

I brought a towel from the bathroom. "Brandy?"

"Thank you, Dick."

We sat in bed with the blanket pulled under our arms.

"At the lab there's a joke about this." Linda sipped her brandy. "Geologists climb from bed to bed," she said. She licked her lips. I rubbed the back of her neck and we kissed. "When I'm gone," she said, "you won't laugh about this, will you?"

I said I wouldn't. And I didn't like to think of her leaving in the morning. "I hope you'll stay as long as you like," I said.

I took our glasses to the kitchen. When I came back Linda sat smiling in the center of the bed, with the blanket around her shoulders.

"I'm being modest."

I looked at her in the faint light. Was she teasing? "Was I too easy?" she asked.

I pretended not to know what she meant. "In bed?"

"To get in bed?"

"I wanted you," I said.

"I hoped you would."

Linda unfolded the blanket and I knelt on the bed to embrace her. We made love slowly and quietly and fully, and fell asleep.

In the morning I listened to her footsteps moving through the flat. Then the smell of coffee reached the bedroom. I found Linda in the front room; one of my sweaters slooped over her shoulders. Her legs were bare and bright in the light. She was looking at the Picasso, one hand balancing her cup and saucer.

"It means something different to you," she said.

"I'm not sure what it means."

I caught a critical glance.

"Is this, by any chance, a trophy?"

When I told her why the picture was there she asked me to take it down: "Until I leave." I put it in the closet and Linda said, "You really are sweet." I'm not. I've never been sweet. She knows that now. But we kissed, and I began to caress her under the loose sweater. Then we went to bed and the picture of those lovers in their solitude and tenderness was forgotten.

By the end of that summer Linda was living in my flat on Stockton Street, rising early in the morning to dress and drive to work. We talked of my moving to Menlo Park if that would be easier, but Linda said no.

"It's much more fun here," she said.

In the evenings when Linda played her flute she asked me to read so she wouldn't feel self-conscious.

She'd open a sheet of music and begin, and stop. "This won't bother you?"

"I want you to bother me," I said, and she'd start again. She played wonderfully. Her phrasing was fine and the tone undulated through the rooms and charmed the air.

Bach, Mozart, Debussy. But if I put my book down and watched her she'd stop.

"Is this too loud?"

"It's lovely," I said.

"But you want to read."

"I can read." I picked up my book. But I kept stealing glances at her. Slender and firm before the spindly music-stand; the oriental lamp filling her red hair with its light, the flute gleaming. Some nights we played records or tapes, we danced on the board floor, then went to bed. Late in September we had a little money left; we went to dinner at a grill on Hayes Street; then around the corner to hear the Symphony.

On weekends we shopped for groceries then set out to see the city. We were both raised in remote places so we played in the city like tourists. We rode the cable car to Ghirardelli Square and browsed the shops. Bringing books and blankets to the Marina Green, we stretched out to read and doze in the sun. Once we rode around the bay on a cruise boat mobbed with tourists; we stood on the cold deck and munched leathery hot dogs while we squinted to see the city shining beyond the water and wished we were back in our flat. When we got there we hurried into bed. "Let's not go anywhere next week," Linda said.

"Some sailor," I said. She slapped at me and we struggled under the blanket.

But after another week at work we wanted to explore the city again. "Ever go to Chinatown?"

"I've seen it," I said.

"I never spent any time there."

"Want to?"

So we went.

We walked through streets thick with the smells of chicken, pork, spices. Midway down one block was an oasis of fragrance, a florist's shop open to the street. Outside a red cart was filled with plants, books about oriental gardening. Linda selected a sketch of a blue iris for her father.

"They're his favorite flower. You'll see where he's planted them in front of the house. And down by the drive."

I thought what it would be like to come to the Pells' home at Lake Elaine as Linda's lover, and visit with her parents. And her uncle, the priest? "I'm much less Catholic than my mother," she'd told me. "But more than my father. I believe there's more to our life than just this world beneath our feet. I'm not sure Daddy does." Suddenly I felt impatient standing in the shop while she waited to pay for the little sketch.

A Chinese couple with a small boy and girl entered the shop. The little girl wore a white dress with yellow ribbons, and a white bow in her hair; her brother wore a dark blue suit with short pants.

"I'll wait outside," I told Linda.

The boy wandered out after me and stared at the cart. Its huge wheels were locked by a chain among wooden spokes. He placed his hands on the spokes, glancing up. Just then Linda came out. When I turned toward her a chain rattled behind me. We heard the boy strike the pavement. He'd tried to climb into the cart by pulling himself up on the spokes; the wheel shook—the rattling that I heard—enough to loosen his grip, and he fell to the sidewalk. Holding his knee, he watched us as tears welled up in his eyes. His mouth was wide open to let out a howl but he made no sound.

Linda hurried over. "Poor little boy. What a nasty fall! That's sore, isn't it?" Cradling his head, she examined the strawberry bruise on his knee. Still his face wore that mask of hurt and betrayal. I ran to bring his parents from the shop.

Linda moved aside when his mother knelt to take the boy in her arms. As soon as we stepped back he began to bellow. Now that he wasn't watched by strangers he allowed himself to howl; his cries soared over the street, bursts of noise like birds shaken from a bush. Seeing what looked like a big bright wagon, he'd wanted to climb in. The next moment he was lying on the sidewalk in pain, under our unfamiliar faces. But worse than the bruised knee was the shock of the fall. His father wiped the boy's tears with a handkerchief and in a few minutes he was comforted, snuffling on his mother's shoulder.

"He wouldn't let out a peep while we watched him," I said. "What pride he has!" Linda exclaimed. "I'd have bawled like a baby no matter who saw me."

In bed that night she began to weep.

"What is it? Linda? Honey?"

"What are we doing?" She sobbed and swallowed. She'd written to her parents when we moved to the city, sending her change of address, a new phone number. But she put off telling them we were living together. Her mother would understand but she was unwilling to tell her father.

"He's so proud of me," she said. "He'll hate me. Or you."

"He couldn't hate you," I said.

"It will hurt him so."

For weeks then we didn't mention it. But when she began crying that night I asked her if she'd told him. She brushed the tears from her eyes with a corner of the bed sheet. "No."

"I'll write to him," I said.

"Don't, *please*," said Linda. "If I don't tell him, he can still believe it isn't true."

"Is that why they never phone?"

Linda nodded, sniffling.

"But your mother must know."

"She guessed from my first letters. The return address was enough, because she brought you here with your luggage. She's sharp, you know. And I've written flattering things about you."

"All of them true." It was the wrong time to tease her and Linda didn't smile.

"Do you know how I've felt? Hiding from them what I feel about you?" She sighed. "I used to think Daddy was the most wonderful man in the world. The most exceptional man–"

"You could be right about that."

"No," she said. "You are the most important man. In my world. But can you understand how I feel, hiding this from my parents? As if it's something sinful–

"Because we're not married."

"And won't be."

"I didn't say that."

"I saw how you turned away in that shop. When I mentioned coming home to see Daddy's flowers. You wanted to walk out–"

"Outside the *shop*."

"Out of any commitment that could keep us together."

"Do you mean a child?" I asked. "Are you thinking about that boy who hurt himself?"

Linda turned her face to the window. The street below was quiet. Then a car screeched to a stop, backfired, sped away. "Yes," she said, "I sometimes think about children."

"But we're both working."

"And it would be such a burden, wouldn't it?" she said. "A little boy like that?"

"When would we be home?" I asked. "Nights? Weekends? What about time for each other? You have your work, too."

Linda shook her head. "It's not important work."

"You're still training at the lab." Putting my arm around her, I inhaled the fragrance of her hair as we leaned together "Linda, your career's just beginning."

"I only enjoy field work."

"But your father's trying to help you."

"Is he? Would he help if I wanted to try something else? I couldn't laugh when you said I'm my father's daughter, because that's what he wants me to be. It's what I always thought I was."

"Linda...I'm sorry."

Her hair shook on my shoulder. "I know doors open for me because of Daddy's name. I'd never have my job in the lab with only my master's degree. Even my assignment at the mountain—"

"If he hadn't brought you to Mount St. Helens," I said, "I wouldn't have met you. We wouldn't be with each other now."

"Why *are* we together?" she asked. You want me—"

"Yes!"

"But you don't want to commit yourself to us. You don't, Dick. Is that because of what happened to your mother? When she died? Are you afraid to love someone and then lose her?"

"I'm not afraid to love you—you know that." But I was speaking over the stunned silence in my mind, in which her words, like a stone thrown into a pond, had startled ripples which were unrolling after the sound had died, leaving this uneasy stillness between us. "I'm afraid of *losing* you."

I got out of bed to make coffee and she pulled her robe on and came into the kitchen. We stood by the sink and sipped our coffee. "So we aren't going to," she said. "Are we?"

I looked at Linda in silence. A siren wailed on and on in the street; then it abruptly stopped. "I mean," she said, "we aren't about to begin a family of our own."

I often think how, at that moment, if I'd had the sense to know that was what I wanted, and if I'd told her so, everything that followed would have been different. And I'm about to offer an excuse—two, actually—knowing no excuse is acceptable. But I'd been working night and day on the NEPA plan for our network of agencies. And I *was* newly in love with Linda and unable to think of sharing her within a family, that mysterious union which fascinated me because it always had been beyond my experience. "I suppose not," I replied, and that, I thought, was the end of it. But it wasn't.

We carried our cups to the table in the front room. To change the subject I asked about Annette: what sort of life had she wanted for Linda? Or did Doctor Pell decide for both of them?

"Mother was disappointed that I didn't study music."

"But you play the flute."

"I mean seriously."

"You play beautifully."

"Thank you."

Linda stood up and tied the little cotton belt on her robe. I inserted my hand into the opening beneath her breast, and the belt fell loose.

"Let's go back to bed."

"Yes, it's late." She stepped away, closing her robe, tying the belt again. "We both have to work tomorrow."

Early in November we brought a bottle of wine onto the roof, and watched, on a rare clear night, the stars blazing above us. If you looked up long enough into the sky, with its rocks and fireballs and vast emptiness, after a sense of isolation you began to focus on a particular star and you could feel its pulse in touch with your own. As if its fire reached down through the cold distance to where we lay together, under that tide of black space. One night Linda put down an air mattress and we spread two blankets over it and lay looking at constellations in the sky.

"Do you have a favorite?"

"When I can make one out," she said, "that's my favorite."

"My father knew many of them," I said. The night sky loomed low where I grew up near the river. We were too far from town to see other lights so the stars seemed close and alive. When people went night-fishing for salmon they brought lanterns onto their boats—small skiffs with their engines shut down, rocking on the water, the lantern in the prow trembling, dipping, flaming up again—and the stars overhead shone as bright as those lamps on the black water. "He showed me the shapes and he knew the stories," I said. "I forgot most of them when I went to school."

Lying on her back, Linda pointed at the center of the sky.

"Is that anything?"

"Andromeda." I showed her where to find the long legs of the constellation. "She was a beautiful princess."

"I'll be that one."

"Dangerous," I said. "A sea monster wants to devour her."

"I'll risk it." We found Pegasus, Aries, then several I couldn't identify.

"That brilliant little cluster?"

"The Pleiades."

"And there. What's that bright line?"

"The belt of Orion." I told her what I could remember about the Hunter. How he pursued the Pleiades, Diana's nymphs, forever.

"He's always chasing girls?" Linda laughed. "Now I know which one you are."

"One of them got away," I said.

"Good for her."

Edna Geyer invited us to dinner, and when Linda met Dorothy they talked horses. Grooming, the cost of hay, shoes, saddles. Both liked riding bareback. "But I'm not allowed," said Dorothy. At the stables in Golden Gate Park the older girls who were instructors and guides would cinch the saddle for her, check the stirrups and reins before she could start onto a trail. A guide always accompanied her. "They never let me go alone."

"They know you too well," said Noah. "When you didn't return their horse they'd come straight here to find it."

"In her bedroom," said Edna. "Lost in all that clutter."

"I'll pick it up. Promise." Dorothy led the world in promises and you wanted to believe all of them. But the idea of hiding a horse in her room made her grin. "We'll keep him in the garage. I'll walk him every day."

"I'll sell the car. Build a cart," her father offered. "You can train him to pull it."

"No—he'll just be here to ride."

"Right." Edna rose to clear our plates. "There's only one workhorse in this house."

Noah hooted but we both got up to help.

Dorothy, following Linda into the kitchen, told her I'd offered to take her to the park. "If you came with me, I could ride wherever I wanted."

"I'd love to go with you. I haven't been on a horse since I left home, and I miss it."

"Will you, then?"

Saturday we packed a picnic lunch and took Dorothy to the park. Eucalyptus shaded the road to the stables. As cyclists wheeled by, joggers plodded down dirt paths past heather and Rose of Sharon. The stables have low mossy roofs of red tile and cream-colored walls daubed with dirt. The police stables stand nearby; blue clusters of cops in uniform, sitting their horses, smoking in the shade. At the rental shed Dorothy chose a horse she'd ridden before. Linda found one that was coal-black. Broad through the shoulders. "Like Blueboy—my horse back home."

Dorothy's eyes flashed. "You keep a horse in your flat?"

Linda laughed. "I meant my parents' home," she said. "At Lake Elaine. I board Blueboy at a stable." That's the last I heard of their horse talk though doubtless there was more as they rode down the trail slowly, disappearing among the trees.

I brought our picnic basket to Spreckels Lake. Ducks wobbled up for handouts. At the water's edge a man and his son launched a radio-powered model boat with guns bristling from turrets. It charged ahead then swung graceful loops as ducks scattered. The boat banked into a turn with an angry whirr. But driving for home it fell still. Moved only by momentum, it careened through the water, quiet, almost adrift. "Better replace our transistor," the father explained. "We don't want to lose our navy."

"No." The boy nodded hard. "We sure don't."

Soon their boat was buzzing through the water again. I watched its maneuvers until Linda returned with Dorothy. She walked with a swinging stride. Her brown hair clung to her forehead but trailed in a braid down her back. Green eyes glowing. In place of her pallor was that ruddy warmth I saw when she came home from swimming. Did her illness cause this ripening? Walking beside her Linda looked radiant. Her hair shone in the sun and beneath her cool eyes was a blush of pleasure. "What fun we had!" She hugged Dorothy. "This little gal can ride."

"This was the best!" Dorothy said. "The best ride ever. We went everywhere and nobody stopped us. Can we come again?"

"Only if we eat lunch," Linda insisted.

I opened the basket, Dorothy spread the blanket, and we laid out sandwiches, carrot sticks, apples. From the water's rim the ducks watched while we ate. When we picked up the blanket Dorothy shook her head to show me her braided hair.

"See what Linda did? Keeps it clean."

"Let's undo that," said Linda, "before we take you home."

"Did your mother braid your hair?" Dorothy asked, loosening the braid. "Did boys try to pull it?"

"There weren't many boys around."

"Just as well," I said and she laughed. "Was your hair long enough to braid? It wasn't, in your father's photograph."

"It never was. Sarah Hack had long blond hair. She wore it like this when she rode a horse. Sometimes I'd braid it for her."

"She was your friend?" Dorothy asked.

"Head down—" Linda's fingers unraveled Dorothy's hair. "If we met at the stables we'd ride out together. That's about the only time we saw each other outside of school. We weren't from town, either of us, so we kept to ourselves. But we liked each other. And we loved to ride." She drew back Dorothy's long hair, letting it fall behind her shoulders. "Your mother will give this a good brushing when you get home."

The next Saturday we took Dorothy riding again and stayed for supper with Edna and Noah. Back in our flat, tired and happy, we went to bed and made love. I woke up late in the night and Linda wasn't in bed. A light shone in the kitchen.

"Have you been up a long time?"

"Seems like it."

Linda lowered her head and the light blazed in her hair.

"I thought you were happy in the park."

She nodded.

I waited. "What is it?"

"I *was* happy. With you. With Dorothy."

I told her I was too. She gave me a cool look.

"That was acceptable, wasn't it? It's all right if I'm happy with Dorothy."

"Jesus, yes! Of course."

"Because she isn't a baby," Linda reasoned.

"No, she isn't. She's more mature than many children her age. I wonder if her disease does that," I began to theorize, knowing it was the wrong time to try that, but playing for time. "If her illness makes her more aware—"

"Dick, don't—we're not talking about Dorothy."

"You said you were happy with her."

Linda looked at me for a long time, her cool eyes not judging me, but simply watching. You might say she was giving me all the time I needed to redeem myself; I believe that, now. And you could say that a better man wouldn't use a dying child to gain an advantage in an argument with the woman he loved. But I did. The words were already out. So I stood there feeling sick about what I'd done but unwilling, or unable, to apologize for it.

"You think it's fine if I like to be with Dorothy," she said then. "But not with that little boy in Chinatown."

"The one who hurt himself?"

Linda sent back her level gaze.

"He was so young," I said. "He was practically a baby."

"And you don't want a baby."

"No. Do you?"

"Sooner than you think. Certainly sooner than you will."

"You've mentioned it. I didn't know it was that important."

"I couldn't tell you–you'd be upset. You're upset now."

I reached for her hand but Linda rushed from the room to stand shivering at the front window. It was almost winter and the window was stained with the weak light before dawn. "This isn't only about having a baby. The point is, I want to have that choice. It's like everything else that I can't do. Do you see?"

In the morning Linda always left before I did, because she had to drive to work in Menlo Park. But that morning she stayed in bed. "Just an hour," she pleaded. "I need more sleep."

"You didn't sleep at all last night."

"Did you?"

"I'll make some toast."

"No, I can't eat. I'll be up soon. See you tonight."

We kissed and I went downstairs into a silver morning of damp streets. Children, wrapped in scarves against the chill, hurried past the Civic Center on their way to school.

When I came home from the agency Linda was wearing a shirt of mine with the sleeves rolled up. "You're early," I said.

"I didn't work today. I called in sick."

"Are you sick?"

"No."

We sat down in the front room between two open boxes. "I'm shipping a few things home."

"Why?"

"Summer things." Folded neatly among the boxes lay pastel dresses. Shorts, sleeveless blouses. A swimsuit. A nylon nightgown. "Winter's coming. I won't need these for a while."

At the end of the week Linda told me she was going home for Christmas. "I miss Mother and Daddy," she said. "It's six months since I've seen them." Which meant she was leaving me.

"The real reason?" I asked, and her eyes brimmed with tears.

"I don't need the lab," Linda said, her voice choking. "And you don't need me."

"But I do."

"You want me. On your terms. That's different," she said. "I'll go home and sort things out. You think you need me. That only makes this more difficult. Because I don't want to accept what's expected of me. However fine it is. I love my mother dearly but I don't want my life to turn out like hers."

I didn't want her to go. We were eating dinner and I left the table, turned off the stereo, and went into the kitchen.

"How long?"

"For the holidays," she said from the front room. "Thanksgiving and Christmas."

"You'll come back after Christmas?"

"Of course."

I brought in a bottle of wine and sat down.

"I've told Doctor K," said Linda. Kurowski, an old classmate of her father's, directed her lab work. "I'm entitled to three weeks' leave. And the lab closes for the holidays."

After dinner she brought out her suitcases and more boxes. "You don't have to take everything."

"I'm packing most of my clothes. It'll be cold up there."

Later we drank more wine, listened to music. We went to bed and made love, and again hurriedly in the morning. I showered and went into the kitchen to make coffee while Linda bathed and dressed. Then she finished packing. The slim black case holding her flute fit easily among her folded clothes.

The last time a woman moved out of the flat we'd looked with sorrow at each other, said things in measured tones; when she left the sense of relief was so vivid I walked for miles; I returned after midnight to fall asleep on the sofa with the stereo playing...I knew this would be different. When Linda began packing her clothes I told myself *you might never see her again.* Now the room was filled with her cartons and her luggage and my heart felt incredibly heavy and at the same time empty.

After toast and coffee we loaded her car. A chill hovered over the street. "If you don't come back," I said, "I'll burn our bed. I'll bring it down here and set fire to it."

"Where will you sleep?" she asked with a large-eyed look.

"On the floor."

"I'll bet." She laughed and we held each other.

"I'll miss you," I said and we kissed goodbye. Traffic crept by; a truck shifting gears groaned in the steep street.

"I'll call you," she said.

Linda never called.

Each morning driving to work I told myself she'd phone that evening, and when she didn't I talked myself out of calling her, growing angry at my own argument: *She's the one who left, let her get in touch with me.* But a week before Christmas I phoned.

Annette answered, and the same anxiety that welled up in her eyes spilled into her voice. "How *are* you, Dick?...I'm sorry, she isn't...Bob's not here, either; I'm alone...How many years and I still worry when he's away...But it's lovely here. Snow everywhere. Though the lake hasn't frozen, quite...I was thinking this morning...when Linda came home from college at Christmas. Will it ever be the way it was? I suppose not...How *very* nice of you to think of us. What fun we had in the city." She remembered the dinner; the priests at their table. "Father Ted was with us this week. He's behaving; he *has* to. And he has the most horrible Christmas present. A motorcycle! That Agape group, those young people in the parish. It's their present to him and he's so pleased. Only...I shouldn't go on!" Another in Annette's string—or chain—of apologies. "I'm sorry Linda isn't here. I'll certainly tell her you called...Oh, I must; she'll want to know...Yes, dear. Goodbye, dear."

On New Year's Eve I brought a bottle of brandy onto the roof. At midnight voices shrieked, horns tooted in the streets below. The glittering city sang goodbye to the past, greeting the future with an explosion of sirens and bells. I looked up at the flickering stars and returned to the flat feeling miserably chilled. I brought the Picasso from the closet to hang in the front room again. The celebration still rang in the streets while the naked couple embraced, their heads bowed in silence. We had another brandy for the New Year, the three of us, and I went to bed.

In the weeks that followed I was still angry with Linda. And anxious to hear from her. But she didn't write, not then, not even to ask for what she'd left behind. Shoes, a light jacket, an umbrella and kitchen things. One night I packed a large box and the next morning I sent it off.

4

Late Spring

I still was hoping to be surprised by Linda. To see her standing in the front room in a pale dress, her narrow chin set, refusing to smile. Or marching through the flat in that determined manner as she left for work in the morning.

Finally I phoned the Geological Survey station. I didn't want to; I expected to learn she'd returned to the lab in Menlo Park without telling me. But Doctor Kurowski knew no more about her plans than I did. It was now more than three months since she'd left; they assumed she meant to resign. Twice Doctor K had placed calls to Lake Elaine, and twice to the university. But he reached only her father, and Doctor Pell was his taciturn self. Except to confirm that Linda was at home and in good health, he remained tight-lipped. All their letters, all inquiries, said Kurowski, went unanswered.

Edna invited me to a Sunday breakfast of cinnamon rolls and coffee. Carrying a pitcher of grapefruit juice, Dorothy padded around the table in a cotton robe like a clown's costume with large red and blue dots all over it. She poured juice for us.

"Aren't you eating?" I asked her.

"Already did."

The scent of rolls from the oven filled the kitchen. Noah unwrapped the newspaper while the dark aroma of coffee drifted through the room. Later as we cleared dishes from the table Dorothy lay on the floor, reading the comics. From the kitchen her mother called: "Get yourself ready, honey."

Minutes later Dorothy appeared in the doorway, tugging at her jeans and sweater. "My suit's under these," she said.

"Dick, we're going for a swim." Kitchen light bleached Edna's hair almost white. When Dorothy weakened she couldn't ride in the park. Her only exercise was in the pool.

"It'll be fun," said Dorothy.

Noah put down a dishtowel and took her hand. "Dick's a fine swimmer. Did you know that?"

"It's been a while since I was in a pool," I said. "I'm probably rusty."

Dorothy frowned. "If you haven't been in the water how can you be rusty?"

"Good question." Edna sent me a glance over her glasses.

Dorothy looked slender and pale. "Will you come with us?"

The silence of my flat was at its worst on weekends. And I remembered an attendant I'd seen at the hospital with Dorothy. An athletic-looking woman with sunny blond hair. "Let's go."

"They'll give you trunks," said Noah, "They even have a pair to fit me."

"An old army tent," Edna remarked and her husband chuckled.

We went down the damp wooden steps to the car. Noah drove us to the hospital and Edna signed in for our lockers and the pool. An elderly nurse left to find an attendant for Dorothy. "You folks go ahead," she said. "I'll send the girl directly."

The pool was warm. In the corners loomed large-leafed plants in terra cotta pots and a green stillness filled the sultry room.

While Edna sat reading in dull light drifting down from the glass ceiling, Noah, after a quick plunge, deposited himself on the edge of the pool. His pale legs dangled in the water as the attendant walked up, tucking thick blond hair under a white cap. "Hi, I'm Joan," her smile announced, then she turned to help Dorothy into an inflated vest. Together they slipped into the tepid pool and dog-paddled around the shallow end. To keep out of their way I swam laps along one side. It felt good stretching out in the water, and I swam until I heard Joan calling.

"Dick?" She stood waist-high in the water, cupping her hands around her mouth: "Dorothy wants you to join us."

I swam over.

Joan's green swimsuit clung to her full figure and the light glowed on her shoulders.

In the moist light Dorothy's pallor looked normal, and the puffed-out vest disguised how thin she was. Earnestly she explained pool-tag: You had to touch someone on the foot, anywhere else didn't count. And no fair swimming into deep water.

Joan listened too but gave her a long look. "I'll be right here, sweetie," she reminded Dorothy.

"I'm fine."

"Yell if you need me," Joan urged her.

"What about me?" I said.

"*You* won't need me." A brilliant smile.

"I'm not so sure," I said.

Dorothy dipped underwater, surfaced, swam a circle, stopping in front of me. I watched to see if she was short of breath. "Stand on one foot?"

"Easy."

I stood stork-like in the water.

But she appealed to Joan: "Is he cheating?"

"Probably."

"I am not. Look."

When Dorothy peered into the water she reminded me of her mother gazing over her glasses. "I can't see down there, it's wobbly," she said. "Show me your other foot."

I lifted my leg so my toes broke the surface. "There."

I'd forgotten the rules and fell for her trick. Carefully her hand approached as if she couldn't believe the evidence of my toes unless she touched them. Suddenly she squeezed my foot, pushing it away. "Gotcha! You start!"

I tumbled backward in the water as she swam slowly away with Joan beside her, laughing.

Joan swam cautiously; Dorothy was more reckless, swerving, splashing, as we played at chasing each other through the shallow water. When we climbed out Joan put her hands on Dorothy's shoulders, water streamed down their legs into a puddle at their feet. Noah and Edna watched the bosomy young woman and their slender daughter, searching for any hint of Dorothy's condition. Joan peeled off her cap, shaking her honey-blond hair. "We did fine, didn't we?" she said. "But that's it for today, sweetie. Let's not overdo."

"Okay." Dorothy had suddenly tired and was relieved that we were finished. She padded over to her mother for a towel.

Noah joined me at the lockers. "Look at her, will you? To see her now, you'd never believe she was ill."

"Her spirit is terrific."

"Her color too. Did you notice, Dick? She has that glow so many kids do."

I'd seen him before like this, grasping at hope. Each time Dorothy came home from the bridle paths or the pool her complexion was flushed, she looked feverish, and Noah told himself it was a sign of her good health. Then she fell asleep, and the next day she was as pale as before.

"She looks just fine. Really," I said, and like her father I wished it were true.

On weeknights I wrote letters and reports. For once I was almost caught up with the paperwork NEPA required. But I hated hanging around the flat on weekends; the rooms were haunted by Linda's voice, fragrance, gestures; I was living alone and not alone, always there was my memory of Linda lingering like a very live ghost. On a Saturday afternoon I drove to Children's Hospital and asked for the therapist who'd looked after Dorothy. She wasn't at work that day but I learned her last name. How could I remind her who I was without bringing Dorothy Geyer into the explanation? I felt ashamed for making the connection in that way, taking advantage of her illness. But that night when I phoned it didn't seem to bother Joan McConnell.

"Do you remember?"

"Yes, I wondered when you'd call. Then I forgot about it." But she sounded upbeat. Breezy. "What took you so long?"

"Shuffling papers," I said. "I had in mind something more interesting."

"I *hope* so." Just as frank as Linda but more forward.

I asked her to dinner and a movie, for Friday night. After I hung up, I remembered what I was thinking when I first asked Linda out; if Friday went well, we'd still be together on Saturday. I was immediately sorry I'd called Joan, for her sake and mine. But we went to dinner and she did her best to keep a conversation going with little help. She was twenty-two; almost the same age as Linda. A pretty woman with a perky smile and bright yellow hair. I missed Linda's tight-lipped grin. We talked about swimming. And Joan loved hiking. Then it was a comfort to sit in the theater for two hours not talking. On her doorstep we politely kissed goodnight. Three weeks later I phoned again to ask her out. She said no. I went up on the roof and drank brandy and cursed the cold.

One morning in spring I found a note from Noah on my desk. *Come by for lunch?* Lately he'd seemed worried and when I arrived I learned Dorothy was back in Children's Hospital, too weak to walk. Her anemia had worsened; her blood cell count was "troublesome." Edna had made sandwiches before her visit to the hospital. While I sat with Noah at the kitchen table his round face looked heavy and a sad stillness filled the house.

"I'm very sorry," I said.

"We can only hope. There are weeks like this. But better times too." Getting up, Noah rinsed our dishes in the sink then dried his hands on a towel. "Want a drink?"

"I'll fix them." The Scotch was on the counter.

"I usually wait until dinner," he said. "It's too convenient when you're working at home. Any problem arises you pour yourself a drink. I promised Edna I wouldn't. But this is a business lunch."

I brought our drinks to the table.

"Remember, Dick, when I asked your opinion of Doctor Pell?" He waited for my reply. His eyebrows lifted and deep lines were etched in his forehead. It was a look of perpetual patience and unanswered hope. A face formed for disaster, for relief, for better luck. I couldn't outwait him, he'd had years of practice.

"No question about his knowledge, Noah. Or his authority."

"Especially in his home territory." Noah lifted his glass. "Lassen Volcanic Park. He's mapped its potential for disaster, right? Not only Lassen Peak erupting. But steam explosions, earthquakes, landslides." He set down his drink. "Think of homes like his at Lake Elaine. And the small towns up there. Isolated cabins. How many people?"

I sipped; swallowed. "About forty thousand."

"In summer? Boating on the lake? Camping; fishing the streams? Say sixty thousand, Dick. Now when Lassen blows—not *if,* but *when*—they come tumbling down the road into Crags Landing."

"Noah—"

"Present population seven thousand," he went on. "Where in that little town do you suppose they'll find shelter? Medical staff? Beds for the injured?"

"For God's sake, Noah, we've tried to alert people. But they don't see any danger until there's smoke in the air."

"We'll change that attitude, Dick. Washington wants an emergency response network in every hot spot in the west. Lives were lost at Mount St. Helens because no one listened. No single authority told them what needed to be done. But if we bring together the right people—"

"The resort owners," I offered. "The water and power firms. The lumber companies."

"Exactly," he said. "NEPA has to tell them: When all hell breaks loose, if you're prepared to help us save lives, we'll try our damnedest to save your property and your resources."

Doctor Pell would bring those parties together. Everyone in the area knew his name. Anyone using the park knew his maps. "But he's a very private man," I argued. "He doesn't get along with people and doesn't care to. He lives in his own world."

"He's a family man," Noah rejoined. "You know his wife and daughter. Do you think he doesn't care about them?"

"He cares tremendously. But that's different. They're in his world with him. And no one else. He sees to that."

"Whether they like it or not?" I was surprised to hear Noah ask the question which had crossed my mind several times since I'd met Linda and her mother: was Doctor Pell's family sustained by his love or by the tyranny of his will?

Down the street someone gunned a motorcycle. Noah sipped his drink. "What we're asking of him is damned difficult. To represent a program nobody else wants. He has few friends, Dick, that's why I was pleased you got along with him. And he does have respect—I'll settle for that. If I wanted someone soft-spoken and soft-hearted I'd go up there and do it myself."

But he wouldn't. Not now. He couldn't bear leaving Dorothy and Edna for weeks at a time, to drive up to the mountain towns and mills and power plants tucked around the volcanic park.

"Have you talked with him? Will he work with us?"

Noah set his drink on the table. "As a matter of fact, I think you might be the best one to approach him." He waved a large hand at the bottle of Scotch. "Want another?"

"Not really."

"Heard from Linda?"

"I don't expect to." I shook my head. "It's over, Noah."

"I'm sorry. Edna liked her too. And she was wonderful with Dorothy."

"If you don't mind," I said, "I will have that drink."

I wrote Doctor Pell at the university but he didn't reply.

I phoned and left a message with his secretary. I wrote again. By the third week in May we still had no answer.

When a reply did arrive it was hardly what I expected. The envelope, postmarked at Lake Elaine, was addressed in Linda's careful script. Inside was a greeting card—a stork stood on a rooftop beside a chimneysweep. A smile lit up the sweep's soot-blackened face and one of his arms rested behind the bird's neck. Above these two, as if to announce an awaited birth, was the message: "At Our House We're Expecting..." Inside the card the chimneysweep pointed at the reader and shouted: "...YOU!"

Under the stork's yellow toes and the sweep's battered shoes Linda had written an invitation. Spring term was over, her father would be at the lake, they were planning a party for the Memorial Day weekend. Saturday was a rodeo in Crags Landing, so the party was set for Sunday at the lake. If I arrived in midweek I could discuss the NEPA proposal with her father. Nothing more personal than that, though she added: "Do come, Dick, please." In a postscript Linda mentioned her uncle was visiting the Trappist monastery in the valley. Would it be too much trouble to pick up Father Ted and bring him with me?

In the mail room Noah poured coffee for both of us. "What do you make of this?"

He smiled at the stork and the chimneysweep but his gaze grew serious over Linda's note, his forehead pinched in a frown. "I'm not much good at reading between the lines."

"I'm not sure there's anything between them."

"Dick, I *can* put someone else on this project. If necessary."

"Absolutely not! I was angry with Linda when she left. But I miss her. I love her. That hasn't stopped."

"Have you told her that?" I was silent and Noah sipped his coffee, scowling. "Forget that I asked. Please. You see what happens when you work at home? I'm more like an old maid every day, living other people's lives."

I'd begun to worry about Noah; he wouldn't be much help to Edna and Dorothy if he gave so much effort that he broke down under the strain. At the door I put my hand on his shoulder. "Take care of yourself," I said.

He looked up from his cup with his brows arched.

"You too."

I brought my coffee down to the office. That afternoon I wrote the abbot at the monastery to tell him I'd be stopping by.

When I left the freeway and drove north, entering the Sacramento Valley, pools of emerald light flashed from the rice fields. At one time all this land lay under water until two ribs of mountain, the Coast Range to the west and the Sierra Nevada to the east, were thrust up from the ocean floor by that leveraging of plates Doctor Pell had shown us on his slides. Today the valley lies at sea level. When you enter it in late spring you feel yourself sinking. Warmth flows over the orchards like water, as if the land is settling back into its ocean bed, and all day glints of color float like motes in the air or like flashes of light seen beneath the surface of the sea.

The road hummed under pickups, flatbeds, freight rigs creaking beneath the weight of packing crates, farm equipment. North of Mingus a shower of birds swooped overhead, veered off, and appeared in the distance like a dark cloud. The cloud changed shape as hundreds of birds hovered, flapping. When the traffic caught up the flock looked like a huge dark hand that was the color of its own shadow, trembling over the boughs of an orchard.

Ahead a horse trailer rolled along toward the rodeo up in Crags Landing.

5

At the Gate of Heaven

Tall grass partly hid the beehives nestled in the field. Above these hives, on the arms of a white cross TRAPPIST MONASTERY was painted in black. The dirt road scuffed through scrub oak to the gravel patch where the fire marshal's red sedan was parked. Nearby, a stone wall was topped by overgrown bushes and trees. At the entrance a wrought-iron arch proclaimed THE GATE OF HEAVEN but I saw no gate, just a gravel path into the monastery. Behind the wall monks stooped over their buckets, picking berries. Others stood on ladders in the cherry orchard, where they'd hung pie tins to startle birds away. A breeze spun the tins, flashing light through the leaves. Swearing like soldiers as they maneuvered behind the tins, blue jays plucked the trees at will. I rang a weathered bell and its clang sounded through the shade. A monk emerging from the orchard wore his robe cinched by a wide belt. The guest master, he explained, was exempt from the rule of silence:

"People call me Brother Bert."

I told him I'd come for Father Ted. With a glance at the iron arch he flung out his arms. "Welcome! As you see, the gate is open wide." His gaze fell to the gravel underfoot. "But our path is strewn with stones."

I laughed. He was in such good humor it hardly mattered how often he'd used that line.

Far off another bell rang.

Monks passed us carrying buckets of blackberries and licking juice from their lips. He pointed out Brother Raymond, the novice master, wearing wire glasses. "Their first day at the bushes he lets them nibble. Tomorrow it's forbidden."

The monks turned down a road between white wooden buildings, the windows and doors trimmed in mud-brown paint. Everybody was heading to the midday meal. "We'll find Father Ted at the guest house." Brother Bert exchanged hand-signs with a pink-faced monk shuffling by. "Our baker. We call him Brother Smudge." Though not because he burned the bread. "A marvelous baker! But no novice ever had such troubles with a censer. First he couldn't light charcoal without poking it until it blackened his hands. Then he was so conscientious about adding incense he buried the coals beneath it. So he'd shake the censer and blow into it. That raised a flame all right, but a face full of smoke as well. Coming from Mass he looked like he'd been stoking a furnace." But the abbot had assured him this was no disgrace. "He cited a passage in Master Eckhart's writings: 'God made this world out of charcoal.'"

Doctor Pell's slides had shown how the earth was born from the fire within it. "This world—" I began.

"Charcoal," Brother Bert repeated. "It makes a dark impression but it quickly rubs away."

As the monks entered the refectory we turned toward a roadside cottage. "Your friend moves slowly these days. You were told about his accident?"

Father Ted, he informed me, was riding his motorcycle down the road from Lassen Peak when a pickup rounded a curve and ran him off. "Smack into a rock wall. He wrenched his spine. He could have been killed. Just like that!" The guest master snapped his fingers. "Still, there's nerve damage, and he's restricted by it. You'll see. There he is."

The door of the guest house swung open and Father Ted appeared in a black suit, gripping a briefcase. The cervical retainer around his neck looked like an oversized clerical collar. I was about to call to him when his raised hand cautioned me to keep silent. He waved and started toward us.

The priest was round-muscled and broad-boned. ("Wait until you see Father Ted," Linda had laughed: "Thank God I got Daddy's body.") Guiding his steps, he looked unnaturally formal. But his thick hair was hastily brushed back, and he'd spent the spring recuperating, a light tan warmed his cheeks. We shook hands and he confided to me: "I follow the fire marshal. The abbot asked me to provide a spiritual reading."

I found a man more firm of purpose, and flesh, than the young priest whose picture I'd seen in Doctor Pell's office. His eyes still suggested humor but he appeared more serious than I'd have guessed from that old photo. I wanted to like him because I knew Linda did. But I couldn't quite bring together two different impressions of him: a straight-forward man of independent action—he'd been warned about that—but a man who took pride in keeping secrets too. He was pleased the abbot had asked him to speak, he wanted to tell me what was in his briefcase, but he wanted even more to keep quiet about it until the meal was finished.

While men in grey robes streamed into the refectory the guest master whispered introductions: Captain Hookins the fire marshal, in a blue uniform, waves of silver hair above his square forehead; and Abbot Stanley, neat-kept, with a sharp look, and tufts of white hair by his ears.

Seated at two long tables with a podium between us, we were served lentil soup, uncooked carrots, tomatoes, mugs of strong coffee. The monks managed a brisk cheerfulness; in the absence of conversation spoons clinked on metal bowls and plates. Brother Raymond signaled a novice to bring Brother Smudge's bread, and we devoured it with a mild cheese. At the podium Abbot Stanley introduced the fire marshal.

Captain Hookins warned the monks that their interest in fire safety came almost too late. From a notebook he read their sins of neglect. Wall sockets were overloaded with electric heaters, fans, clocks, power drills. His silver head swinging right and left, he voiced his fears for their future: Inadequate ventilation in the maintenance garage. Exposed wiring in the hen house. “Except for the stone hut out back, every structure is made of wood. Your household could go up in flames any minute. Where are your fire extinguishers? When were they last inspected?”

Captain Hookins left them with praise for the one safety procedure they did practice, the fire watch. Each night a monk inspected the monastery by flashlight, alert for fire hazards. A spark from wood shavings, smoke rising from a rag-pile. “Be vigilant,” he concluded. “If there’s ever a night when you forget, when you’re careless, some of you won’t live to see the morning.”

Then, while the monks exchanged guilty glances, Abbot Stanley admonished them: They must recognize their responsibility to each other. What if the dormitory itself should burst into flame? Were they not a family? Each man must set an example for the others. They must heed Captain Hookins’ warning and replace old plugs and worn wires. They *must* be vigilant.

Chastened, they watched Abbot Stanley and the fire marshal return to their seats. Without introduction, Father Ted approached the podium. His hands shook as he withdrew a manuscript from his briefcase. His brace wouldn’t allow him to survey the room; he kept his eyes lowered while the pages trembled before him.

The abbot, he explained, had asked him to translate a text written in French by Jules Beauregard. It was the language Beauregard had learned as a boy in New Orleans and later spoke among fur traders on the frontier. A trapper in the Sierras for forty years, at the turn of the century he came to The Gate of Heaven, where he lived until his death. Most of the manuscript consisted of his soul-searching in those final years, but the opening pages told a tale which the priest suggested might be called “After Innocence.” In a rasping voice he began reading:

“I say this in the silence of my hand…”

Pausing, the priest remained ill at ease. “You’ll notice this was Brother Beauregard’s metaphor for writing: language spoken by the hand. He respected your solitude, which I fear I’m violating now.”

I glanced at Abbot Stanley, composed, meticulous. From behind his wire glasses Brother Raymond looked on, little noticing the novices at his side. He rested his chin on one hand, his arm crooked on the table, a bird about to bury its head beneath one wing. Brother Smudge wore a long-suffering smile. In each face I saw this charitable nature, more in some than in others;

a willingness to undertake even the task of listening with a kind expression. It was their labor as much as their worship that brought them together. Certainly no visitor to our NEPA offices would see anything like this—men working quietly in the orchards and fields until they became the crop that was cultivated. Then harvested. Still it was hard to imagine that same smile on the solitary trapper. He'd been dead for seventy years, yet his anguish survived. Listening with the others I hardly understood his torment; later, when I saw his face, I knew who he was. But can we ever claim that what we learn is worth what it cost?

What Father Ted read to us now in his quavering voice was the old trapper's account of events in this region more than a hundred years ago. Beauregard, who had no friends but the Yahi tribesmen who shared his territory, was hired by two white men to guide their hunting party into a canyon. They befriended him, offering him food, liquor, lodging, a young woman. Their real purpose, which he'd failed to perceive while accepting these favors, was to discover the large cave in the canyon wall where much of the Yahi tribe were living. The men hunted, returned to town, treated the trapper to dinner in the tavern where they'd first plotted this campaign. Each was a rancher, and they visited their families now. Later, when they knew the young men of the tribe were away from their dwelling, some on sentry duty and others fishing the salmon creeks, they took the trapper's trail into the canyon, arrived at daybreak at the mouth of the great cave, and massacred the old men, the women, and children sleeping there. The trapper, wakened by the gunshots that shattered the stillness of the canyon, knew he'd betrayed his only true companions. Years later, unable to tolerate his shame and rage, he'd come to the monastery to live as a hermit. The hut mentioned by the fire marshal, set apart from the other buildings, had been his home.

I said at the start this was Doctor Pell's story; and Father Ted's, and Linda's, and mine. We're all part of it. But I have to tell you, the old trapper who tried to remove himself from the world is involved in it, too.

After hearing his story the monks trooped out to the sheds and barns and the orchard. Men with pails followed the novice master to the berry bushes. Father Ted held back in the shop road where our voices wouldn't violate the silence of the others.

Did he see himself in some measure in Jules Beauregard's confession? A maverick holy man, an outsider, straining to make contact with others, and failing. Feeling inadequate, perhaps foolish. Is this what made him so nervous when he began reading, the pages trembling as he turned them?

There was something shameful about the trapper's participation in the massacre. No wonder his guilt drove him nearly mad. But the story of those hunters was troubling too. Because they killed with a clear conscience. They'd saved their families, hadn't they? And their ranches. But the young Yahi who weren't at the cave that morning—who survived the killings—what became of them?

"And Beauregard saw that happen. He had to."

"He still lived in the canyon. He was a trapper—that was the only work he knew. They began to use hand signals. He'd learned their signs." I'd seen the monks use a wave, a lifted eye, to communicate with each other. "Yet he wasn't allowed to *speak* to the survivors," said the priest. "He was never able to reveal his role in the massacre. It's not surprising that his manuscript developed into a confession. And because he'd suffered to write it, many monks believed he was a saint. *He* felt he was a murderer."

"But he didn't know what the hunters were planning."

"He knew his motive was to help himself. And he saw what that had led to."

"Then how did he live? After what he'd done?"

"Like them, he set his traps and nets. He never fired a gun; a precaution to keep the silence. At times he left them the carcass of a fox or cougar. It was too little. The tribe was dying. He kept watch and he'd signal when whites entered the canyon. It didn't matter if settlers knew he lived there—an eccentric figure from the old days, wild in the head. Woodcutters came. Vaqueros chasing stray cattle. Land surveyors. He let them get a look at him, and he made sure *they* were seen by the survivors, in hiding."

"Then he would vanish."

Supported by the cervical collar, he dipped his shoulders in nodding agreement. "Into the quiet of the canyon," he said. "He practiced the silence of a Trappist for thirty years before he walked through that gate and met one."

The sun baked the road and the white buildings gleamed. As we walked Father Ted slapped his briefcase against his leg. "What do you make of this business?"

First, I'd been impatient for him to finish. Linda was waiting for me. But as preposterous as it seems, I'd felt there was an obscure purpose in my hearing this story. But I had no sense of foreboding. I told him plainly: "I was astonished."

That pleased him. Again the priest slapped his leg. "The hermit," he said, "was tormented by horrible memories; if he hadn't written these pages he'd have gone mad. What you heard was the preface to his *Meditations*. Since his death they've kept his manuscript here in the only structure that can't burn. Beauregard built it with the same stones you saw in that wall out front."

"No, that's volcanic tuff. It's too coarse. He'd have to seal the walls or the cold and rain would blow right through."

"Wait!" said the priest. "You'll see how he solved that problem. And one or two others." He wiped his face with a handkerchief, and 1 held his briefcase while he slipped out of his suit coat. He'd worn his brace long enough to accomplish this by shrinking his shoulders and straightening his arms, hardly moving his spine. With a grimace he reached for his coat, his briefcase. "Abbot Stanley will tell you Beauregard has something to say to us in his *Meditations*. I'd been here a week when he showed me the manuscript. Next day he stopped by the guest house with an inspiration: I should attempt a translation, to be printed here in the monastery; visitors could purchase copies. The monks sell their brown bread, cheese, honey. Why not peddle a bit of their history? That was the bait and I swallowed it."

"You don't believe they'll print your work?"

"Oh, it could be done." He showed me a narrow shed. "That's a print shop. And one brother used to be a bookbinder."

"What more do you need?"

Father Ted shifted his shoulders. "In ancient Africa the Desert Fathers wove straw baskets day after day. At year's end they burned all those baskets. I suspect Abbot Stanley thinks I need a project during my convalescence. If only to keep me from disrupting the peace of the monastery. The *Meditations* are my straw basket, Dick, and I doubt that I'm the first newcomer who's been asked to weave that manuscript into English. I expect my pages will be delivered to the fireplace, not to the bindery."

Behind the blacksmith's shop sat an igloo-shaped shelter with a pipe poking up from its roof. Two window holes stared over a garden surrounded by a wire fence. "To keep out rabbits," said the priest. Though the monks cultivated broad fields on the valley floor, a few still worked this green patch. Cornstalks rose above the tomatoes, carrots, beans. "Vegetables they can cook for a meal one day then put into the next day's soup. This little plot was never meant to feed multitudes. They work it in memory of the hermit. It's an exercise for the body and the soul."

He unlocked the door and we ducked into a room as cool as a cave. In that cramped space we blinked at the light seeping through the two holes. Poles soaked in creosote formed a ceiling under the rock dome. A pale mortar sealed chinks among the volcanic rock. Wait and see, he'd said, but now that I felt the slick substance I couldn't guess what it was.

"Beeswax," said Father Ted. "He'd lived poor long enough, he knew not to waste anything."

Beside the wall a broad rock had served as an altar. On its crown a wooden candlestick stood next to a two-foot cross. Father Ted passed me his matches. When I'd lit the candle, he reached, careful of his spine, to seize the cross.

"He carved this himself. It's valley oak. Hard, durable wood. You can feel how he chopped away at it."

He laid the cross in my hands. The whole work was sharp-edged, irregular, as if it had been hacked out by a hatchet and a hunting knife. A task done not with painstaking care but with the ferocity of the man's remorse.

The priest replaced the cross exactly as he'd found it, propped upright on the rock. "Now and then a monk will come here to pray. I've knelt by that rock myself. But look at this." I lowered the candle over an oak chest. "A gift from a family of settlers. The abbot brought it here for Beauregard when he'd finished building his hut. This was his desk and his table."

The priest sank to his knees and grasped the lock on the chest. His face gleamed in the candle's glow as he lifted the lid. Inside was a garment that looked like burlap. A few books with covers cracked. And a cluster of small wooden figures. He scooped them out. Woodcarving had been a hobby of my father's; I examined the pieces with interest, and, after seeing the crude cross, with amazement. An owl smaller than my thumb had ruffled its feathers, ready to plummet toward its prey. A bear stood with one foreleg firmly planted, the hindquarters giving support should it need to rise up, or run. A hawk extended its wings to glide on thermals over the valley, a scene from my childhood. A cougar gave us a curious look, wondering why its creator had abandoned it in a world of bare stone with no ground cover. Two deer raised their heads, listening. The simplest piece was a plump bunny, a work of such childlike love that I suspect the rabbit fence was the work of monks who toiled in the hermit's garden after his death. It wasn't surprising that the old trapper observed these animals with attention. But it was remarkable that the hands which hacked out that cross had worked these figures with such patience and love.

Father Ted gathered the carvings into a corner of the chest. Then he brought into the candlelight a packet made of an animal's hide, one side stitched with a leather thong. As he settled onto the floor, Beauregard's manuscript fell open on his lap. "In the guest house I work from a copy. But here we have the original."

He opened his briefcase to show me, side by side, the title page of the French text and his own translation:

THE MEDITATIONS

of

Jules Beauregard

"As you see, his text is in two parts. The first is his confession; you've heard that. Then he describes how he lived after the massacre. And he realizes how inadequate this is. He still has to confront the questions that hound him day and night." The priest patted the pages of the manuscript. He'd translated three questions, listing them in a table of contents:

I. After Innocence
II. Why Did I Come Here?
III. Why Did I Bring the Child?
IV. Why Do We Punish Desire?

The child?

I imagined a young face watching us from the shadows. Candlelight rubbed the belly of a black stove. A few feet further it fell across two planks laid over stones.

"This is another bed. A smaller one," I said "He didn't live alone."

"No."

"Who was the child?"

Seated on the floor, the priest rested his back against the chest. "The night Jules Beauregard arrived at the gate in a cold rain and rang that bell, he carried a small boy in his arms. A half-breed about a year old. He was wrapped in fox furs badly sewn—undoubtedly Beauregard's work. He'd trapped fox for years but he sewed skins poorly. He carved his needles from bone—they're kept in the tailor's shop today—but never learned to use them like the Yahi could. In any event the monks must have been astounded when their lanterns revealed a bearded man in his drenched furs holding an infant. But every Trappist community has a guest house. They welcome anyone who asks for their charity; even someone as troublesome as myself. However, Jules Beauregard wouldn't part with the child, and they couldn't occupy the house permanently. So he built this hut. His love for the child impressed the monks. And his habits of silence, poverty, and hard labor suited him to the community."

I thought of my quiet father; he'd cared for me, surely, but I never comprehended his silences. Had he always been that way? Or only since the death of my mother and their second child. He'd tried to have a family, and he, too, ended up with a child to raise by himself. "He carved those animals for the boy."

"They were toys," said Father Ted. "Constructive ones. You saw the care he took with them."

It was craftsmanship as careful as my father's. "How long did he live with the child?"

"Eleven years. When Beauregard died they buried him like the others. A cross to mark his grave. No name on it."

"The boy was twelve then."

"It's anybody's guess. But the monks looked after him. It was years since the cave killings. Still you couldn't ask a valley family to adopt a half-breed from that tribe...If that's what he was."

"You don't know?"

"It's more likely his mother was a ranch Indian who ran away. Or she was chased away when her pregnancy was discovered."

The candle glowed between us, lighting the pages of the manuscript. "You believe he was Beauregard's child."

"I've written to a woman who knew him. Hannah Bascomb was born in Crags Landing, but they met when she was a young lawyer in San Francisco. They were lovers until he died. She claims when he spoke of Jules Beauregard he always called him 'father'."

"People call you 'father' too."

"I doubt if he thought Beauregard was a priest. Many men live in monasteries, but few of them are priests."

Now that I knew the old trapper had a son I couldn't let go of his story. Abbot Stanley had asked the monks: Were they not a family? The answer meant more than I expected. "The boy left when his father died?"

"Yes," said the priest. "The monastery hadn't yet built its dairy. Milk had to be brought to a creamery in Mingus. A rig arrived and monks loaded the milk for the old driver, who hauled it into town. First he'd sit talking with the boy about the world beyond these stone walls. One morning the abbot asked if the boy might help him make his deliveries. In time he'd have to learn a trade. So the driver let the boy ride with him on the rig. But a month later something remarkable happened. A survivor from the old Yahi tribe appeared at a slaughter-yard in the valley. The crowd that gathered to gawk at him could see he was starving."

"It was Ishi."

"Yes."

"I went to school in Mingus," I said. "In history class Ishi was called The Last Wild Indian in North America.

"Well, he'd walked in naked from the canyon, you see, and a butcher in the slaughter-yard put his apron over him. The news swept the valley like a grass fire: the old driver heard it, and the boy, too, when they brought the milk to Mingus. So they went to see the wild Indian. Who was actually a mild-mannered gentleman. But by this time the sheriff had him housed in jail for his own safety—so many people wanted to touch him."

"The hermit's boy must have been fascinated."

The priest bobbed in agreement. "Ishi was trying to answer questions from the crowd. But no one understood his strange tongue so he fell silent. The boy watched his hands. To his amazement he grasped the Yahi's gestures. He was reading Ishi's sign language—the same signs Jules Beauregard had taught him—the old trapper, after all, had communicated in silence with Ishi's people all those years in the canyon.

"Then Ishi signed that he wanted to take off the butcher's apron. It was soaked in the blood of cattle. It stunk, and it stuck to his skin. But it was a gift and he wished not to offend his hosts. Once the boy understood he removed his own cloak—the kind the monks wore—and traded with him. Ishi put on the cloak and the boy rode home wearing the bloodied apron. Not all the monks appreciated it, but he wouldn't wear anything else."

I remembered the Yahi's story. "Linguists and anthropologists identified him. They took him away to their museum. And a medical school in San Francisco."

"When the boy learned Ishi was gone he was heartbroken," said Father Ted. "He refused to ride on the rig. He ran and hid when he heard the horses approaching. Then one night he slipped out the gate on foot. The abbot and the old wagon-driver searched the valley for him: *Had anyone seen the half-breed boy?*

"Did he have no name?"

"Beauregard called him 'the boy'; a name wasn't much use in this place. But the abbot and the driver found someone who'd seen him—that man who'd given his apron to Ishi in the slaughter yard. Yes, he said, the half-breed had asked him where the Yahi could be found. The boy had called himself Jim Beau. So, going into the world, he took his name from Jules Beauregard. He ran off to San Francisco searching for Ishi. Some years later he died in a fight between striking workers and the National Guard. I imagine only Old Hannah knew him well. After his death she came home to Crags Landing to practice law. Old Hannah's a grand lady and an institution in that town. But whatever else she knows about Jim Beau she's kept it quiet.

"Exactly as he'd want it," I said.

And Jules Beauregard? He'd lived his last years here, among the only family that would have him. Here he wore his memories the way the boy wore his blood-drenched garment. From his manuscript I'd learn that every day he remembered the Yahi slaughtered in their cave. And he blamed himself. After dark, when the work in the shops and fields was done, they came to visit him in this stone cell. Ghosts that inhabited his heart, they nearly drove him mad with guilt. In his solitude the hermit's grief—and his love for the boy—became the meaning of his life. He might have worn that butcher's apron himself.

6

Why Do We Punish Desire?

The priest sat with his briefcase across his knees as we drove down the dirt road through high grass to the freeway, slipping into the speeding traffic. We passed a cattle ranch, an almond orchard, then a range too dry for farming or grazing. To the west stood dusty groves of olive trees and the dense green oaks over by the river. Between the river and the mountains the valley stretched bare, sun-struck. We swung around a chartered bus to Crags Landing; hundreds of people were heading north with us and the traffic thrummed along, flashing in the sun. East of the freeway a hawk glided across a deep gorge where a canyon gaped. The chaparral was bleaching out and dark oaks clung to the rocky slopes. It was desolate country, as silent today as when the Yahi lived there in hiding.

"If a child like Jim Beau was brought to Mercy House today could you take him in?"

"I'm sure we'd have found a home for him." Father Ted fidgeted with the briefcase on his lap. "Linda told you about our efforts?"

"Linda and her mother. The first night I met Annette." I said nothing about Annette's fear that he'd cause a scandal.

"Really?" His surprise seemed genuine. Also, his delight, which he attempted to mask: "I expect they meant to warn you about me." I remembered his reputation for trouble with the bishop in Sacramento; his banishment to the little parish in Crags Landing; the charitable operation he was directing without the blessing of the church. "It hardly matters now," he said. "Mercy House is closed. By order of Bishop Moore. I've had to disband our staff and turn everyone away."

"But why?"

"Should Bishop Moore allow a renegade priest to direct a charity for his own interests? He had no control over our funds or priorities. Why put up with that? Well, he won't. I was told to close the doors of Mercy House and cease its services." Smiling, he concluded: "Which I refused to do."

"You defied the bishop? And you were suspended," I said. "That's why you were sent to the monastery. To learn obedience."

"Abbot Stanley hasn't much hope for me. However, he permitted this visit to my family. And I'm allowed to offer Mass on Sunday, before I return." Father Ted removed a cigar from his coat. "Do you mind?"

I said I didn't.

A stream of smoke slipped out the window. "God, but I've wanted one of these."

"Was smoking forbidden?"

"Not strictly. But the abbot disapproves."

"He can't be everywhere."

The priest laughed. "There now, you see, you don't have the proper attitude."

I laughed. "That's true."

"Anyway, I owed Abbot Stanley a favor or two. This was the least I could do for him." He drew in and savored the smoke then let it out with a sigh of satisfaction. A motorcycle buzzed up. A girl in jeans and a t-shirt pressed her chest against the boy driving. They swerved ahead.

"Do you miss it?"

"The bike?"

I laughed. "Yes."

"I do," he said. "I like to get into the mountains. At every opportunity. For the air. And the solitude."

"You go alone?"

"I did," he said. "Or with young people from the parish. They're the ones who gave me the motorcycle. God knows how they raised the money for it. The straight kids wash cars and the others sell pot; I don't ask too many questions."

"Is this difficult for you?" I asked. "Coming home?"

"They're like a family, Dick. You hope they'll love you. But they don't have to. Still you go back to them." He turned his shoulders so he could speak to me. "I'll say Mass and give communion in my own church. I can talk to these people," he said cheerfully. "How do you talk to a monk? If he isn't stooping over a row of beans he's down on his knees in prayer."

I laughed because I knew he admired the monks; he might even have been a little afraid of them. In any case, his humor wasn't malicious, he was just happy to be going home.

"Still," I said, "it won't be easy for you."

Ashes dropped onto his coat. He tried flicking them off but only rubbed them in. "True. But it's harder for you."

"I had to come. NEPA has a project for Doctor Pell."

"And?" He went on brushing his coat.

"And I have to see Linda."

"How long has it been?"

"Six months," I said quickly.

Entering Caliente County, we passed thick green walnut orchards thriving in the heat. As we drove into Crags Landing a billboard cowgirl twirled her lariat around the words: *Cocktails, Beer,* and *See You In The Chute!* Red-white-and-blue streamers decorated the fairgrounds for the Memorial Day rodeo. "If your family wasn't putting me up," I said, "I'd never find a room."

"Not a chance," he agreed.

"It's very kind of them." I hoped it meant more than kindness. How would Linda look? After these months. This was what I wanted, wasn't it? Yes. This opportunity to let her know I loved her more than she thought. More than I'd thought.

Overlooking the plaza, the courthouse was flanked by tall junipers; an aged stone building fronted by oak doors, stolid pillars, a resplendent dome. Across the plaza stood the more somber Church of the Immaculate Heart. Like the dark old church with its black trim, the rectory beside it had been built of coarse red brick. As we climbed from the car the door swung open and out flew a dark-skinned girl wearing a white blouse and black jumper. She came running toward us, sandals slapping the sidewalk.

"Father!"

"Teresa, dear."

Setting down his suitcase, he pressed her to his side in a light embrace. She blushed, then beamed extravagantly like a favored child. Father Ted told me Teresa Espinosa did all the sewing in the rectory: the priest's clothes, vestments, the altar cloths. She ran errands for Mrs. Muller, the housekeeper, as well. Teresa looked perhaps sixteen; dark hair, a wide nose, and dark wet eyes alive with happiness. Her delight was more at seeing him safely home, I thought, than listening to his litany of her virtues. She seized his suitcase with both hands and carried it up to the door. "I'm not an invalid," he called after her. "And I won't be unpacking all that. I'm going on to the lake with Dick Darwin. Thank you all the same."

Seeing a troubled look in Teresa's eyes, the priest tucked his briefcase under his arm and went up the walk to join her. On tiptoe she whispered something in his ear. I waited in the parkway, watching this scene, until he returned. "Dick," he said, "it seems I won't be riding up to the lake with you. Sorry. I really don't want to disappoint Annette. Or Bob, either. Please tell them I'll come tomorrow."

"A problem in the parish?"

"More or less."

I've mentioned that the priest enjoyed keeping secrets. But he wasn't enjoying this one. He looked worried, indecisive. As I climbed into the car he took an envelope from his briefcase and let it fall on the seat beside me. "You might look that over while you're at the lake," he said. "Thanks for the lift."

Teresa had brought his suitcase inside. In the doorway now the blue-haired old housekeeper flung out her arms in glee. She was about to hug Father Ted to her bosom but saw his brace. She kissed his cheek instead, took his arm, and led him in.

There in the shade I could have opened the envelope and read its contents in a few minutes. But I was in a hurry to drive up to the lake to see Linda.

The road out of Crags Landing crosses an iron bridge over the Sacramento River. At each end the bridge is anchored on the crags that gave the town its name when the riverbank offered a landing for steamboats pushing upstream. In the era when my great-grandfather, Thomas Darwin, built his loading dock along the river, fifty miles to the north Crags Landing was a sprouting village of cabins, sheds, stables, two churches, a gallows, and a station for the overland stage. Today I watched a family fishing from a patio boat as I drove across.

A mile beyond the bridge I passed Sawyers' Stables. Horses were pastured in open fields. Beside a small house a silver ranch wagon blazed in slanting light. Quickly the road rose into the mountains. I eased ahead of a truck struggling up the grade into the pine forest. These were yellow pines, tall and lean, and dusk gathered among the trunks.

From the turnoff to Lake Elaine an access road led onto a wooded peninsula. It was dark among the trees until my headlights struck the sign on a steel gate that closed the road.

PRIVATE PROPERTY
DO NOT PROCEED
BEYOND THIS POINT

A security guard with a flashlight checked my driver's license, wrote the number, and my name, in his notebook, and waved me on. "Enjoy your visit," he said, and I drove into the dusk.

From the road I saw lights in the vacation homes set back among the pines. Most were cabins with peaked roofs; some had been converted into full-size houses with a porch and garage. Owners' names appeared on signposts. Far out on the peninsula I found the small iron sign by the Pells' driveway, a black schooner in full sail over the family name. Here the pines had been cleared away and the last of the twilight clung to the lawn.

The Pells' driveway, where I left my car, was bordered by stones that must have been brought up from the lake; they were worn smooth and sprayed with white paint. Down the sloping lawn a flagstone path led to the water, where two men towered over a small woman at the end of the pier.

"Dick! Come down!" Annette ran to meet me. In her billowy blouse and skirt she shivered in the evening air. She wore her perpetually worried look but the warmth of her embrace surprised me. "I'm so happy you came." She tucked her head beneath my chin. "It's awfully good to see you again."

"And you," I said. "You look wonderful. Where's Linda?"

"Working late." Annette offered her arm and I walked her down to the pier. "I'm sorry, Dick. She phoned about last-minute chores. She'll stay the night in Lassen Park."

"In a cabin?"

"I think she'll camp out. That frightens me. But I could *not* talk her out of it. She can be as bull-headed as her father." She pulled my arm. "I imagine you *know* that."

"I expected to see her tonight."

"She promised she'll be here in the morning, dear. And the rest of the week." She gave my arm a gentler tug. "And Father Ted?"

I told her how the girl had whispered her message in his ear. "I'll bet he loved that."

"He seemed unsettled."

"Teresa's a darling."

"You know her, then?"

"Through the church. And she's done some sewing for me," said Annette. "For Linda, too."

We walked onto the pier where the Pells' boat lolled against a piling. Ahead of it was a park ranger's boat, a 20-foot craft with red lights mounted on a bar over an open cabin and a V-8 engine that could rocket that hull across the water. A yellow lamp glowed at the end of the pier where two benches faced each other. The ranger rested one foot on a bench as he held a notebook on his knee. Doctor Pell gave me his firm handshake. "Dick works for NEPA," he said, introducing us, though he refused to look at the ranger when he spoke to him. "And this," he informed me with a note of contempt, "is Danny LeFevre."

LeFevre, blond, broad-shouldered, wore a cap with a brim—in the valley we'd called it a hunter's hat—and a khaki shirt with his silver badge pinned to his pocket. When he turned to greet me his leg swung off the bench and the pistol holstered on his belt slipped down, resting on his hip.

Their dispute was about a duck blind Doctor Pell had anchored offshore. As twilight flickered out the lake turned violet and the first stars appeared. "Ought to write you a citation," LeFevre's voice boomed. He'd been drinking and he wanted to bully Doctor Pell, I thought; but not too much. Not so much that a complaint could be made against him. He turned to me with a beery cheerfulness. "No two ways about it," he said.

It only made matters worse that he was right. I looked over the water. "You don't leave the blind offshore like that," I asked Doctor Pell. "Do you?"

"No, no." He'd hauled it out with his boat this morning. "For the party on Sunday," he explained. "It's just a raft. A clump of brush. People might want to swim out. Young people especially."

"Water's awful cold for that. All the more reason to hang a proper light. A caution lamp like this one on your pier." LeFevre had a deep resonant voice, he enjoyed using it, loudly, and his words filled the dusk around us. "You hang a light on that blind or I hang a ticket on your ass. That's the law."

"Watch your language!" Doctor Pell flared. "And don't lecture me. I know the law on this lake better than you ever will."

"Swear to God," LeFevre laughed, "I bet you do." But he realized he'd gone too far. "Hey, no offense." He flashed a smile. "I go by the book, that's all. Take a look at your blind out there. Hardly see it, can you? And this isn't full dark."

"I'll light it," said Doctor Pell. "You have my word."

"I have your *word?*" LeFevre laughed. But he accepted his victory with a hearty gesture, slapping his notebook shut, pocketing it. "Well, sir," he smiled, "that's good enough for me."

"It will have to be," said Doctor Pell.

Annette joined us and he put his arm around her. I hadn't imagined how they might fit together; in my mind Linda's parents lived separate lives. But his hand rested on his wife's skirt as she leaned closer, sniffling into a handkerchief, and I saw how they comforted each other. Two people who could never be content outside their small family.

"Sorry I missed Linda," LeFevre said. "She always liked this lake. And the trails. Didn't she?" He turned to me. "We were friends in high school."

"Is that so?"

"You bet." He smiled broadly. "She was so smart. But I was real fond of her."

Danny LeFevre was handsome and arrogant. Was he ever a friend of Linda's? I didn't believe it. And I wasn't jealous. Not all that much, anyway. "For your daughter's sake," he told her parents, "I won't write a citation tonight. This is just a warning. We've had our little chat. But I'll be back to look for that light."

"What a dear friend you are." Annette's gaze lingered on LeFevre. "All this fuss is for our party. And you've been so kind–we'd love for you to come."

Doctor Pell looked stunned. "What in the name of hell?"

"I thank you." LeFevre retrieved his notebook and flipped it open. "Sorry. Sunday night's my shift again."

"But that's perfect! Tie in here and come join us. For an hour if that's all you can spare. In return for your kindness."

LeFevre's full attention shone on Annette. A tall young man, he bowed and thanked her in a tone suddenly without a trace of arrogance. Does she do this to other men, I wondered. Does she have this humbling effect on her husband too?

Doctor Pell stiffly shook LeFevre's hand; he disliked the ranger but he respected his duty. I think, too, he felt relieved that LeFevre hadn't taken advantage of Annette's invitation. We watched him climb into his boat, the engine throbbed, a headlight threw its beam on the water. The twin lamps over the cabin brightened, blood-red, spinning round and round.

As the patrol boat churned into the night and we started up the path, Doctor Pell turned to his wife. "Why in God's name did you do that?"

"Do what, darling?"

"Invite LeFevre to our party."

"He did us a favor, didn't he? And I imagine he'll enjoy himself. Lake patrol must be lonely work."

"Danny LeFevre is a horse's ass."

"I only meant to be polite."

He looked at her. Was she serious? Yes. But he'd made his objection and now he relented, he put out his arm and Annette slipped alongside as we walked up the lawn. He asked about his brother and I told him what I'd told his wife. "If it isn't Mercy House," Annette offered, "I'm sure it will be all right. His heart's in the right place."

"Yes, but his mind wanders," Doctor Pell quipped. "That's why he's in trouble. It's why he was sent away, isn't it?"

"If people need him, darling, he has to help them." Annette sniffled, dabbing with her handkerchief.

"Damn it, dear, must you do that?"

"It's turned chilly."

"Nonsense," he insisted.

"I have a cold." Annette, pulling free, fled into the house. Between a pair of white pillars the door slammed shut.

It was a solid house built of smooth red brick. White shutters framed the windows, and the lamplight from over the door spilled into beds of iris. Bordered by pines and flowers, like a snug fortress the Pells' home overlooked the lawn and lake. We stepped into a foyer where a white banister, curving like a swan's neck, rose to the second floor. Halfway up the stairs sat Annette with her ankles crossed. With panic in her eyes she clasped the banister like a child frightened by a carnival ride, afraid to let go. When her husband saw that look he turned away.

"I'll fix our drinks, dear."

"None for me. Please."

He glanced up. "No?"

"You know what I want, dear."

"There isn't any more."

"Where have you put it?"

"Never mind. You don't require medication. I've told you that."

Annette, with only a hint of her lingering terror, smiled agreeably. "I'm off to bed, darling."

"I'll be along soon, dear."

In the bright kitchen light glimmered on the wall clock, on the chrome sink, the tile counters. Doctor Pell opened the liquor cabinet bristling with bottles and splashed Scotch into two glasses. "Let's take these onto the porch, Dick."

We passed Annette still sitting on the stairs.

"I thought you went to bed," her husband said.

Behind the bars of the banister her eyes were alive with a fearful excitement. Unable to move, she gripped the banister so hard her hands were as white as the wood. "The guest room is ready, Dick." She gave me that fetching look that had flattered LeFevre. "I've turned back your bed."

I wanted to ask her husband what the hell was going on, but there wasn't time, and in a few minutes I wouldn't have to. From somewhere in Annette's blouse her handkerchief dropped into her lap, and Doctor Pell leaped to her side. She let him pry her hands free, the handkerchief blossomed in her palm, and she dabbed her nose as if inhaling a flower's fragrance. When he lifted her in his arms her fingers dug savagely into his jacket, clawing his shoulders. She writhed, struggling to secure her grip. At the top of the stairs they stopped. Annette, sobbing, wrapped her arms around him, and he walked her down the hall.

I brought our drinks out to the porch. A blue blanket covered the back of an old leather sofa; on the wall behind it was that picture of Doctor Pell's parents I'd seen at Mount St. Helens, the smiling seaman and his wife in Hawaii, the big warship looming behind them. I looked out past the pines where the surface of the lake was scratched by stars. Doctor Pell came downstairs in his shirtsleeves; sinking into the sofa, he drew the blanket beside him. "I slept under this when I was a seaman. In the Aleutians years ago. I'll say this about the Navy, Dick, they give you a damn fine blanket." I suppose it was a relic from a time when his life, however hazardous, was more easily managed. With Linda away and his wife suffering he looked strained, drawn. "I'm not having much luck tonight with the women in my family."

"You know Linda can take care of herself."

"Yes, sir." He lifted his glass.

"But you worry about her."

"I do. And Annette is worried sick."

"I can see that."

"What you saw tonight is not Annette." His voice fell to a whisper and for a moment I was drawn into his confidence. "It's her damn medicine. As she calls it. Why, hell, it's that damned coke she's putting up her nose. For her nerves. No, sir. I won't have it in my house. In our home. Never again."

I can't say I was surprised so much as I was weighed down by sadness when I thought of Annette's eyes, fraughtful and excited, as we stood on the pier. Her panic on the stairs. "You love her–," I began, but he cut me off.

"With all my heart," he said. "My wife is not an addict. She can stop. I can stop her. But the truth is, Dick, we're both dealing with some difficulties just now. You know how that is." His face broke into that excruciating smile. "You and Linda have had your troubles."

I set down my drink. "We have."

This seemed to please him. He settled back on the sofa. It had grown dark beyond the porch, the pines blending into the blackness. "Linda's bright, she's young," her father volunteered. "But look what's happened to her. She has no prospects for a career unless I can be of help to her. And you know that's what she wants, Dick. That's why I want it for her."

"We were in love. For a while that's all she wanted."

"Yes, that was all." He paused in mid-thought with his glass raised as if to honor a memory lost among the years, a forest more impenetrable than the dense pines crowding the lawn. After a long drink he slumped forward, looking weary and oddly sympathetic. "She was devoted to her work," he confided. "In school. In the lab. It meant everything to her. I'm sure that made it difficult for both of you."

"I made life difficult for her." I finished my drink. I thought of Linda's wanting a child. Wanting to start a family. Which was what I longed for, and hardly knew it, and was in any event unable to accept. "I failed her," I said.

When I saw him flinch I began to understand how thoroughly he wished to possess his wife and daughter. Under the burden of his concern Annette had broken down, and Linda was threatening to break free of him. He was worried about them, I suppose he was worried for his own sake as much as theirs, and he was tired. In the long days we'd worked at Mount St. Helens, Doctor Pell rarely showed his fatigue. I told him I was going to bed and he lifted himself heavily from the sofa. We climbed the stairs and he went down the hall. In the guest room Annette had left a light on, a pot-bellied brass lamp with an amber globe. The room stood midway between Linda's bedroom and her parents' room, and I closed the door against the murmured quarrel at their end of the hall.

I walked over to the window. The moon was up and tall pines latticed its light against the screen. Out of the stillness an owl called. Suddenly I felt awful; I felt that sadness that weighed me down when I was a child and my father forgot himself and spoke about my mother—just a remark about how she used to enjoy a boat ride in the evening, her azaleas, anything that pleased her—then he'd remember I was there and he'd stop, but already I was filled with a death that I carried inside me. I suppose we all do that, don't we? Carry our loves and our deaths among each other and think we're alone with their company. Christ, you're feeling sorry for yourself, I thought. Linda isn't here and you want her. She isn't dead. Nobody's going to die. Just go to bed. All right. Put your things away and go to bed.

I thought of Jules Beauregard in his hut, tormented by guilt, but that night I didn't care how he faced his final questions. And on the porch with Doctor Pell I hadn't brought up the NEPA proposal. I was only waiting to see Linda. I put some things in the dresser and shoved my bag into the closet. I was angry because she wasn't here; angry with myself because I was here without her. Sitting on the bed, I opened Father Ted's envelope and removed the pages he'd left me. They contained an interrogation but the questions and answers both came from Beauregard; it was like hearing the old trapper talking to himself:

Why do we punish desire?

We're afraid to love.

Don't try to be clever. Just be honest.

I mean it! Love changes me. And I fear my desire will lead me to love. Then what will I be?

God knows!

Listen, old man. God knows only what we know.

Men, women, children. The weasel, the lark. This fog—its droplets of light—are these not the eyes of God? The hyacinth, the grasses, too, all are

God's body. It is by my body I learn this world. By my eyes, hands, tongue. By my cock, by my blood. Every living thing—coyote, worm, flea, poppy—all touch this creation, taste it, sing to it.

Many refuse it. I think they fear it.

And they suffer for it. When the hunters came to the cave they massacred the women and children and the old ones. These were the ones they feared.

Why were these helpless Indians dangerous?

The whites were afraid to love them.

Crazy! How could they love them?

Because the Yahi were too proud to flee. Peaceful if not provoked. Skilled at hunting bear, cougar. Fishing for salmon. Fond of their families. These were the enemy? Yes; they feared they might love them. In the tavern I heard men swear all the squaws were whores. They said this with loathing and desire. For the hunters wanted to bed those women. And could not. So they slaughtered them.

Because they were afraid to love them.

Yes.

They were not judged guilty. They murdered so many but were never punished.

To go unjudged is not to go unpunished.

How can you say so?

Listen, old man. Did I not lead those hunters into the canyon? Always in my soul is the sight of those corpses. Every night they visit me. Stop. No pity. Begin again—

Why do we punish desire?

We punish its cunning, its persistence. Like the coyote it thrives without reason.

The abbot says faith is without reason.

And it's punished, too.

What's the punishment for faith?

Poverty.

You've always lived in poverty. Have you always lived in faith?

No.

Why do you live with a child?

I don't deny my love for this child. When I see him about the hut or in the fields my heart is glad. I'm aflame with joy. Listen, when lightning strikes the dry meadow there's no boundary to the blaze. But from that black ground comes a fresh green growth!

I was astonished by the hermit's passion. It rose up like a flame—the candlelight illuminating the hut where he'd written his confession. I put these pages on the table under the lamp and I remembered a cold night when Linda and I were lying under a down comforter, nearly asleep. I touched her hair behind her ear and she put her hand on my shoulder. I caressed her hair and we kissed; she brought my hand between her legs, I brought her hand between mine. She moved beneath me and again we kissed. Her tongue was in my mouth when I entered her. "Oh yes," she whispered. She hooked her legs over mine, pulling me further down. We rocked wildly on the bed, Linda was moaning, and then we rested. We made love again, we rested, finally we fell asleep in each other's arms.

7

False Color

When I met Doctor Pell the next morning I felt he was trying to win my friendship. Not that he approved of me—he couldn't approve of a man who wanted to take his daughter from him—but I think he wanted my allegiance in his struggle with his family. He was already in his flowerbeds, Annette said, as we sat down to scrambled eggs and toast. Coffee.

"Did you sleep well, Dick?"

I hadn't. I'd gone to bed tired but I was anxious about Linda and I slept badly. I didn't want to explain. "The air is wonderful," I said.

"It *is* lovely," she said.

"The night was very still."

"It usually is." She buttered a slice of toast but ate nothing. "Unless I get carried away," she said. "Then it isn't so peaceful, is it?" Her glance fled around the glimmering room. From the chrome sink to the glass clock. "I'm afraid you saw me lose my dignity." She set down her cup. Trembling, she rose. "It must be dreadful when a woman behaves like that."

"You haven't lost your dignity." I saw again how intense she was. "I've always thought you were very restrained."

Her palms flat against her skirt, she looked at once eager and helpless. "Only wild things need restraint, dear."

"You're more civilized than the rest of us."

"I pretend to be. But you mustn't believe it. Pell women are wicked." Annette, smiling, turned away. It was a smile meant to put both of us at ease, and I went out to find her husband.

Doctor Pell knelt among the iris, his hands in the soil. A pale green still enfolded their buds but dozens of others were in bloom. Some were the white and blue bearded iris I'd seen in the valley. "These need only a little attention now," he said, weeding among them. "Keep their beds clean, that's the main thing. And let them see the sun. It's worth the effort for colors like this. Don't you agree?"

Iris bloomed across the front of the house in beds set one below the other, and a small bed was in blossom down by the lake. "Linda told me they'd look terrific. And they do," I said. "But I need to speak with you about the NEPA project."

"I'll just wash up."

"Fine," I said.

"I can come back to this," he said, but he didn't get up. From his knees he pointed out the orchid-like blossoms of the spuria iris with white and violet petals. It towered over others with their delicate tongues of bronze, marble, lavender. He'd mixed bark into the soil, and when he finally stood up he brushed it from his knees. "Lovely, lovely. So healthy I'll need to thin them out. Strange world, isn't it? The strong kill each other off and the weak sprout up like weeds. Look over here." He dragged a hose down to a bed of flat blossoms, pink and purple and rose, embossed with thin stripes. The Japanese iris, he said, was unlike any other. "It drinks like a fish. This downhill drainage helps but I still have to soak them." He looked up. "I'm keeping you waiting? All right. Let's go around to my study and we'll discuss Mr. Geyer's project."

"That's why I'm here."

"Is it?" He stood up. "I did wonder, Dick, if you came to see me or my daughter." It wasn't exactly a question so I chose not to answer. He set the hose at the edge of the border, letting the water seep into the soil. We walked around the porch to the back. A piano sounded where a window opened onto the woods. Annette's playing was fitful and jittery rhythms rushed through the stillness of the morning.

In his study her husband had arranged rock samples on his bookshelves; the only furniture was his desk, with these photos of his wife and daughter in their double frame, and a swivel chair.

"Please sit."

"No," I said. "I'm fine."

He sat on the edge of his desk, bolt upright, ready to rise. Did he expect to be interrupted, or joined by someone? Maybe his daughter.

"Have you heard from Linda?"

"When I phoned the ranger station this morning," he replied, "I left a message from her mother."

"Her mother?"

Doctor Pell frowned; he didn't like his tactics to be questioned. But he revealed his temper only in his dead-level voice: "I don't want Linda to think I'm hounding her. Or following her every move." He was; but I didn't know it at the time. "I'm sure you understand," he said. "She's not a child anymore."

"Do you expect her this morning?"

"I think we can count on it."

I sat down.

He switched on a lamp, throwing light over a huge picture above his desk, a photo of Lassen Volcanic Park and Lake Elaine. Shot from a high-flying jet from NASA using film sensitive to infrared light, the picture was printed in false color. It showed green forest in fire red, as if this entire region had burst into flames. Dark red for the conifers; lighter reds for hardwoods. The coolest color, purple, indicated rocks. The hottest was white. Patches of white among purple meant steam escaping between rocks. Volcanic areas with potential for erupting or exploding were numbered with pins.

"Where are we?" I asked.

He pointed out the lake region. In the midst of a flame-colored forest Lake Elaine was light blue, like a fragment of glass. "Our house is right about here," he said, tapping the shore of the lake. The NASA flight had passed over at dawn when the ground was cool. The camera had seen into the heat emitted from growth and decay in the forest; from the magma, mud, steam, and gas of the volcanic field. "There's a fly-over every month to check the hot spots."

While that picture in false color dominated the wall above his desk, his whole study was a gallery honoring his family. Or something else. On the walls around us were the photographs from his office at Mount St. Helens and more: a half-dozen photos of his parents in black and white or a sepia tint; that picture of Father Ted I'd seen at Mount St. Helens; and at least a dozen more, in color, of Linda and Annette. "My parents. My family," he said, pushing off from the desk to point with pride to one picture after another, walking about the room. Linda in a stroller. In her mother's arms, frowning; in her father's arms, grinning. In a cowgirl costume. "Six years old," he said, "and she wanted to ride a horse." Linda in a graduate's gown. Annette, quite young, in a ball gown. Later, in jeans and a blouse, seated in the boat by the pier. Between the pillars at the front of the house with her husband's arm around her, smiling. Down at the pier again looking frightened as she held a large fish. "What a lovely lady," he said. "I'm a lucky man."

"This is one I remember," I said, finding among the photos the sketch of a blue iris Linda had bought for him in Chinatown, that day when a small boy fell from a cart and hurt himself. Next to the iris was Doctor Pell's gun rack; his rifle and a 12-gauge shotgun with a deeply polished walnut stock. Duck decoys rested on one bookcase, and on the other were trophies Linda had won for riding. Propped among these was a framed snapshot: Linda, her arm around a girl with braided blond hair—her friend Sarah Hack?—both girls holding trophies, the blond girl smiling. Glossy ribbons were hung above the trophies. Twice in her teens, her father told me, she'd won prizes in barrel racing in the rodeo; the others were second and third place awards for sprints, riding Blueboy.

I was told all of this by Linda's father in a confiding voice. If he was boasting it wasn't about his wife's fragile grace or his daughter's horsemanship. The point I was meant to see was that these people enclosed him; he was here at the center, always within reach of each of them. The family photos then were trophies too. Prizes he'd won. Turning away, I went back to the gun rack to admire that burnished walnut stock.

"Do you shoot with this?"

"In season," he said.

"This is wonderful work."

"Do you know woodcraft?"

"Only what I learned from my father."

"He was skilled?"

"Yes," I said. "I thought so."

"You'll appreciate this." From the bookshelves he brought a wooden model of a battleship. The same ship I'd seen in that photo of his parents, the *U.S.S. Arizona.* Working in Hawaii with Kurowski, he'd bought this model on a visit to Pearl Harbor. "Not far from where we lived when the war began." Carefully he set it on the desk. Its detail was extraordinary: the guns in their turrets, a towering foremast, intricate rigging, tiny flags. I thought first of my father's fondness for carving. Then I remembered those figures Jules Beauregard made for his son: the owl, hawk, and deer. "This is splendid," I said.

"My father died on that ship," he said.

I returned to the chair and sat down. "I'm sorry."

"The day the Japs bombed Pearl Harbor. I was nine. Ted was two." He paused. "I want to tell you this," he said.

"It's all right," I said.

"The *Arizona* was moored at one end of Battleship Row. It was destroyed in the first-wave attack. The Japs threw everything at those ships. They bombed them to hell, then strafed the survivors."

"Your father had no chance."

"None. The bombing and strafing had begun. The ship already was on fire. He was at his gun station, here," he pointed to the model, "when a bomb hit this forward magazine and the ship exploded. The concussion blasted him into the air—blew his clothes off, all but his steel helmet. He came down, struck the deck, somehow got to his feet. His back must have been broken; I don't know how he did it. A pharmacist's mate told a reporter he landed in a pool of flaming oil. He leaped up but he was burning alive. He stood there while the flames ate everything but his helmet. Just burned him black. Then he fell into the water. Next day when his body was hauled from the harbor—they roped it; dragged it in behind the boat—it was a charred pulp. Like many others. They recovered his helmet and his wedding ring."

"I'm very sorry," I said.

"Of course." Reticent, he looked at the photo of Linda and her friend. "Why do I tell you this? You aren't one of us."

"That may be the reason."

"I suppose it is."

On the far wall was his map of the hazard zones in Lassen Park, like the one at Mount St. Helens with its colored circles and its list of hazards: hot mud, avalanches, ash, scalding steam. It looked like thorough work and I told him so.

"My work *is* reliable," he said. "Whether Lassen is reliable is another question. That volcano hasn't read my map." Next to his map was a Department of the Interior poster:

SCENES OF DEFORMATION

The upper half showed volcanic domes raised by the pressure of magma and steam beneath the earth's surface. The lower half was a photograph of surveyors at work in a rock-strewn area of Lassen Park while a small girl watched from a distance. One of the men was a younger Doctor Pell and the girl was Linda. "I brought her with me that day so she'd be in the photo. She was tickled when those posters were printed. Nine years old, and her picture was sent to universities all over the country."

"You're awfully proud of her."

"Yes." His blue eyes were quick and confiding. "Proud, but terribly disappointed. I've wanted so much for her. You know, Dick, when Linda left for Stanford I wept. I watched her car pull onto the road, I started to cry, I couldn't stop. I thought of what I'd wanted to do for her. All that I'd wanted to give her: love, education, confidence. But there was no more time."

"Linda knows how much you care."

"But it breaks my heart that she's abandoned her training. She won't go on to earn her Ph.D., I've given up on it. I don't blame you—she'd made her decision before you met her. Maybe when she first went to work in the lab and saw she could do something on her own, besides her riding. I don't know. It's a damn shame, Dick. She's thrown away every opportunity I've given her." With the Forest Service she was clearing trails in the park as snowmelt allowed crews to open the roads. "Anybody can do that. And it's seasonal—it only lasts through the summer."

"Will she come back to the lab?"

"If she wishes. Do you know Kurowski?"

"I phoned him when I was looking for Linda."

"We're old pals," he said. "We met in grad school and we've worked together two or three times since. In Hawaii. In Mexico. He'll be glad to see Linda come back, I'm sure."

"If she does. She told me she enjoys field work."

"And you remembered that." His eyes beamed approval while he sat with his arms straight, his hands covering the stains on his knees. "Dick, you want what's best for her too."

"I do now."

His quick eyes looked wary.

"You didn't until now?"

"I'm still learning."

"Aren't we all," he said. "Tell me what I need to learn about NEPA. What does Noah Geyer expect from me?"

"The voice of authority. When you go before the public," I said. I saw his eyes fill with surprise. "That's what he wants."

"He believes I'll bring authority to the project." He half-smiled. "What do *you* think?"

"Noah's judgment matters more than mine."

"I'll decide that."

"I think he's made the right choice," I said. "I'm here to help you think so."

"Thank you, sir."

I told him what Washington wanted: an emergency response that included the lumber companies, resorts, power plants. A coordinated effort to save lives and property. "We need that one individual who can speak out, in a practical, forceful way, for the scientific community."

"That person doesn't exist." His face tightened; the idea was distasteful to him. "No one scientist speaks for another."

"It would help if you did."

"I don't agree."

"If an eruption occurs," I argued, "we have to avoid the chaos of the past. And the deaths."

"For safety's sake," he conceded, "it *is* better for science to speak with one voice. If we can save one life."

"Then you'll consider the appointment."

"I'll consider it. But I don't see why Noah Geyer has selected me, of all people."

"You'll be out front—talking tough to the public and the media. We need a person who commands their respect."

"I'm flattered if he thinks I do." He riffled pages in a desk calendar next to his photos of Annette and Linda. "I'll give you my answer before you leave."

"Do you mind if I tell Linda? She'll be pleased that her father was our first choice."

"Tell her if you wish." His gaze found her bright ribbons on the wall. "But everything in this world changes. You know that as well as I do."

"Is she riding again?"

"She is."

Linda boarded her horse, Blueboy, at Sawyers' Stables. "You passed it on the way up," he said with that unhappy smile. I remembered a small house, and horses put to pasture. "The Sawyers were good people. They've turned it over to a young hand who used to muck stables. Akira Jagao." He pronounced the name with a delicate precision and waited for my response. I said nothing. Casually, he added, "We call him A.J."

"He looks after Linda's horse?"

"He manages the whole place now. The Sawyers retired to a trailer park in Sacramento."

Until that moment I'd thought nothing about the fact that Linda and her uncle both were unexpectedly absent last night. Now her father, who did most things deliberately, was telling me about a young man he obviously disliked. I didn't want to see a connection but he'd put the thought in my mind.

"Father Ted knows A.J.?"

"We all do." Frowning, he got to his feet.

Then we went outside and everything was fine. A graceful melody flowed between the house and the close-standing woods. In the shadows and sunlight whatever stirred—the dark boughs or bright grass—was moved by that music. Not Annette's nervous energy now but the charm of the piece she was playing. Its rhythms, its serenity, had become her own. Tipping his head, her husband listened with appreciation. "She loves Chopin," he remarked.

As we came around the porch he stopped.

Two people had stepped from the woods, walking quickly across the lawn. Linda wore jeans and a purple sweater, and her march-like step kept pace with the young man striding beside her. He moved in a jaunty way, arms swinging freely, down to where the water was running among the iris. He shrugged off his backpack and dropped to one knee beside the flowers. As he bowed his head his black hair blazed in the sun. Kneeling over the gleaming blossoms, he picked up the hose and began to drink.

8

Making Plans

Turning the tap beside the porch, Doctor Pell shut off the water. "I see A.J. came with her," he said.

Gulping eagerly, Akira Jagao suddenly watched the water fall away from his mouth. He knelt by the flowerbed staring at the empty hose. Then he glanced over his shoulder and saw us approaching on the stone path. He sprang up with a sunny smile as if Doctor Pell had played a prank on him and he meant to show us that he enjoyed the joke.

"Good morning," Akira offered but he received no reply. He smiled at the hose lying at his feet. He kicked at it with the scuffed toe of his boot. He had high cheekbones and straight black hair down to his shoulders, and his brown eyes continued smiling. He wore jeans and a leather jacket that hung open, the leather soiled and scraped and the sleeves crinkled at the elbows. "We went for a hike in the woods, Doctor Pell."

Linda's father ignored him. His joy at seeing his daughter—joy and relief—leaped into his eyes, though he suppressed any greeting. The breeze off the water brushed his sandy hair while his face flamed in furious silence.

I was watching her with my heart slamming under my ribs. She looked so small there on the lawn with the wide lake behind her and the mountains beyond the lake. But vivid as a flame with the light of the lake and the morning sun in her hair. I came to her and put my arms around her and she hid her face in my chest. "Hello, love," I said. "It's been a long time."

"It's been too long." Linda looked up and we kissed. "Sorry I wasn't here to welcome you. I thought this would be best. Now our time is our own."

"It's all right," I said. "It's fine."

We kissed again. Linda wore no makeup, only sun lotion, and I noticed the resin scent of the pines. Holding her for the first time in months, I smelled that fragrance in her hair. "I've missed you," I said. "What were you doing in the park?"

Linda stepped back gravely.

"I want you to meet Akira."

I went on looking at Linda, at her red hair in the sunlight, her mouth firm with purpose. In the silence of her eyes I was looking for the letters we didn't write and the time we'd lost. When I realized I was being rude I put out my hand to her friend.

Akira Jagao stood by the flowerbed, grinning, letting me wait. His air of contentment suggested he was certain to accomplish something important. Meanwhile, he found life so fine and amusing because of what it promised him. Finally he grasped my hand. "Happy to meet you, Mr. Darwin."

"It's my pleasure."

Even that amused him. Full of good spirits, he stood smiling in the sunlight. "Not at all. The pleasure is all mine, Mr. Darwin."

I waited for an explanation. What was he doing here? In an awkward silence Linda came over and put her arms around her father. "Good morning, Daddy."

He held her at arms' length. His hands clenched her shoulders. "Your mother has been worried sick." He said nothing about himself; he pretended it was only Annette's anguish that mattered. "You know how she worries when you're alone in the park."

"I wasn't alone."

"A.J. was with you?"

"And Father Ted."

"Ah—"

"And Teresa. She drove A.J. and Father Ted."

"The four of you were there last night?"

"Yes," said Linda.

Doctor Pell frowned while the breeze off the lake tousled his hair. "Tell me—what was the idea, anyway?"

"I was working late and I decided to spend the night. I explained that to Mother. I told my crew boss. And I told Wally Hack where he could find me. Sarah, too.

Hack was the chief ranger in the park and his daughter, Sarah, had been Linda's best friend. Doctor Pell sent me a questioning look. I'd been piecing together a picture of the four of them in Lassen Park last night, and it began to make sense. Only later did I learn how much of it was a lie. A tactful lie to placate her father. I can't say I blame Linda for that, but I wish I'd understood it at the time.

"A.J. phoned and he wanted to join me. I said not just the two of us." She glanced at A.J. and he quit grinning. "So he called Teresa and she brought him to the park with Father Ted."

"I know you can manage by yourself." Her father released Linda from his grip. "But your mother doesn't quite believe it. You ought to have told her Father Ted was with you. She was nearly out of her mind. You can imagine the scene she made."

"I'm so sorry." Stricken, Linda clutched her sweater.

"She's at the piano now. Let her know you're home."

"I'll go in and see her."

"Good girl."

Linda stiffened, she didn't like that. If she meant to be his obedient daughter a moment before, now she wouldn't budge. She swung around to A.J. and touched the elbow of his jacket.

"Do you want to come in and wash up?"

"I'm going down to the boathouse," he said.

"What for?"

"A swim to cool off."

"That's crazy. You'll freeze."

"Look at that water." He smiled. "It's beautiful." Lake Elaine was radiant in the broadening sunlight.

"I mean it," said Linda. "You'll turn blue."

"It's okay." He was lean and his jacket slipped across his shoulders as he walked away. The boathouse was an old stone structure at the far end of the lawn. A.J. sauntered down to the shore, shedding his jacket as he went.

"I'll go cheer up Mother," said Linda.

Those twin benches at the end of the pier had been freshly painted in preparation for the party. When we were here last night I'd seen the safety lamp but not the bell suspended from the opposite post. Guests who came by boat tied in at the pier, then announced their arrival by clanging the bell. Now we drew the Pells' boat alongside the pier—it was an old motor launch maintained in fine condition—and climbed aboard. Doctor Pell slumped comfortably behind the wheel and gauges; on my side was a clock that actually ran, and I found a toolbox beneath the windshield.

"Let's have a look in that box," he said. "We just might need to fix something. Like this damned day."

I snapped open the lid. Inside was a pint of Scotch and two cups. "Keep any tools in here?"

"Why should I?" He laughed. "They'd just get wet." He'd stocked plenty of liquor for the party, he said, but he kept one bottle on the boat, always. "For my friends," he said.

A strange comment from this solitary man. Was I his friend? Apart from Kurowski, and perhaps Wally Hack, did he have any others? I broke the bottle's seal and poured our drinks.

The duck blind that had worried LeFevre was built of brush and wire on a raft anchored on the water. Over by the boathouse A.J. had stripped to his shorts. Two rows of boulders were thrust into the lake for a breakwater; he strolled onto the boulders and looked down at the shining water. I thought he might dive from there but he walked back onto the grass.

"Lost his nerve," said Doctor Pell.

From the shore he waded out slowly. Holding himself against the chill, he inched into deeper water until the cold ripples reached his thighs. Immediately he flung himself forward, hacking at the water, thrashing toward the bobbing clump of brush.

"He's not very good, is he?"

"No." I watched A.J. lunging through the water. "But he seems to enjoy it."

"Tell me something he doesn't enjoy," said Doctor Pell. So he'd noticed that unflagging happiness and he resented it as much as I did.

"He's so damn cheerful," I said.

Doctor Pell sipped his drink.

"Is he always so respectful?"

"Dick, that doesn't mean he respects you or me. What he does respect," he said, "is the distance he keeps between himself and us. That's why he calls me *Doctor* Pell though I've known him for years. He'll call you *Mister* Darwin for the rest of his life."

Halfway to the duck blind A.J., rolling onto his back, flailed at the sky. But he gave up his backstroke when his face dipped underwater. He rolled again, thrashed out, and with his awkward overarm stroke he started swimming back.

"He didn't last long, did he?"

"No."

"Linda says you're an excellent swimmer."

"I grew up in the water." I told him about our boat dock outside of Mingus.

"Abner Darwin was your father?"

"Yes."

"Darwin's Dock!" He finished his drink. "I didn't know that was your family's place. It's been there for ages."

"Thomas Darwin built it. My great-grandfather."

"At the start of the gold rush."

"That's right."

In the spring of 1849, after gold was found down at Sutter's Mill, my father's grandfather built a dock on the east bank of the Sacramento River. For two generations the landing thrived as wheat barges and sternwheel passenger boats moved up and down the waterway. But railroads and trucking killed off river traffic. Now people drive out from Mingus for fishing and boating, bait and tackle. On weekends couples come for lunch or supper on the deck, or a party on the houseboat alongshore. I told Doctor Pell why I sold the dock; the landing and store.

"But it gave you an education," he said, his hand on the wheel of the boat as he watched A.J. laboring through the water. "And you learned to swim. A hell of a lot better than that—"

"I suppose so,"

"Hell, sir. You know you can."

"Yes."

Doctor Pell first looked puzzled. Then pleased. "You ought to race each other. See how he takes to competition."

I kept silent. Later I wondered if this was the moment he first saw how he might save what he loved and destroy what threatened it? Today I tell myself I suspected nothing. This much at least is true: that morning as we sat in his boat I had no idea what was forming in his mind. I poured him another drink and tried to ignore his agonizing smile.

"Why not?" he asked.

"I don't race anymore."

"From the boathouse to the blind. That's not too far."

"No, it isn't too far."

"But you won't do it."

"No." I thought of my father. Both of us at supper in the kitchen of our house above the river. On a winter evening when the dock was deserted and we'd brought up the small boats from their moorings. We could hear the walls creaking while a cold rain swept downriver, drenching the valley. "I don't want to race anyone," I said. "I wouldn't enjoy it. It doesn't mean what it used to. Anyway, I don't think A.J. would go for it either."

"I say you're mistaken about that."

A.J. had reached shallow water and stopped swimming. He stood hip-deep in the lake, sunlight glistening on his black hair, his narrow chest, the rope-like muscles of his arms.

"You don't like him much, do you?"

"Not especially." He watched A.J. wade to the shore. Linda had come down from the house with a towel. "We get along, you and I," her father said. "We see things for what they are."

"What do you see over there?"

"Trouble."

Doctor Pell put aside his cup and started the engine. It coughed, then caught; he let it idle. His hands trembled on the wheel as the hull throbbed. "Go for a spin?"

"Another time." I didn't want to leave A.J. alone with Linda. I stepped out and tossed the lines into the boat; it lurched from the pier and roared away.

A.J. had followed Linda back to the house and I went up the path to wait. Coming out between the pillars, with A.J. behind her, Linda carried a cloth shoulder bag. They started toward her car. "Mother wants her medication." Linda stood with her hands at her sides, helpless. "And I need to take A.J. home."

A.J. grinned and said nothing.

He managed the stables where she boarded her horse, that was all. It was stupid to think she shared his infatuation.

But I didn't like to see them together. "I'll drive," I said. Smiling with relief, Linda took my arm. "Would you, Dick?"

"We'll go through the park. I need to see Wally Hack. I'll tell him what Noah has in mind and how the Park Service can help."

"He's in his office until noon."

"I won't be long."

"You're very sweet."

"You know I'm not."

"We'll have a picnic. I'll make sandwiches and coffee."

"Will you bring your flute?" I said.

"Oh yes!"

At her warm look A.J. turned to me, pushing his hands deep in his pockets. "I'll bring my guitar. It's in her car."

We'd made our plans, then Linda went into the house and I walked down to the pier with A.J. Waves lapped at the pilings. The sun was well up, glaring on the lake. "It still looks cold."

"Cold?" He laughed. "I froze my ass."

That's when I began to wonder about A.J. Beneath his carefree manner was a deep pride, I thought, and a fear of shame. He'd kept up his clumsy effort in the water so he wouldn't be embarrassed in front of us. I had to admit a grudging respect for him. It occurred to me that Linda must have told A.J. about us. All right, I understood what had happened: She'd gone to the stables to work her horse. And A.J., without encouragement, fell hopelessly in love with her. When she told him I was coming to visit her it hurt him to learn we'd been living together. He must have regarded me with the same attention—curious, distrustful—I'd been giving him. I didn't like to think she meant so much to him. But in a small way I tried to make peace with him. "I know the water's cold. I wouldn't have cared if you quit."

"That didn't worry me, Mr. Darwin."

"Really? I think it did."

"No." A.J. shrugged. "Not at all."

"Then why did you go on?"

"You weren't the only one watching," he said.

Gulls picked among the stones near our feet. Looking up, we saw Doctor Pell's boat cut across the water. Turning for home, it veered toward the blind, and for a moment it was out of sight. The blind pitched sharply as the boat droned behind it.

9

The Ring of Fire

The woods were aspen and pine and from the park road we saw deer standing in deep shade. Where the road made a right turn a fawn sprinted across and Linda cried out. We drove up to the Visitors Center. Linda sat taut, withdrawn. It wasn't only the danger of running down that deer. Something else troubled her but she couldn't say what it was.

I found Wally Hack in his office; a short, tightly built man, almost bald, with a brown mustache. Not everyone is happy to sit listening to a NEPA agent, but Hack seemed reasonable. A good listener, he was patient with others but impatient with himself. He let me lay out Noah Geyer's project with a nod of understanding. But once he began to respond he picked up a pencil and started bouncing its eraser on his desktop. Was Washington committed to emergency funding? "Yes." *Tap. Tap tap tap.* Did NEPA understand the Office of Emergency Services had first call on equipment? "Yes." *Tap; tap tap tap.* Our focus was on coordination and safety? "Exactly." *Tap tap...*The walls were pine, and on the door was a calendar photo of Lassen Peak, like those of Mount St. Helens I'd seen last year. Hack promised his cooperation. All he asked in return was that Washington protect his budget. *Tap tap tap.* I stood up to leave.

Wally Hack dealt with stranded hikers, drunk drivers, boating accidents, a range of folly and disaster. So I wasn't surprised to find him willing to help. But I couldn't see Danny LeFevre on his staff. Stopping in the doorway, I asked about that. He set down his pencil: "You know Danny?"

"I met him last night. He had boat patrol."

"Thursday," he recalled. "Why, yes. He did."

Hack impressed me as fair-minded and I wanted his opinion. "What do you think? Does he do credit to that badge?"

"He's been a big disappointment. Well. Actually. A pain in the ass," he added harshly. LeFevre must have exhausted his patience. "He has time for everything but his job."

"You've told him this?"

"Many times." He put down his pencil. "His weakness is booze and babes. That's what he says: 'It's booze and babes.' He's proud of it. I've chewed him out." He laughed softly. "Cussed him out when he came around to see our Sarah."

"Your daughter?"

"Winnie and I were worried." His hand brushed his mustache. "But Sarah saw through him. She's known him for years. Or known about him. She turned him away. But he's always on the make."

"He'll transfer out of here."

"Actually, we're stuck with him. He'll get no recommendation from me so he isn't likely to apply anywhere else. But he's so fond of himself I doubt if he cares what I think." Wally Hack seemed resigned to deal with one more folly. He pressed his pencil with both thumbs. "If you ask me he's a natural-born salesman who got lost in the woods. Damned if I know what he's doing here. But, then, neither does he."

I met Linda and A.J. outside the Visitors Center and Linda looked anxious. "You haven't seen our exhibit, have you?"

"No," I said. "And I want to."

A.J. sprang to open the door and Linda went in. I noticed how doggedly he remained beside her, anticipating her every step. I did not know then that such constant courtesy—because it's not quite natural—is a sign of kindness, and a mark of imagination. For he had always to imagine how he might be helpful or courteous to someone in an unobtrusive way. And he was, unfailingly. Impetuous, charming, he was so polite he seemed to unnerve Linda. She paused to speak but changed her mind and marched through the lobby in silence. He held the door as an older couple entered, and while we had a moment alone I took her arm.

"What is it?" I asked. A.J. was eager, attentive, and Linda was upset. "You're very tense," I said.

"I'm quite all right."

"You're not all right. You were here last night, weren't you? In the park. And something went wrong. What happened?"

"Nothing has happened. I'll be fine. If he'll just leave me alone for a while."

A.J. caught up and we walked through the lobby together. The Center was built of pine and stone and the rooms were cool. Parents led children through the exhibition wing with its photos of the surrounding lakes and mountains. On one wall were posters like the one Linda appeared in when she was nine. The older couple stood before the first poster; the woman was reading the caption aloud: Lassen Peak sits in a field of steam vents and lava ducts, she explained, and all the mountains around us are volcanoes. Her husband nodded thoughtfully.

Chunks of lava were displayed on one table, on another were arrowheads and Indian baskets. This was where the Yahi came in summer when they left the oven-heat of the canyons to follow the deer into the forest. Ishi came hunting bear and deer with bow and arrows, trapping raccoons with snares. Under a glass cover lay the shafts of arrows; a quiver made of an animal skin; a snare of braided hemp. I thought of Jules Beauregard with his heart full of guilt living his last years in the monastery. *Love changes me,* he wrote: *And I fear my desire...*

A.J. followed Linda everywhere as we moved among the exhibits. I used to hold her hand when we walked in the city, but A.J., for all his constant attention, hadn't touched her since we met on the lawn. But he often gazed at Linda as if he was waiting for her to answer a question he hadn't dared to ask. Even with that unspoken hope in his eyes he looked happy.

What if he *was* in love with her?

It was ridiculous to be jealous of this avid young man who was too easily happy; too pleasing. His undaunted eagerness had made him appear even younger than Linda. And made his fine manners seem antiquated, a courtesy at times so solicitous it grated on her. She stepped briskly from one exhibit to another without comment. But I'd known that stiff silence, her jaw firm, her mouth set, when she couldn't bring herself to speak about what troubled her. Not until she broke down and cried. Sitting on the bed at night, trembling, weeping.

Now, suddenly, she sat down before the main exhibit. A map of the Pacific Ocean and its coastlines was painted on a panel. Red bulbs marked volcanoes around the ocean rim, the Ring of Fire, an irregular oval that a string of Christmas lights might make if you laid it down on the face of a map:

1. KATMAI	7. LASSEN	13. TARAWERA
2. BAKER	8. PARICUTIN	14. LAMINGTON
3. RAINIER	9. COTOPAXI	15. KRAKATOA
4. ST. HELENS	10. EL MISTI	16. MAYON
5. HOOD	11. CALBUCO	17. FUJI
6. SHASTA	12. EREBUS	18. SARYCHEV

Press a button and a bulb brightened where each volcano stood on the Ring of Fire. A screen presented the volcano's history.

Linda pressed the first button. High on the map, at the edge of Alaska, Katmai flashed on. She pressed the next button. In the state of Washington a bulb burned, fire-red, as Mount Baker erupted.

"Don't start this," A.J. urged, and I'd soon see why.

She pressed the next button and Mount Rainier flamed up.

"Will you stop?" he pleaded.

She pressed the next one. Mount St. Helens. The massive eruption we'd witnessed together. Linda worked down one side of the ring into Oregon:

Mount Hood. Down to California for Mount Shasta. Next was Lassen Peak. The pines, the deer. This building itself. Buried under simmering ashes.

Over the South Pacific a light flashed for Tarawera. Now a bulb burned for three thousand killed in the blast as Mount Lamington heaved up a hot cloud over New Guinea. In the Philippines the deadly explosion of Krakatoa. From Mayon the destruction rose to Fuji, then to Sarychev. From Russia it crossed the Aleutian chain to Katmai on the North American coast, completing the ring.

Linda's face was flushed. On the map all eighteen bulbs were blazing. "What do you think?"

"It's s tremendous exhibit," I said. "Your father's?"

"Daddy's design."

She flipped the switch and the map went dark. Behind us the children had held their breath at the huge display of destruction. Now, on a sigh of relief, they drifted away. When she rose, A.J. was at her side.

"You enjoyed that," he accused her.

"People find it interesting," she replied.

"If you think about it," he said quietly, "it's terrifying." Linda looked startled when he corrected her. "Forgive me."

I left the car beside a large snow-rimmed rock. The sun was strong but the air felt cool. Linda had her flute and her father's blue blanket, and I brought the basket with our drinks and the food.

Above the timberline the slopes were white. Below us the snow had melted from the meadows, the grass glistened, wild flowers bloomed in clusters of purple, blue, yellow. The whole region looked unmarked, but Linda's crew had been clearing trails down there for weeks and she found a path. We hiked around the rubble of an old avalanche, into a valley of hot springs. Clouds formed swiftly over the grass, then they vanished.

From the edge of this valley you could see Lassen Peak, solid and blazing white, a wisp of steam above the crater, the scars of black lava on its flanks. The trail led out of the valley onto bare slopes where steam billowed up from cracks in the earth. A warning was posted:

<u>DANGER</u>
Mud pots, fumaroles
and pools are hot,
ground crust is thin
<u>Stay On Trails</u>

Murky pools seethed beside us. Water boiled beneath rocks and the sulphurous air smelled like rotting eggs. Mud swirled up, splattering from festering holes. Around us these mud pots bubbled. But under the steam and stench the minerals flushed to the surface had cooled, painting the earth in pastel yellows, greens, and a delicate copper color.

Crossing a creek, we hiked through lupine and scarlet paintbrush. Beside a small blue lake A.J. dropped to his knees. "Mr. Darwin, did you ever see anything like this?"

Bubbles rose as if the water was boiling but I couldn't feel any warmth from it.

"It's gas," said Linda.

"Is it hot?"

"Put your hands in."

I knelt next to A.J. and plunged my hands into the water. Bubbles rose around my wrists but the water was so cold my hands stung when I pulled them out; I rubbed them hard before I could pick up the basket. I saw Linda's little smile. "This is Cold Boiling Lake," she said.

"It's crazy."

"Daddy says this park is a tourist's view of hell. Boiling hot in one place. Ice cold in another. But it's beautiful."

It *was* beautiful. We pushed through meadows and thick hemlocks until we came to a creek. Alpine shooting stars had opened violet petals and their fragrance floated on the grass.

While A.J. spread our blanket Linda unwrapped sandwiches. I opened the thermos and poured the coffee before A.J. could offer to do it. Or Linda. I didn't want to witness any intimacy between them. Did she make coffee for him this morning before they came to the lake? Did he hand her a cup like this, watching her, waiting on her with his impeccable manners?

As a hawk glided overhead I remembered that photo printed in false color. The plane passing over to map the earth's energy. Here the evidence of a violent creation was all around us: mineral deposits beside mud holes; a scarred and steaming mountain; rock scattered by eruptions; the green pelt of trees ripped by an avalanche. The world before the first man and woman walked in these meadows. I went down to the creek and knelt to drink. The water was clear and cold and walking back I felt the bite of the cold water on my teeth.

We ate sandwiches and drank coffee. Linda unwrapped the cheese and A.J. unsheathed his knife to slice it. He handed her the first piece. He gave me a larger one, leaving the smallest portion for himself.

Lassen Peak was a brilliant white against the blue sky. After we rinsed our cups in the creek Linda sat looking at the glowing mountain. I poured our wine. "Would you still push the button?" A.J. asked. She was silent but he persisted: "Why did you do it?"

"Just nerves. It was foolish." She shook her red hair. She picked at the grass beside the blanket. "I had to do something."

"For no reason," A.J. said. I was mistaken to think he cared about nothing. He certainly cared about what had happened in the Visitors Center. "If that mountain blew–" he said.

A woodpecker hammered in the grove behind us. Linda put down her cup. "Please don't," she said.

"If it blew, this minute, what would you do?"

"Please let's talk about something else."

"There *is* nothing else." Sitting with his back to the mountain, he'd taken on that easy manner again. "What about you, Mr. Darwin? What would you do?"

"After the blast?"

"Yes."

"No one knows until that happens."

A.J. laughed. "And then you know nothing."

"Please let's not talk about this," said Linda.

"How much time would we have?" A.J. asked.

"Not much," I replied.

"Not enough time to run."

"Where could you run from the gas?" I asked. "Or the ash?"

"Then what do we do when we see it coming?" He smiled. "Do we sit here drinking wine?"

Linda clenched her hands in her lap.

"You heard Mr. Darwin. There isn't a moment to waste."

"I suppose there's time to pray," she said.

"Would you pray?"

Her fingers probed the blue blanket. "I don't think so." The woodpecker hammered again.

"It would be exciting," A.J. suggested softly, "to make love then. In the last moments. *Our* last moments."

He waited eagerly but Linda was silent. She looked up and I knew that cool gaze. "We should comfort each other," she said.

I was suddenly ashamed, remembering that family in the camper at Mount St. Helens. The fisherman with his temper. Trying to bully the young trooper. In the end he did what he could for his family. And died. His boots were scorched onto his legs.

"How do we comfort each other?" I asked.

"We might sit quietly together."

"Is that all?" A.J. asked. "Is that all we can hope for?"

"When there isn't any hope," Linda said, "at least we can set an example."

"Who will see it?" I said.

"Anyone who survives."

I found myself asking A.J.'s question: Is that all? But perhaps Linda was right. The fisherman set an example and in the end you overlooked his bad temper; what lasted was the painful memory of his love. His effort to save his family. This was Abbot Stanley's message to the monks at The Gate of Heaven, wasn't it? After the fire marshal's lecture. Are we not a family? he'd asked. Then he urged them to set an example for each other.

"Nature calls," A.J. announced. "I must ask you to excuse me. Please." He crossed the meadow to the grove behind us.

"Your friend is terribly polite. He's charming." Linda, gathering the wrappings from our lunch, didn't reply. A.J. had left his knife. The handle was carved from steer horn with his initials burned into it. "Does he ever use his name?"

"Akira Jagao? Not often."

"I see."

"*Damn* you." She could see I was jealous. Bunching the wrappings in her hands, she dropped them into the basket.

I didn't see why she thought he was so charming. He was cheerful and god-awful polite and obviously in love with her. It must have been a relief to find such devotion after she'd left me in the city. I closed my hand on A.J.'s knife and opened it again. The blade, heavy and cool, had been honed from an iron file.

"He made this?"

"His brother made it for him. When they worked together."

"At the stables."

"No." Linda's hair was full of warm red light. But her mouth was firm and her eyes were like ice. I saw her struggling and I wanted to help her, to hold her, but I wondered about A.J. "I don't want to discuss him," she said.

"I'd like to know more about him."

"Would you?" His family were farmhands near Salinas, she said. After his father died, A.J. went on working the lettuce fields with his mother and his brother. It was stoop labor; he lasted two seasons. Then he told his brother he was determined to leave. And he was given that knife. He hitchhiked to the tomato fields near Sacramento. The next year the peach orchards. Then he helped to harvest an almond crop near Mingus, working his way up the valley to Crags Landing where he was jailed as an alien. He had no papers, no green card, he hadn't needed any, his parents had been Japanese but he was born in California. Still, when the court learned his mother had died he was held as a vagrant. Father Ted heard of his predicament and intervened. "He knew all the kids in Crags Landing. All the young people. He knows when they're in trouble. He called Old Hannah. She had A.J. made a ward of the court; then Father Ted had him placed with the Sawyers."

"And his brother?"

"He went into the Forest Service."

"Where is he now?"

"He was pruning trees at Mount St. Helens. Planting, pruning. Clearing trails. They wrote letters. They never saw each other again."

"He died in the blast."

"Yes."

"Linda." I took her hand. "I'm sorry."

"He was much too close. He never had a chance."

All those dead. We saw them. Their orange hair and shrunken bodies. Corpses brought down to us by the helicopters and left in green bags beside the road. Any one of those that had passed through my hands might have been Akira Jagao's brother.

"I'm very sorry," I said. "Christ, that's awful."

"It hurt him terribly."

"It was a terrible time." I wanted to tell her it was too bad he'd lost his brother. Christ, it's very bad. But she shouldn't let him fall in love with her because she felt sorry for him.

"It upset him terribly when I lit the Ring of Fire. You saw that," she said. "It was a cruel thing to do."

"What I see," I said, "is that he's devoted to you."

"And you're jealous."

"That's a hell of a thing to say."

"Tell me I'm mistaken," Linda whispered.

But I knew it was true. Linda lowered her head in silence.

I reached for the bottle of wine. "He loves me because I'm here," she said then, with so little breath in her voice I could barely hear her. "He was in love with Sarah Hack—he used to see her at the stables—but he never spoke to her. He's told me so. Sarah says she never had a clue. Not one hint from him—he wouldn't, would he? But he told me, and because I listened, he decided he was in love with me. At least we talked. That meant more than I'd realized. He's very shy." Linda put our napkins in the basket. "I won't be cruel again."

"Tell him I love you. Or I will. He'll recover."

"What makes you say so?"

"Because he's so cheerful."

"Dick, that's his way of hiding from people. Let me tell you a little story." I poured more wine. Linda sat back on the blanket. "One Sunday when I went to Mass he waited for me. He wouldn't enter the church, he waited until I came out. I wore a white dress and we went for a walk by the river. It was early April and families had gathered there. A few children knew him; they'd had riding lessons at the stables. They called, and he called their names, waved back. People were enjoying picnics with their blankets spread like this." Linda stroked her father's woolen blanket. "We hadn't planned anything. I didn't bring a blanket. He wanted me to sit with him the way the others were. On the grass above the river. I didn't want to stain my dress. For an hour we walked back and forth past those parents and their children and he wouldn't speak to me. He was offended because I wouldn't sit with him. As if I was ashamed of him. He tried to hide his feelings. He swung his arms as he walked, smiling at everyone, but he couldn't speak, he was so upset. He has so much pride. Finally I gave in; I said I'd sit on the grass with him. Then before I could sit down he slipped off his jacket and swept it under me in that courtly way of his. He'd planned to do that, to protect my dress. But he couldn't say so because that wasn't the issue in his mind. The issue was whether I was ashamed to sit with him." Linda looked across the meadow toward the trees. "He's as proud as my father but he isn't so obvious about it."

A.J. emerged from the grove zipping his fly. He ambled over with a big grin.

"Feel better?" I asked.

"Much."

"Men have it too easy," Linda said.

"How can you say that?" He was smiling.

"I mean it," she said. "Nature makes that business too easy for men. It's harder work for women." She handed him his guitar. "Will you play something?"

The creek cut across the meadow, then slipped beneath the trees. The damp grass was sweet-smelling. Above the dark fir forest Lassen Peak stood massive and misshapen, the sun on its slopes. When my father was a child the volcano erupted repeatedly. For seven years, he told me, it went on spewing smoke, ash, cinders. Now the snow-hooded mountain glowed above the trees, the quiet creek, and the meadow where we sat.

A.J. strummed a chord.

He tuned his guitar and looked at the forest. "Allow me to play, in this place, a very old piece. *Wilderness Variations* we'll call it." He smiled at Linda, or at himself, as he thrummed the strings with a nervous hand. He bowed his head. "So—"

He began to play.

It was a lovely, lonely piece, and the silence between notes filled the meadow like water forming a pond. Soon each note was a pebble dropped into the pond. A sound heard once and lost. Then its reverberation, the after sound, ringing through the air. To tell the truth, I hadn't wanted to watch A.J. playing; I didn't want to listen. But everything was listening. The cold water. The firs. The mountain. A red bandanna, knotted at one corner, hung from the throat of his guitar where it fluttered, pulsing, as he played.

Linda leaned her head to one side, the way her father did when he was listening to her mother playing Chopin, and her red hair rested on her shoulder.

A.J.'s eyes brimmed with pleasure. "Will you join me?"

Linda took up her flute. Together they played *Greensleeves* wistfully. When they stopped the meadow was still. "Soon it'll be summer in the valley," A.J. said. He nodded toward me as if to say: We share this, you and I, we grew up in the valley. And he was right. "But it's just spring here. Let's play *Sakura.*"

"Oh yes!" Linda beamed. She told me, "It's a song to welcome spring."

A.J.'s guitar at first sounded sad. Then Linda's flute added its silver tone. Together they made a poignant music which turned playful. It rose into the shadows among the firs and the light on the mountain where the sun glared on the snow. Finally a counter-melody was heard, the great breathing stillness of the mountain.

When the song was finished I longed to be alone with Linda. On the blanket in the meadow. But A.J., constant as her shadow, followed every movement, watching for his chance to help her. Had I ever wanted anything for Linda's sake alone? We'd often talked about my assignments, she read my reports. But we never discussed her lab work; she assumed, rightly, that I had little interest in it. And when she wanted to have a child I refused. I'd wondered once about her mother: how could Annette live with Doctor Pell?

A prisoner of her husband. Was that why Linda left; was she afraid her life would be like that? Yes. I watched her close the black case on her flute and again I ached to hold her in my arms.

Everything changes, her father said. Still, I loved Linda and, as I said, I began to see why she'd left. Then A.J. put away his knife and slipped his guitar over his shoulder. I helped Linda shake out the blanket, fold it. It was like this when we made the bed in our flat. She held her side of the blanket, I held mine, but all the while our eyes were on each other.

I drove us down the road to the clearing where the woods ebbed away from Sawyers' Stables. Grass from the pasture spilled through the fence. A path led to a small wooden house. An apricot tree hung its leaves near the porch and bluejays hopped from the limbs onto the roof and back.

Beneath a lean-to A.J.'s winter wood lay under a tarp and beyond the stables sat a mound of manure. The tack room smelled of leather and saddle soap; a cabinet with no door held bandages; a liniment bottle. Bridles and harness were hung on the walls. I saw Linda's saddle and a bareback pad. Her name was engraved on a metal band on a bridle her father had given her.

"Here's my darling." Linda led Blueboy into the sunlight, patting his nose. "Did you miss me?" With a bashful swipe his head brushed her cheek. He was a large glossy horse with eyes like live coals. Linda put down her bag and circled him, picking and tapping at his shoes. "Yes, you're fit as can be, aren't you? You can hardly wait for Saturday. You want to run the race of your life, don't you? You always do. But look who you're stuck with, poor dear. It's lead-butt Linda again." She turned to me, smiling. "Did I tell you I've entered the rodeo? In the sprint. Will you come?"

"I wouldn't miss it."

She brushed the black horse and at each stroke his flesh rippled. "I wish Dorothy Geyer could be here. I'd sit her on Blueboy and we'd walk the pasture. Wouldn't she love him?"

I saw Dorothy gazing down from the dark horse with that serious regard she gave to everything, from small talk at the kitchen table to the question of her death. "She'd love him," I said. "But her parents would never risk it."

"I think of her every day." Linda went on stroking Blueboy. "How is she?"

"She was in the hospital when I left."

"Oh dear." Her hand stopped.

"Her blood count was slipping."

"Oh, the poor girl."

Linda brought the brush into the tack room. A.J. had led six horses to pasture and he joined us, walking through the high grass to the house. "I'd better fix up this place," he said. "It's grown scruffy," said Linda.

We went up the stairs and Linda followed him into the house. A porch swing creaked as I sat down to wait. Then Linda came out carrying her shoulder bag. Putting it down, she sat beside me on the swing. "How long have you known A.J.?"

"We met when he handled horses for the Sawyers. We boarded Blueboy here. I saw how hard he worked but I hardly knew him."

"Until this winter."

"Spring," she said.

I must have looked surprised.

"You don't want to hear this," she said.

"I asked you."

Linda sat so still the swing was silent. "It was Easter Sunday. And cold when we went to Mass in the morning. Mother and I. Daddy declined, as usual. Father Ted had been banished to the monastery. When we drove back—it was a bright day—I went for a walk by the lake. It was all ice but there were patches of thaw. I had on heels and a fake fur, and I was crunching along on the crust when I felt someone was watching me.

"I turned around and I saw this dark figure by the boathouse. I don't know how long he'd been there. But I felt his eyes on me, as if he could touch me with his sight, and for a moment I was frightened. Then I saw who it was.

"I waved and Akira waved back. I walked over. He was shivering. I invited him up to the house for a cup of coffee. He said he couldn't do that. Then I noticed the doors to the boathouse were unlocked, one door stood ajar. 'Wait in there,' I told him, and I ran to bring Daddy's blanket from the porch. Then we snuggled down in the boathouse. We sat in the boat, looking out the open doors at the ice on the lake, and I said he should come into the house and I'd make a warm lunch for him. Mother was preparing dinner, I was about to help her, and I could easily find him something to eat. But he refused. Politely, of course. 'No, thank you, you're too kind.' He learned his manners from his parents, a point of pride with him, and he would accept no favors. So we sat.

"I was so dumb; it must have been another ten minutes before it dawned on me. When I first saw him standing by the shore those doors to the boathouse already were *open.* Finally, I asked him: 'Who gave you a key?'

"'Your father,' he said.

"He was dealing a little coke in Crags Landing and for a few families around the lake—the Sawyers had leased the stables to him but he needed money through the winter. Daddy would leave an envelope full of bills in the boathouse. And he'd given A.J. the key. That's his way, isn't it? Daddy has to control the situation. If he couldn't make Mother do without, he could limit her supply. If her source was someone he knew. I'd thought she bought her own in town, discreetly. But Daddy was buying it for her. We were in church on Sunday mornings when the buy was made. So I never knew, and Mother never had to hand over any money. He was protecting us."

I remembered Annette on the staircase with panic in her eyes. "She calls it her medicine," I said, sadly.

"Yes," said Linda. "I felt bad about A.J., his sneaking around like that. I told him I'd bring Mother's money each time I paid for Blueboy." She leaned forward, I put my arm around her, and the swing rasped, sending a blue jay flapping from the roof into the tree. "I urged him again to come up to the house and this time he accepted. We climbed out of the boat. He gave me the key as he went out and I locked the doors.

"When I turned around he was gone. I saw him running across the ice. I called. I started after him and stumbled in the snow. I knelt there in my coat and watched him run away. When he reached the pier he stopped and flung his arms around—I knew he was freezing, I thought he was trying to get warm. Then he started back. I thought he wanted to tell me something so I walked toward him. Then I saw why he was hurrying. He'd dropped something. He hadn't missed it until he stopped running. Then he felt for it and it wasn't there, that's why his arms were flailing like that, and now he was racing back to retrieve it." Linda glanced up, reluctant to go on. "It was his knife. I found it lying on the ice."

"The one we used today."

"He saw me put it in the pocket of my coat. He came up and he didn't ask for it, at first. We just walked off the ice and stood among the pines. That's when he told me about his brother. The Forest Service had sent him a letter. He drove up to Portland, he identified the body, he read the autopsy. He gave him a Buddhist burial. When he returned to Crags Landing he felt so alone. He'd lost his parents and his brother was dead. The Sawyers had been like grandparents but they've moved to Sacramento. He had a friend in Father Ted but Mercy House is closed and his friend was in the monastery. He'd loved Sarah Hack but how could she know that? He'd never told her. He felt desperately lonely. He kept thinking about his brother: what his last moments must have been like. Finally it was unbearable.

"He drove up to the lake. He meant to make his last delivery for Mother then hike over to Lassen Peak. To honor his brother he meant to take his life in the snowfield on the volcano. Then we met and suddenly I had his knife.

"He was so miserable I knew I shouldn't give it to him. He could have pulled it from my coat but he didn't. He pleaded for it but I wouldn't give in. We went back to the boathouse. He asked me to come into town the next day to have coffee with him. That was the least I could do, and when I met him in town he seemed at peace with himself. I returned the knife. Now he says he's alive today only because I kept his knife that day."

"He thinks he owes you his life," I said. I heard the contempt in my voice and I was ashamed of it.

"Yes," she replied softly.

"You don't owe him anything."

"No," said Linda. "I don't."

"What does he want?"

"He says he's alone in the world. I'm the only reason he's alive. He doesn't want to live without me."

"If you believe that–"

"He meant to kill himself. If I walk away from him now he'll do it; I know he will."

"You can't allow this," I insisted.

"You can see how he's attached to me. What am I to do?"

Then A.J. came onto the porch. We stood, and the swing screeched. He handed her a foil packet and Linda opened it. The cocaine glistened with a cold light.

"How good is this?"

"It's fine."

"Don't disappoint her."

He smiled. "She'll love it."

"I don't want her to love it. But I can't bring her a cup of sugar."

"It's real," A.J. said. "But it's been cut a little."

"Quinine?" I asked.

"It can't possibly harm her."

Linda took her wallet from her shoulder bag and paid him. He went into the house and the door slapped shut.

"Why is he angry?"

"Because you're here. He's afraid you'll spoil everything for him." She pushed the packet deep into her bag then put her wallet on top. In the car she placed the bag between her feet. "I haven't thanked you." Linda laid her hand on mine. "It was kind of you to bring Father Ted."

"I was happy to do it."

"But you went out of your way."

We followed behind a truck struggling on the incline. I swung wide, pulled ahead. "In his condition he couldn't drive himself."

"No," she conceded.

"There's something I don't understand."

Linda looked over.

"At the rectory Teresa whispered something to him. Then he said he couldn't come to the lake. And she brought him to Lassen Peak last night."

"That's right."

"To see you."

"Well, yes."

"Why wouldn't he tell me that?"

"He loves me. He thinks you do too. And you might worry."

"I *am* worried."

"So am I," said Linda. "That's why I asked him to come."

"Why did you ask me?"

"When we met at Mount St. Helens you wanted me," she said slowly, thoughtfully. "And in the city."

"I still do."

"You wanted a bright girl and an easy lay."

"That isn't fair."

"Darling, you can't say it isn't true."

I said nothing as the road rose among the pines.

"I wanted one life for both of us. My life and yours to be lived together. That's why I was eager to have a child. Our child. But you didn't want to be as close as I thought we could be. So I had to leave. I was ashamed of how I'd loved you."

"And now?"

Linda measured her words. "I think you want me to be in your life more than you did before."

"I do."

"And I need you now," she said.

It wasn't an admission Linda could make easily. I reached for her hand then let it go. The forest crowded toward the bending road and I braked for a sharp turn.

10

Swimming with Doctor Pell

A small white car sat in the Pells' driveway. A front fender was dented, the dent had rusted, the trunk was sprung half open. Teresa had driven up from Crags Landing to help Annette with her dress for the party, and she brought Father Ted. The priest was in the kitchen making a sandwich, Doctor Pell told us. In his swim trunks, a towel over his shoulder, he lowered the garden hose into one of the flowerbeds. "You took A.J. home?"

"Yes," I said.

When he stood up he noticed Linda's shoulder bag. "You've been to the stables."

"Yes." Linda slipped indoors to find her mother.

"I'm going for a swim," her father said. "Care to join me?"

I went upstairs to change clothes and when I came down he was waiting. We took the stone path. "I'll string lights over the pier. People can walk out to the water with their drinks."

"I'll give you a hand."

"Tomorrow," he said. "Or Sunday. It won't take long." By the boathouse he slipped off his sandals. Leaving our towels on the grass, we waded into the lake.

"Christ!" I said.

"Isn't this great?"

The cold gripped my legs but Doctor Pell seemed invigorated by it. He was in his element—the icy water broke into chips of light as he splashed handfuls on his face and shoulders. White hair was mingled in the sandy thatch across his chest. "This is terrific. So glad you could be here, Dick."

I ducked into the water and emerged with my face stinging. "Dick, when you swam for Cal, what was your best event?"

"The 400-meter freestyle."

"It's about 400 from here to there." He was judging the distance to the blind, the clump of brush and wire rocking on the water. "Maybe a little more."

"Yes, it's a little more."

"Can you reach it?"

"Swim to the blind?"

"That's right."

I was sure I could do it, though I remembered how A.J. had thrashed through the water halfway to the blind but gave up and turned back. As we crouched in the shallows I wondered if Doctor Pell remembered that, too. "It's maybe 420," he said. "You could be right about that."

"Yes, it's at least that far."

"What do you say?"

"Why not?" I said.

We plunged in. Struggling at first because of the cold, we pushed ahead. Doctor Pell had a good stroke, cleaving the water with that economy of effort you see in a trained swimmer. Then he let himself lag behind. I pulled on through the low waves, he drafted behind me, and whenever I caught sight of him he was swimming easily. I was slow to warm and didn't feel comfortable until a hundred meters out from shore. Swimming in the river taught me to breathe on either side, and now I could stretch out with a full rotation of my shoulders. I'd learned sighting too, keeping a target in view so you don't waste strokes. I sighted on the clump of brush; drawing near, I saw the raft that supported it. I waited for it to tip toward me, then I grabbed hold and pulled up, resting on the edge. Doctor Pell followed six or seven strokes behind. Catching hold of the blind, his hands looked unnaturally white, spotted with dark freckles.

"So it isn't too far," he said.

"When the water's this cold it takes more effort. It wrings something out of you."

"You made it look easy."

"We did all right, didn't we?"

"Dick, when I hang a light out here, suppose I use three or four of those colored lanterns that we string over the pier. I'll attach them to that wire frame above the brush. Just use another battery. What do you think?"

"They'll look fine after dark. They'll throw their colors on the water."

"Annette will appreciate that. A very nice effect." As we bobbed in the water, riding our corner of the raft, he looked pleased with his idea. Then, pushing off, we swam back. He kept pace all the way and together we climbed up, chilled, dripping, onto the breakwater.

On our way to the house Doctor Pell stooped to draw the hose toward a bed of iris taller than the others. "You see these?" Around him the petals swayed on stems three and four feet high. "These sturdy ones are Siberian. Did you ever see such beauties?"

Each scalloped flower was as wide as my hand. I was impressed by their delicate texture. And the vivid colors: white, purple, sky blue, and the deep blue of the lake. "I've never seen any like this," I admitted. "They're magnificent."

He sloshed a little water into the bed. "You soak them the first year. After that, they only rarely need a drink. Which is more than I can say for myself." Doctor Pell squinted into the light. "What about you, sir? A drink?"

"Yes, let's have a drink," I said. "After I change clothes." We went around to the porch and brought our towels indoors.

"Dick, I'll meet you in my study. I enjoyed our swim."

I told him I felt better now. "Frankly," I said, "I've been worried about Linda and A.J."

"I understand."

"I think she'd like to be free of him."

"So would I." Doctor Pell settled heavily into the old leather sofa. "Every single day I feel his influence on my family. In one way or another. Look how he follows Linda everywhere. For God's sake! At the stables he has ample opportunity to see her. Is he satisfied with that? Hell, no! He has to hold her attention even when she manages to slip away from him. I'm certain that's why he writes so often."

"A.J. is writing to Linda?" If he heard the alarm in my voice her father was too preoccupied to mention it.

"Three letters every week. Sometimes four or five." He met my stare and answered it.

"Trust me, sir."

"Love letters?"

"Yes."

"How do you know that?"

His face flamed with fury. "I have a right to know."

"She shows them to you?"

"Certainly not."

"But you've read them."

His blanket was draped over the sofa and he leaned back, wringing his towel in his hands. "Dick, it's no mystery. When his letters first arrived I made it my business to find where Linda kept them. A little white purse in her bedroom, in plain view of anyone. Linda is a straightforward girl. Deception isn't natural to her. She doesn't welcome his letters."

"How can you be sure?"

"He writes the usual nonsense. He pleads with her to answer his declarations of love, so I assume she *doesn't* answer them. Still the letters arrive. And I read them. I have to protect our only child. But I can assure you his devotion doesn't mean much to Linda. I notice she keeps only his most recent letter and tears up the others."

"Does Annette know you're reading Linda's mail?"

"Certainly not."

"You don't discuss it with her?"

"She'd never approve." He rose from the creaking sofa, twisting the towel in his fists. "I take that into account. And I consider how overwrought that poor woman has been. I won't let him distress her any further. I have my family to think of."

"If you ask me—"

"I don't ask you. And I don't ask Annette. Where Linda's welfare is concerned I rely on my own judgment."

"I'm sure you do." I was about to storm out of his house in anger when I stopped. Halted by a sudden revulsion. It sickened me to see Doctor Pell was attempting to control Linda just as he'd dominated Annette's life. Yes—I was intrigued by his cunning. But I resented it and I despised what he'd done with it: his invasion of Linda's privacy. Still I couldn't simply pack my bag and drive back to the city. I tell myself that wouldn't have changed anything. The truth is—apart from obligations to Noah and NEPA—I was unwilling to leave him because it meant leaving Linda and her mother, as well. We faced each other with nothing more to say. Then, still seething, he pushed by me with a mumbled apology, on his way to the kitchen to fix our drinks.

You may say he was an irascible son of a bitch, and that's the truth, or it's what survives of the truth, which comes to the same thing. I won't defend him as a friend. It's too late for that. But I'll insist that his most consistent virtue and failing, his love for his family and his quiet rage, made him the man he was. Standing in the doorway, I saw for the first time that this ever-ready anger in Linda's father was the shadow of his love; the two were always together in him, and would be to the end. And the end was nearer than I knew.

I went upstairs to shower and dress. When I came down I brought the envelope to return it to Father Ted. *Love changes all of us,* Jules Beauregard had written. Does it? From deep in the house I heard the tentative notes of Annette's piano. Then her daughter joined her and I stood at the foot of the stairs, listening to Linda's plaintive flute.

11

Day and Night

I told Doctor Pell I didn't want that drink after all, I meant to call Noah Geyer. "Use my phone." He stepped out, closing the door. I opened the window and sat behind his desk. Sunlight fell through the window, missing the desk, warming a patch of carpet. Outside, his brother greeted him and he replied sharply. I picked up the phone but their voices continued beyond the window, hard-edged, unyielding. I put down the phone. I remember sitting back in his leather chair looking at those bookshelves, rock samples, the model of the doomed *Arizona*; and the gun rack where reaching daylight rubbed the barrel of his rifle and burnished the walnut stock of the shotgun. The argument grew more intense, Father Ted defensive, then urgent. Doctor Pell's voice, low, angry, had remained strictly controlled until the priest questioned him.

"Don't you trust your daughter?"

"You've no right to ask that." For the first time I heard in Doctor Pell's voice the pain of a bitter injury. "And you had no right to bring him to Lassen Peak when Linda was there."

"Teresa brought him, Bob."

"Teresa brought both of you."

"Linda asked for my help."

"I don't believe you."

"He's made these threats before. You know that. If she failed to stop him—"

"If Linda needed help she'd have asked me for it."

"Perhaps she couldn't ask you."

"Why not?"

"She knows you hate him."

A pause.

"You left them *alone.*"

"I had to return to the rectory. Teresa had to get home to her mother. She's upstairs now. Call her down. Ask her."

"Damn you!" said Doctor Pell. "You left them together in the park. For the rest of the night."

"They had a problem," said Father Ted. "We settled it before I left. Do you think I'd let Akira kill himself?"

"Is that all you care about?"

"Bob, please don't disgrace yourself."

"He thinks he's in love with her. *That's* the problem. And it *hasn't* been settled. You're a fool if you think it has."

"Give him time to let go. He'll find another girl and he'll forget Linda. He's never been so alone as he was this past winter. Or so depressed. I'm sorry I wasn't in town to help him through it. I know Akira; I understand a little of the turmoil in his mind."

Harsh laughter.

"How can you understand a young man who wants a woman? I know what he has in mind. And I'll put a stop to it."

That was the end of their argument. In the sudden stillness I went over to stand before Linda's trophies and glossy ribbons. I glanced around, my eye catching the photo of Linda with Sarah Hack. A.J.'s first love. I wished I'd met Akira in other circumstances. His pride was unmistakable and he possessed a gritty determination. At Mount St. Helens he'd have been an asset to any search and rescue crew. And I wished he'd not been so tongue-tied with Sarah Hack. Though I wasn't much better when I first met Linda, was I? Among her father's gallery of family photos I saw one I'd missed: he was a child gravely holding a model boat while his parents stood beaming behind him. I'd begun to believe A.J. was no threat to anyone but himself. But Linda's father? Here, among his family, he was more complex than the man I'd known; capable of more passion and severity. I picked up the wooden battleship, surprised at how light it was. I thought of Doctor Pell's account of his father's death when the Japanese bombed his ship. The flaming oil. Back at his desk I reached for the phone. Noah Geyer had misjudged him and I'd better tell him so.

I dialed Noah's office, learned he was at home, then phoned him there.

I told him I'd talked with Doctor Pell last night. And today. "We went for a swim this afternoon. He can't commit just now. But he's interested. If we are."

That's all I needed to say. Noah heard my uneasiness and asked: "What is it that worries you?"

I thought again how his taking on other people's pain year after year had taught him a sensitivity for suffering. I saw how unlike him I was and how much I had to learn.

"It's Doctor Pell," I replied. Turning his chair, I faced the photo of the volcanic park with pins marking the danger spots. "He commands respect. But he won't make us any friends."

"We buy that risk," said Noah. I imagined him slouched behind his desk in the front room, the phone against his round chin. "We know he has a quick temper."

"I've seen it before," I said.

"His anger doesn't bother me particularly. He's strong-willed, he doesn't suffer fools, but those are not the worst of qualities."

"It may go deeper than that."

Noah maintained a patient silence. Beyond the window the sunlight cast a trellis of shadows among the pines. Into Doctor Pell's study drifted the resin scent of the trees, the dusty smell of their fallen needles, the fragrance of the spring grass in the lawn, all of it mingled in the mountain air.

"I don't know that we can rely on him in a crisis." I could hardly have told Noah anything more damning. He waited to hear if I wanted to retract what I'd said. I didn't. "I ask myself, is he emotionally stable? If we face a disaster at Lassen Peak is this the man we must depend on?"

"You found no fault with his performance at St. Helens."

Sitting forward, my elbows on his desk, I looked at the picture of the iris Linda had given her father. Across the room was his map of the hazard zones around Lassen Peak and the *Scenes of Deformation.* In my silence Noah heard uncertainty. "Something has happened," he concluded. "It's personal?"

"A personal difficulty. Yes."

"Family?"

"Yes."

"I have his complete dossier."

"It doesn't help," I said.

I'd wondered about that dossier. Washington would have sent it to Noah before he suggested we approach Doctor Pell. I'd found it on file before I left the city. But who prepared it? FBI? Interior? Someone with little knowledge of the man. Whoever it was had spent a week scanning newspaper files, back issues of *Time, Newsweek, Scientific American,* then questioned his colleagues. But hadn't taken the time to visit with the subject himself.

"Does this difficulty affect his professional life?"

"It hasn't," I admitted.

"Maybe he'll work it out."

"I don't see how."

"He's a determined individual," said Noah. "Resolute. Assiduous."

The language of the Pell dossier; he remembered it as well as I did. During a stillness on the line I heard squirrels outside the window chuckling as they scrabbled among the pines. Behind me the Pells' front door was flung open then slammed shut with such force the sound carried to the back of the house. Noah said in a husky voice: "Do you want to come home?"

"Give it up?"

"Just give me one solid reason."

"I can't do that," I said. "Not yet."

"Then keep in touch," he said. "When you know something."

I shouldn't have phoned. It was a mistake to worry Noah with a problem for which he could give no help. He made an effort not to let his voice reveal his frustration: "Do you see Linda?"

"Yes."

"Splendid!"

A pause.

"Or is it?"

A long pause.

I asked, "Is Edna well?"

"As sweet as ever." He laughed.

I hesitated to ask about Dorothy. I heard a rapid thumping across the floor of the Geyers' front room. "Guess who's come to the phone? She wants to say hello." I listened as he told her I was calling from Lake Elaine.

"Have you seen Lassen Peak?" she asked, breathless.

"Today," I said.

"Will it blow up?"

"Someday," I said. "Not soon. I hope."

"Why are you there?"

"I blame your father for that," I said.

"Okay," she responded cheerfully. "How's Linda?"

"Linda misses you," I said. "We talked about that today."

"How's her horse?"

I mentioned the rodeo in Crags Landing. "It starts tomorrow. Linda will ride Blueboy. In a sprint."

"You stinko." She laughed.

"What's that about?"

"You get to see Linda and her horse. And the race," she said. "And I don't."

"I'll bring pictures."

"Really?"

"I promise."

"Thank you so very much," she said solemnly.

As I put down the phone I heard a motorboat. Someone had gunned the engine, then it backfired. People called out, laughing; boaters or skiers out on the lake. I'd left the envelope on the desk. Now I brought it with me to the kitchen, looking for Father Ted.

Light darted about the kitchen, glinting off the clock on the wall. Four-thirty. As I went out I heard a voice so vibrant and soulful that it made its way through the stillness of the house. The French doors stood open to the music room where Teresa Espinosa, a white blossom in her black hair, Annette's lavender gown draped over her arms, sang in Spanish about a girl who lived on a sheep ranch long ago. She was a lovely girl, *la flor del valle,* the flower of the valley. We remember her beauty and her kind heart, she sang. But the girl died young and her death cast a spell on the land, and to this day no one visits that place...As I entered the room Teresa glanced up, embarrassed, and stopped. "You have a marvelous voice," I said. "Don't let me interrupt. Please."

I waited for her to continue but she wouldn't. Cautiously she threaded a sewing needle. "The ladies are upstairs," she said,

"They're changing?"

Her eyes were large and dark and she looked baffled.

"They try on their gowns upstairs," I said. "You make the alterations here."

Her answer was a nod toward the wicker basket perched at one end of the piano bench. In the basket were pin cushions in various colors, pink, violet, green; a tape measure spilled over its side. Linda's flute lay on a cane-backed chair beside a music stand. I put Father Ted's envelope under my arm, picked up the flute, and sat down. I held the flute carefully across my knees. Teresa wasn't wearing the black-and-white outfit of the rectory, but a denim skirt, a russet blouse, a silver cross on a slender necklace. "Is this your day off?"

"Yes." She hid her hands in a fold of the gown.

"And you spend it sewing for the Pells."

"For the ladies." Her hands twitched under the fabric. "They hire me to help them."

"They're fortunate," I said.

"I, too, am fortunate." She bowed her head and the flower gleamed in her black hair.

"And you sew for Father Ted."

"For the church," she corrected.

"Especially for the priest."

She was fond of him and I shouldn't have teased her about it. She looked up with her large eyes filled with pride. She said nothing but bent over her work again and I felt ashamed. Angry with myself. Angry with the priest.

According to Linda he'd been Akira's first benefactor. Perhaps he was Teresa's too. That's to his credit, isn't it? But I'd had enough of his schemes. His secrets.

"I'm looking for the priest," I said.

"Here?"

I laughed. "No."

Teresa, seating herself beside the wicker basket, drew the gown across her lap. I was imposing on her, I was being tiresome, we both knew it. But thinking of Father Ted gave her pleasure. "He walked down to the lake," she offered.

I stood up to leave.

"He wanted to smoke his cigar," she went on. "Mrs. Pell asks him not to smoke them in the house. It's the smell."

"Do you mind it?"

"No." She shook her head. "But he never smokes in the rectory either." Needle in hand, she wagged an admonishing finger, imitating the blue-haired housekeeper. "Mrs. Muller won't allow it."

"I'm not surprised."

"Mrs. Muller was surprised this morning," Teresa said. "He told her he is quitting his cigars."

I laid the flute on the chair.

"He will do what he promises," she assured me. Smiling, she turned back the hem of the gown. "Perhaps today," she said.

"Or tomorrow," I said.

"Mrs. Muller says it's a wonderful thing to do."

I looked at the envelope the priest had given me. "I'm going to meet this wonderful man down by the water," I said. "Or perhaps he will have walked across it."

She laughed at me as I left.

Father Ted sat on a bench at the end of the pier, smoking a cigar. I walked out and the boards bent beneath my feet. I sat facing him, the bell rope dangling between us.

"Teresa said I'd find you here."

A Hawaiian shirt, open at the throat, left room for his cervical collar. The sky-blue shirt had green fronds and scarlet and yellow flowers splashed over it. He knew it looked awful and he seemed to enjoy it. "I'm off duty," he said, smiling.

"You look comfortable."

"I'm healing. Slowly."

I gave him the envelope with Jules Beauregard's manuscript in it. "I read this last night."

"Why do we punish desire?" the priest said. "Do you remember his answer?"

"Fear."

"Of what?"

"People are afraid to love each other," I said. "Or that's what he came to believe."

"Exactly." He drew on his cigar, expelled a bluish cloud of smoke, and watched as the breeze carried it away. "We betray each other, we even kill each other, because we're afraid to open our hearts. Then he learned that love could change his life if he let it."

"His guilt taught him," I said.

"His guilt prepared his soul," the priest said, "so the child could teach him what he needed to learn. Jules Beauregard lived in torment because of his conscience. But a bad conscience can be a blessing if it makes us examine what we've done."

"Was that your message to me?"

Holding his cigar between thumb and finger, he studied it as if it might suddenly explode or sprout wings and fly into the woods. He tapped it with a heavy finger and a clot of ash fell, breaking apart on the plank between his feet. "You feel guilty about Linda."

"I've loved her since the first day I met her."

"But you drove her away."

"I miss her every day."

"You want her to come back to the city with you. You want to atone for what you did. Or what you neglected to do."

"You're a smart man," I said. "Aren't you?"

A boat pulled a skier far down the sunny water, the drone of its engine fading in the distance.

"Are you pleased with yourself?" I said.

"Almost never," he said.

"But you figured everything out."

"I didn't figure on Akira Jagao," he said. "I didn't know how he felt about Linda."

"What happened last night in the park?"

A clot of ash from his cigar landed in his lap. He brushed it away, leaving a grey smudge. When he knelt to rub out his cigar on the pier it burned a mark like a dark knot in the wood. "When I was a child," he said, "1 was taught that sin made a stain like that on my soul. It wouldn't come clean unless I made a good confession."

"What happened last night?"

Two weeks ago, he said, A.J. had asked Linda to spend a night with him in the mountains. She turned him down as kindly as she could. He began pressing her for one night together. She wouldn't. He convinced himself that she'd sleep with him if they were married. And he proposed to her. Still, no. "Then he told her that he can't live without her. Which is nonsense and she knows it," said Father Ted. "But it's a threat that she has to consider." My visit to the Pells made him more desperate. When he learned Linda would stay overnight in the park he told her he'd be there too. Not unless the priest was present, she said. "That was the message you saw Teresa give me. Linda asked me to join her for a campfire supper. She said it was urgent."

"And you went."

"Teresa took me," he said. "And Akira."

At Lassen Peak A.J. begged Linda to marry him. The priest, he reasoned, could perform the service at the foot of the mountain. Teresa would be their witness.

"Linda refused," I said.

The priest moved his upper body in a stiff shrug as if he wore a yoke across his shoulders and he was taking up the burden of it. "He looked devastated," he said. "So she asked if he'd like to come to her parents' party on Sunday. Her father, he said, already had phoned to invite him. But he hadn't wanted to come unless Linda asked him too."

"Doctor Pell invited A.J.?"

"Incredible, isn't it?" said Father Ted. "But he's coming because Linda asked him."

"That's why he was so cheerful this morning."

"She's afraid he'll harm himself if she turns him away."

"He has a knife," I said.

"He worries you, too."

"Yes.

"Then help him."

"You expect me to help A.J.?"

"He doesn't threaten you. Or Linda. Help him through this. He has no one else."

"I believe you."

"And Bob is furious with him."

."I've wondered about that."

"It's the truth."

"Your father's death at Pearl Harbor. He carries that with him. Even today."

"Always." Father Ted sighed.

"But you don't hate A.J.?"

"I was two years old when Dad died. I hardly knew him. And that was forty years ago. I can't hold Akira responsible for what happened to my father," said the priest. "He needs a friend as much as he needs a woman. Or more."

"He trusts you."

"Yes," he said, "but he knows my limitations."

Shifting so one shoulder was braced against the bench, Father Ted saw her first. He gazed at the woman walking down the lawn. Lacking Linda's assurance, less at home in her own body, Annette advanced down the path with a hesitant step. Then halted. She wouldn't set foot on the pier but looked across the water, arms at her sides, hands in the folds of her lavender gown. Her hair was drawn back; her gown cut low. Sunlight glowed on her small shoulders and above her breasts and on her bare feet in the grass.

From my seat by the bell I rose and applauded her. Father Ted joined in, both of us clapping. Annette's sudden smile told us this was all the response she'd hoped for. Her gown was a success, she'd be a stunning hostess, she had no reason to doubt her ability to charm. She'd ventured down the lawn seeking our support, satin shimmering about her, uncertain as a flame, but now she was here no words were needed. She wanted to be admired and she was. Lifting her gown almost to her knees, she turned and walked briskly back to the house.

Ripples lapped at the pilings with a persistent *plash, plash.* "My brother married an extraordinary woman," said Father Ted. "It's a crime that he can't appreciate her."

"He loves her," I said. "I saw that last night."

"I'm sure he does. In his way."

"You sound disappointed."

"I know *they're* disappointed. When they eloped they were hoping for a miracle, each of them, but they've had to settle for an ordinary marriage."

"Linda never told me they eloped."

"They met at just the right time to misunderstand each other." said the priest. "Bob was an ensign. Handsome. Anxious to be admired. And already he had that air of authority. But no experience with women. He used to ask *me* what to do on a date. I was sixteen; I'd slept around a little. He'd ask how to kiss a girl. Would she think he meant to go to bed with her? And if he did? What could I tell him? He'd known Annette less than a month when he was calling her his angel because she'd appeared in his life and made him feel wonderful. Important. He was a young sailor; he had a month's pay in his pocket and nothing else in the world. She'd been dominated by her parents and their money. They threatened to disown her if she didn't give him up. She wouldn't, or course; they ordered her out of their house. They shut the door on her and locked it, thinking she'd give in. She was kind and vulnerable, pretty, needy; she wanted a hero to rescue her. There he was. She'd kept the spare key to her father's car. One night they went to her parents' house and swiped the car from the driveway. A red Chrysler convertible. They drove to Reno that night and were married the next morning. They've labored ever since to make it work."

"My God!" At the time I was happy to hear this story; happy that Annette had eloped with Doctor Pell. Probably it was the most desperate thing she'd ever done. "This morning she said she was wicked."

"In the first years of their marriage if Bob wasn't at sea he forbid her to leave the house unless he was with her. If he left for any reason he locked the doors and took the keys. He said he meant to keep her from harm. What he meant, of course, was to *keep* her. Well, she knew how it felt to be locked out. Now she was locked *in*. But she *allowed* it! For a while. That changed when Linda was born. She wanted more of the world for both of them. And he's loosened his grip. But only a little."

Was that why she needed drugs? To open a door she could pass through no matter who'd locked it? I saw a second boat plow across the water pulling a pair of skiers, a boy and girl. The girl let go, sinking in backwash until I saw only her head bobbing there. The boy knelt over his skis; then released his grip, easing into the roiling water. They called out. The boat whirred around and was throttled down as it drew near. Someone fished the girl out, the boy sprawled aboard, and they sped off. Their wake thumped the pier.

"Annette is actually a strong-willed woman. Married to my brother," said the priest, "she'd better be. Most days she keeps it under control. But it will break out."

"You know she's doing coke," I said.

"If I were a woman married to Bob," he said, "I'd use more than a little coke. I'd use a gun."

It was just past six when Father Ted wedged himself into Teresa's car, she turned a tight circle in the driveway, and they sped down the road toward Crags Landing.

I went upstairs to invite Linda to dinner in town. She came to the door of her room wearing a burgundy blouse and beige skirt. In a rocking chair by her bed sat a doll dressed in a satin wedding gown. Milky blue eyes gave a wide open stare. The doll's hands held a white purse and I wondered if the latest letter from A.J. was in it.

"Give me a minute. I only need shoes."

It was more like twenty minutes. From my room I looked at the shadows lengthening in the woods behind the house. I came back into the hall. I was waiting for her with one hand on that swanlike banister when I heard something shatter downstairs. I heard it again. Again. Shattering sounds that broke through the house like an electric storm starting at full force. Each crash like a thunder clap but closer. Linda flew past me, red hair bobbing, her hand slapping the banister as she ran downstairs.

I caught up with her in the dining room. The drapes were open and the dusk of the mountains pressed into the dim room. Only the kitchen was splattered with light. Doctor Pell blocked the doorway but beyond him the chrome sink gleamed and shards of glass sparkled on the floor.

Linda edged past her father and I joined her in the kitchen. The ceiling lamp flung light over the sink, the faucet and handles. The toaster. A cabinet door hung open; liquor bottles, some of them empty, crowded the counter. The tiles in the floor looked like brickwork—squares of sandy browns and earthen reds—but all of it sparkling. Fragments of smashed bottles littered the floor with chips of light.

The sleeves of her blouse pushed above her elbows, her hair loose about her face and shoulders, Annette emptied a bottle of vodka into the sink. She swung around, smashed the bottle on the floor, and turned back to the sink.

"Please stop," said Doctor Pell.

"It isn't *fair!*"

She opened another bottle and upended it. A gummy orange liqueur slid into the sink.

"Dearest," he said.

"It *isn't.*"

She reached for a bottle of sour mash. A moment later the bourbon gurgled down the drain.

"Mother!"

"It isn't fair!"

In brooding silence Annette bowed her head.

Suddenly, spinning, she hurled the bottle across the room. It struck a spice rack, the rack tipped, vials and cans spilled out, clattering across a cutting board. That same impact jolted the wall phone; the receiver leaped free and dangled by its cord.

Already Annette was emptying another bottle, speeding the whiskey into the drain with angry jets from the water faucet.

As her husband approached glass crackled beneath his feet. His voice was soft, furious, controlled: "Have you thought what this will cost?"

Turning, she hurled a bottle and the clock above the doorway exploded. Glass sprayed as it dropped to the floor. It continued ticking behind a dented face; the batteries were intact, arms twisted, pointing at the ceiling lamp. Over the doorway was a ghostly moon, a pale circle where the clock had been.

Annette emptied another bottle. Lifting it overhead, she swung down, let go, smashed it on the floor. Each time she threw an arm across her face to protect herself from the shattering glass, and smashed the bottles blindly.

I started forward but Linda held my hand.

"Don't interfere," said Doctor Pell.

"Let her be," said Linda.

Annette's lips moved and she cried out. Then her hand clasped her mouth, she bent over, sobbing. Doctor Pell dropped to his knees in the glass at her feet. He wiped her face with his handkerchief.

"She bit her tongue," he said.

Gasping for breath, she rested her head against his and her dark hair covered his shoulder.

"You did this," she said thickly.

"I'll clean it up."

"You did it!" she insisted.

"I'll pay for it," he said.

Annette sobbed.

Doctor Pell climbed to his feet and leaned Annette against the sink. "Rest," he said. "You're exhausted."

"Do you see–"

"Yes," he said.

"I'm not sorry."

"Can you stand?" he asked.

She slumped against the counter. Leaving her there, he approached us, glass crunching underfoot. "Is it all gone?" Linda asked.

"About half." He opened his wallet.

"How much?" I asked.

"A dozen bottles. Scotch. Bourbon. Vodka. Never mind the liqueur," he said; "we have plenty."

"Whiskey City?" Linda asked.

"Yes, the store by the river," he said. "Will you?"

"Certainly," I said.

Linda wouldn't take his money. "I'll put it on your account," she said.

"Good girl." He brushed flakes of glass from his knees.

The road was bright in the moonlight but it was blackened, briefly, by shadows of outcrop, tall crags, clusters of pines. Then it glowed again. Once, when the shadows fell away and the car filled with a cloud of ghostly light, I looked at Linda and I remembered that first night when we lay in bed in our flat in the city and the traffic in the street below us threw its jittery light across the walls and we were happy.

"You mustn't think badly of her." Linda told me her father had taken away Annette's coke. He wouldn't tolerate her doping, not now, though he promised to return it to her after the weekend. But not while I was staying at their house and Father Ted and Teresa were coming and going and fifty guests were due on Sunday. Where had he hidden it? "Probably on his boat," Linda suggested. "Mother wouldn't look there." Annette took her revenge on his supply of liquor laid in for the party, and he didn't blame her. He'd carry her up the stairway, wash her face and undress her. He'd help her into her nightgown and put her to bed before he came downstairs to clean the kitchen. I listened with difficulty as Linda told me about her parents. I was sorry for their pain. Especially for Linda's. But I welcomed this time alone with her. I saw her face luminous in the moonlight. Her hand rested on my leg and I put my hand on hers.

We ate at a coffee house at the edge of Crags Landing. Crowded, but not like the crush of people downtown. Afterwards I drove past The Chute; a neon bronco was bucking above the door. The crowd from the bar filled the doorway, backing onto the sidewalk, where cowboys and tourists passed, awash in country music wailing from indoors.

At the Whiskey City store near the park business was brisk. We brought the bottles out in two boxes and locked them in the trunk of the car. Then we left the traffic and the crowd swelling in the street and walked among the trees where the land, dipping between two crags, forms a grassy shelf above the water. The boat rental was shut. The Sacramento flowed under the iron bridge and shimmered in moonlight.

The wind buffeted Linda's hair. "We can't stay long."

"No," I said.

"I'll get up early to help Mother. She'll be cooking all day. And then I have to ride."

"Will your father come with us?"

"To the rodeo?"

"Yes."

Her hand brushed at her hair but fell away. "No."

"I don't believe it," I said.

"I've asked him."

"He's so proud of you."

"He knows Akira will be there."

"He invited him to your house," I said. "To your party."

"That's what Akira says."

"You don't believe him?"

"It doesn't make any sense," she said. "Akira must have made up that story. Why would Daddy ask him? He hates him."

Did he hate Akira? Father Ted thought so. The river pushed past us; lamplight from the bridge scattered on the water. "He won't miss your race. You mean too much to him."

"He never has," she said. "But he'll miss this one."

Lighted buoys marked a navigable channel beneath the bridge. For all its beauty it can be a hazardous river, winding, flood-prone, with treacherous currents and snags. Tree trunks surge beneath its placid surface. Clumps of brush swirl in the shadows.

"Your father's going through hell," I said.

"And dragging us with him." Linda folded her arms, rubbed them, and looked down at the water. "He's afraid I'll behave the way Mother did. I'll run off and marry Akira the way she ran off to Reno with him."

"A.J. did ask you to marry him."

"Oh yes."

"He writes to you."

She looked around sharply.

"Your father knows," I said.

"Yes." She brushed at her hair; then gripped my arm. "Akira writes to me. Passionate letters. I blush when I read them. Sometimes I wish they were written by you. I know that's foolish."

"No, it isn't."

"I made no attempt to hide his letters. I never thought my father would come looking for them. But he did. Now I save them so he *can* find them. God knows what he'd think they said if he couldn't see them."

When we came back to the house it was quiet and the kitchen floor was mopped clean.

12

Saturday Afternoon in the Arena

After breakfast we cleared the table while Doctor Pell carried paper lanterns down to the pier. "I'll be along," I said to his back as he walked out the door. Annette set her wedding ring on the counter where the gold band glimmered with intimate fire, before she ran water in the sink. Suddenly I saw her as she was last night, turning from the sink, in a pool of smashed glass, frail, tormented, the lines about her eyes bright with sweat and tears; a porcelain figure that's been finely shattered. This morning she was subdued. And the kitchen was immaculate–not one shard of broken glass. The only sign of destruction was the pale moon on the wall where the clock had hung–and soon the room sparkled with fine crystal. Linda stacked dishes and dessert plates while Annette, hair drawn back, sleeves rolled to her elbows, hands trembling, cautiously arrayed rows of water glasses, cocktail glasses, wine goblets, each row glittering in sunlight streaming through the curtains above the sink. "I have to inspect these first. Then the silver," she said. "For tomorrow."

While Linda tallied the crystal for her I walked down to give Doctor Pell a hand with the lanterns. Delicate globes of yellow, lime green, Chinese red, sea blue, orange. We strung the lights overhead the whole length of the pier. They were powered by two batteries secured beneath the benches.

"We're leaving soon," I said. "Come with us?"

His fingers closed on a light bulb as if he'd crush it in his hand. "No."

"You do want to see her ride."

His head bowed over his hand; his sandy hair brushed by the breeze off the water. "I don't want to see her Jap lover."

"He isn't her lover."

"So she says."

"Why did you invite him to your home?"

His shoulders snapped back and he lifted his face with a look of astonishment. "I was doing my daughter a favor." Water slapped the pier underfoot. "He'd show up anyway. I can't keep him away from her."

I was about to remind him that A.J. was too polite to crash his party but it was pointless: Linda was right. Her father wouldn't come to Crags Landing to watch A.J. follow her around the arena. When she walked out to tell us it was time to leave he ignored her, fitting the light bulb into a green globe while she waited. Finally he kissed her cheek but said nothing to either of us.

We left him waving to us from the lawn, the sun bright on his forehead as we drove off. Linda waved, then her head sank as she began to cry, filling the stillness with deep breaths. I was angry, thinking her father was a stubborn fool. Yet she quieted when she remembered how he'd cleaned up the damage last night. "Did you notice? He scrubbed the kitchen spotless."

She brushed her cheek with the back of her hand, and a note of pride lifted her voice. "I knew he'd do that for her."

Yes, he would.

Tell me, is this love too? This need for each other's frailty and acceptance. This bond of breakdown and repair. What did I know of their struggle to live each day in pleasure and pain? Life with my father had taught me little of this. It fascinated me—it still does—and it baffled me. But while Doctor Pell had traveled the Pacific rim, lecturing on its volcanic hazards, his wife had remained at home where she understood, if anyone did, that the family too is a ring of fire.

Linda wore jeans and a teal-colored sleeveless blouse and while we drove to town she peered into the mirror on the sun visor to pin back her hair. I glanced at the downy light on her neck, wanting to touch her there, unable to reach across the silence: "Are you worried?"

"About the race?"

"Yes."

"I'm anxious. I wish it was over."

"You'll be terrific."

"I've run Blueboy so little. I haven't really pushed him."

"He'll be rested."

"Will you stop being so reassuring?"

"You know how much he can give," I insisted.

Linda needed only a moment to think about that. Smiling, she patted my leg. "Thank you."

We picked up the priest at the rectory then fought traffic to the fairgrounds, pulling into a parking lot nearly filled with cars and pickups. Akira would be with Blueboy out back, in the lot reserved for trailers bringing stock to the pens and the corral behind the grandstand. A van from KMGS, channel 5 in Mingus, was parked outside the entrance. The TV station's logo was a large eye over the slogan *We're Watching the Valley with You.*

A camera crew was filming pickets holding signs in support of animal rights: "Say No to Rodeo", "Animals Are Our Friends", "Calf Roping Is

Cruel". And two placards shaped like high-rearing broncos: "The Buck Stops Here". It was an informational picket line, members shuffling through the crowd, side-stepping to let people through to the ticket booths. Father Ted, in his black suit, wedged toward a rail-thin man wearing glasses. They spoke briefly, then the priest returned through the throng of cowboy shirts and neon blouses. The man he spoke with was David Williams, he said, pastor of the Unitarian Fellowship in Mingus. He'd driven to Crags Landing with two carloads of protesters. The governing board had ignored their letters, and the arena director, Angelo Costa, refused to meet them. So Williams phoned KMGS and they sent this crew with camera and tape recorder.

Bulling his way through the crowd, Angelo Costa shouldered aside a picket, planting himself in front of David Williams and the KMGS woman with her recorder. He wore a rancher's hat, a bolo tie secured with a lump of turquoise, a sport jacket with leather trim on the pockets. Short, broad-shouldered, he looked solid enough to carry the belly squeezing over the buckle on his cowboy belt. His two-tone boots, brown and white, gleamed with polish. "Get your rabble out of the way," he told Williams. "You've no business here."

"Animals aren't a business," Williams countered. His high reedy voice carried above the heads of the people around him. "Or they shouldn't be."

Angie Costa's face was heavy but he had quick dark eyes, a black mustache, thin, neatly trimmed, under a broad nose. Hands on his belt, he thrust his jaw at the pastor. "Where's your permit for this picket line?"

"It's not a line. We're not stopping anybody."

"Damn right you're not! I'm calling the cops. We'll throw your skinny ass in jail."

"No need to do that." William's thin voice rose higher. He didn't look frightened–just embarrassed about being the center of attention. "We want people to know there's another opinion about this activity."

"I got an opinion for you," Angie said. "You want it?"

The cameraman pushed forward; his partner held her tape recorder between the two men. *They* wanted it.

"Get that goddamn thing out of my face!" Angie told her. Father Ted forced his way through the crowd. "Angie, you can't run these people out of here."

"About what I'd expect from you. Weren't you put away?"

"Sent away," said the priest.

"Who let you out?"

Pickets tried to join the pastor but at the sight of the camera the crowd swelled and they couldn't reach him. "We're leaving," Williams called out. "We don't want anybody hurt."

"You hear that?" Angie asked the cameraman. "It's over. Go tape the rodeo. That's something people want to watch."

"We have cameras in the arena," the man replied.

"Our sports crew." His partner clicked off her recorder.

"You have cameras everywhere, don't you?"

"We do our job," the man said curtly.

"Tell you what. Why don't you stick a camera up your ass," Angie suggested. "Show people what kind of brains you got."

The woman clicked on her recorder but Angie lowered his head and plowed through the throng, disappearing under the grandstand.

For years Angelo Costa, principal owner of the Pacific Lumber Company, had been Arena Director of the rodeo. In three of the past five years he'd had the pleasure of presenting the winner's ribbon for the saddle horse race to his daughter, Marcella. Twice Linda had finished second to her. Last year at this time she'd just left Mount St. Helens, returning to her work with USGS, and she didn't come to Crags Landing to compete. "I just want to whip Marcella once," she said.

"You will." I took her hand as we joined one of the lines shuffling toward the ticket booths. A boy selling programs worked the line. On the second page we found: "Ladies Saddle Horse Race—5 Furlongs—Purse $275." Nine riders including Linda, Marcella, and Linda's friend, Sarah Hack, were listed with their horses. "How good is this field?"

"They're more ready than I am."

A hand on the brace beneath his chin, Father Ted read the list. "Marcella Costa," he remarked. "Didn't she board a show pony with Akira? And a speed horse. Both well bred."

"The best that money can buy," said Linda. Our line nudged forward; stopped.

"I remember Reaper," said Father Ted. "She won with him. What—two years ago? That horse was a nervous wreck. Antsy every minute of his life. I'd drop by to see Akira and Reaper would be prancing in the corral. He was even edgy in his stable. Like he ate coffee beans for breakfast."

"He's gone," said Linda. "You can't compete in this event on a horse that's already won it. The board made that rule so one good horse won't dominate. Then Angelo bought Fair Weather and they won with him last year. I've seen him at the stables. A beautiful bay."

I checked the list. "She's riding Fair Weather today."

"This used to be a four-furlong sprint." Linda frowned in frustration. "Angie persuaded the board a five-furlong race appeals to more spectators. I think he's right about that. But after they agreed, he announced that it's a new event. So until there's a winner at this distance, all entries are eligible."

"So Marcella can ride Fair Weather again?" Father Ted raised his eyes. "Good Lord! And Angie Costa's a Catholic, too. How did the Jesuits overlook a mind like that?"

"How did they miss *you*?" Linda asked.

The priest, a cigar at his lips, puffed and laughed.

Red-white-and-blue bunting was draped around booths offering souvenirs and drinks. Kids flocked to the American Legion stand for cotton candy, popcorn. The Moose Lodge kept a beer booth, the Lions Club sold barbecue ribs and soft drinks across the aisle. Women dressed as old-time temperance marchers sold lemonade for the Methodist Church. A full-figured woman glowing with the rouge of a frontier saloon madam—her high school drama teacher, Linda told me—handed out coupons for half-price drinks at The Chute, a Chamber of Commerce badge pinned to her scarlet gown. From a man in a tattered vest I bought a green bandanna with *Crags Landing Rodeo* in golden lettering and gave it to Linda.

"For luck," I said.

"Thanks." She smiled tightly. "I'll need it."

Linda looped the bandanna around her neck, lifting her hair in back, then tied it in a loose knot above her breasts.

In one booth two teenagers, a boy with a crewcut and a girl with a ribboned ponytail, sold straw cowboy hats. The priest tried one on. It was too small, it rode high on his head, but he bought it anyway. He walked off beaming with satisfaction.

Behind the grandstand stood the stables for the broncs, a corral held the other horses. White-face calves were penned nearby but the bulls were kept to themselves. Flies swarmed in warm air that was heavy with the leathery smell of the animals and with a sweet acrid mixture of urine, manure, sawdust.

Leading Blueboy to the corral, A.J. looped a rein around the top rail. Sarah Hack left her horse, Thrifty, and came over to say hello to Linda. I said I'd met her father and she smiled in a bashful way. She swiped at a fly. Father Ted asked: Was she nervous about the race? Yes, a little. "But Thrifty's ready to run." She laughed softly. "He always thinks he's ready." He looked it. Blueboy waited obediently by the rail fence, a big quiet horse dark as night from nose to tail. Sarah's mount, so fit and eager, rippled constantly. A mottled grey, he stood in the dusty corral looking like rain coming down.

Linda and Sarah discussed girls they'd known in high school. Which ones were married. Working. Or both. Asked about each other's parents. Their horses. Sarah admired Blueboy. "So handsome. So good natured," she said.

But it was A.J. she was watching. "You're lucky you can leave Blueboy with him." She flashed the smile I'd seen in a photo in Doctor Pell's study: Linda with her arm around Sarah, the girls in their teens, holding trophies. Today her smile was for A.J. as much as Linda. He looked surprised and pleased.

We wanted a few photos for Dorothy Geyer, Linda explained. This girl in San Francisco who loves horses. "Akira? Over here?" She posed A.J. with Blueboy just over his shoulder. I focused. *Snap.* "I'll be in this one," she said. When I saw him standing beside her, posed there, I felt something small and mean. Father Ted had told me A.J. could use a friend. Can't we all? I focused on Blueboy brushing against Linda's red curls. *Snap.* "Dick, here," she said. "Dorothy's going to want to see you too. And you," she told Father Ted, motioning him to join me.

"Happy to." He flapped his hat at a fly.

"Let me snap this picture," said Sarah. "So you can all be in it." She examined the camera; sighted it. "Easy," she said. Taller than Linda, she was lean, thoughtful, with her blond hair in a braid down the back of her shirt, and faded jeans tucked into her boots.

We lined up against the corral. I put my arm around Linda. Father Ted stood on the other side of her and A.J. took his place beside the priest. Blueboy nuzzled his hat. "He wants to eat it!" Linda laughed. "He had no supper last night. He never eats before he runs." Father Ted, chuckling, removed his hat.

"Stand closer," Sarah directed us. "I want to include that handsome gentleman."

A.J. laughed guardedly, giving his hair a swipe.

"I meant the *horse*," said Sarah, and we laughed.

"Say 'beer'," she said. We laughed and she caught us just right.

"Can Dick take a shot of you with Thrifty?" Linda asked.

"Would you?" said Sarah. Thrifty stood rippling and twitching in a rope halter and she handed the rope to A.J. "Please? He'll be quiet for you." A.J. smiled, happy to be asked. First I shot just Sarah and her horse. *Snap.* "One more?" She moved next to A.J., Thrifty nuzzling her palm, and I caught the three of them. *Snap.* As she took the rope from A.J. she squeezed his hand. "Thank you," she said.

Her attention pleased and unsettled him. Turning to Linda with an uncertain look, he asked if he could saddle her horse.

"I'll do it," said Linda. "Later."

"I can use a hand with Thrifty," Sarah volunteered. "You see how jumpy he is."

"I'll be happy to help you, Sarah," A.J. said with his antique courtesy. They crossed the corral together while Thrifty scuffed at the dust, impatient with his short halter.

"Poor Sarah. She's saddled her own horse for ten years." Linda shook her head. "I guess she forgot how it's done."

"You did tell her that he cared about her," I said.

"Yes, and it's about time she took notice of him. But Akira can be so proper. Will he let her know he's interested too?"

"Do you mind?" I didn't; I was relieved to see Sarah reaching out to A.J. But it might hurt Linda's pride.

She laughed ruefully. "Only a little."

I left her at the corral and went up in the grandstand with Father Ted. We settled in with the early crowd. From our seats we looked across the track to the arena, the dusty infield surrounded by a green fence. A flagpole rose over the reviewing stand draped in bunting. Two cowboy clowns tumbled out of a chute, chased each other around the arena, then scrambled over the fence. Merchants rented space for advertising on the fence and their signs were hung around the track:

BARBARA'S TACK SHOP
Complete Saddlery
& Western Wear

———————

JESSUP'S FORGE
Horseshoeing & Ironwork

———————

HANSON BROS. FEED SUPPLY

———————

WHISKEY CITY
Beer, Wine, Liquor
Sodas–Snacks

"Bob should be here," said the priest. "How can he miss her race?"

"I'm to blame for that."

"Not as much as you think."

"Tell me he didn't order her to quit her job. To leave the city and come home."

"Dick, it wasn't because of you—it wasn't personal. He couldn't believe his bright little girl was a young woman living with a man. My guess is he still isn't ready for that."

"He'll force her to break away."

"Yes."

"Or he'll shut her out of his life."

"It'll break his heart if he does that. But he might. I wonder, how much obedience can he demand? At what price?"

The precision of the color guard quieted the crowd. Into this stillness spilled a Caliente County Vigilance Committee, twelve ranchers and merchants on horseback wearing broad hats, leather vests. They fired a volley of pistol shots into the air.

Instantly the man who'd supervised this ceremony bounded up the stairs to the reviewing stand, his two-tone boots taking each step firmly. On the platform Angie Costa turned, offering his hand to the old woman laboring up the stairs behind him. Shoulders slumped, dark suit glossy from wear, she paused, caught her breath, and joined him at the podium. At the foot of the stairs another man fidgeted with the watch-chain on the blue vest of his three-piece suit. For a long moment he leaned forward, as if straining to escape from his body, to become the naked energy burning inside it. Now the stairway was clear he sprinted up the steps, taking his place with the others.

Father Ted found photos of all three on the celebrity page of the program: Angelo Costa, Arena Director; District Attorney Leonard Mix; and Hannah Bascomb, Honorary Marshal for the rodeo. At the podium Angie introduced her as: "Old Hannah, the first woman from this valley to earn herself a law degree." Often in her years of private practice she'd served on review boards and advisory panels throughout the state, and lectured on legal ethics, rewarded with honorary degrees from Berkeley and Stanford. At eighty-two she still practiced occasionally in the courtrooms of Mingus and Crags Landing. With a pale hand she acknowledged our applause—a plump woman in a rumpled suit, string tie, silver belt buckle. A soft-eyed smile under a hay-pile of white hair.

Would Dorothy be interested in Old Hannah? *Snap.*

When the color guard presented a flag to the DA, Leonard Mix ran it up the pole, the stripes rippling in the breeze. A murmur rolled through the stands as the Sheriff's Posse paraded by. Mounted deputies in green hats, tan shirts. They rode escort for the Rodeo Queen, a sun-pinked blonde all in white; hat and jacket caught in a hailstorm of rhinestones. She rode her sorrel into the arena, the posse looking protective at a respectful distance. Dorothy would love this. *Snap.*

The drum and bugle corps struck up a brassy "Star Spangled Banner." At the rousing finish we clapped, stomped, whistled.

Old Hannah, the sun ablaze on her white hair, carefully descended the stairs. She was accompanied to her seat in the grandstand by a young man Father Ted identified as MacArthur Landis, junior partner in the firm of Bascomb & Landis.

Vendors hawked refreshments through the stands and I bought myself a beer and a lemonade for the priest. The day continued to be warm and dusty and the beer was sharp and cold.

A chute opened. The first horse and rider bolted across the arena after a white-face calf. The cowboys came from ranches in California, Idaho, Montana, Oklahoma, Arizona, Colorado. Now and then there were Blackfeet or a Ute or Pomo or a local man from the Pit River tribe. Top prize for roping was a thousand dollars, which Angie Costa presented from the reviewing stand. When a Texan rode off with the check not many cheered.

For bareback riding a string of bucking horses had been brought down from Alberta: Captain Jack, Mr. Lucky, Red Moon. "A mean little eliminator," said the announcer as Mr. Lucky twisted, leaped, and his rider landed at the base of the fence. The riders spurred high, hard. Noise and dust mingled in the air until the last bronc was led to the corral. Final round tomorrow.

Steer wrestling quieted everyone as we watched to see contact made. Each cowboy coasting alongside, sliding across the steer's back, wrestling the animal to a stop. Wrenching the horns, twisting the steer to the ground, doubled over in the dust. Finals tomorrow

Intermission brought us the Saddle Tramps, a team of trick riders. Young women wearing gold earrings; fringed vests; spangled blouses, a bare midriff, pink hot-pants. They rode in standing up; pivoted; stood backward. They lay back on their horses; rising onto their shoulders. They scissored their legs, then arched into backbends that turned into handstands as their mounts trotted around the arena accompanied by our clapping, whistling.

"Good pictures? Or weren't you paying attention?"

"I saw it all," I told the priest. "Great stuff!"

He laughed and I left him the camera and went down behind the fence past the first stock pens.

I found the paramedics still in their tent. Brian, a strong-looking young man with curly hair, lounged in a canvas chair, hands in the pockets of his white jumpsuit. Erica sipped orange juice through a straw. Her white outfit was baggy around her waist; she tucked it against her stomach, bending to set the juice carton in the grass. She rose smiling. "I'm from NEPA," I said, looking from one to the other. "You've heard from us."

"Her brother, Rob, he's the manager," said Brian. "He mentioned some letters."

"That's all?"

Erica scowled. "What do you want us to do?"

"It would help if you'd answer your mail."

"I'll tell Rob to get back to you. What's the worry?" Brian asked. "Lassen come alive?"

"It never died." They looked so fit and comfortable, so friendly but ungiving, it made me irritable. "We've told you we need to coordinate emergency services. All through this region. A network of names, phone lines, vehicles."

"Looks like you'll be busy." Brian shrugged.

"We want *you* to get busy before it's too late." How did Noah Geyer manage meetings like this for twenty years and maintain his easy nature?

Erica stretched her long-muscled arms. "Nothing we can do without money."

"Money isn't the vital element."

"*You* can say that. You're government."

"We'll find the funding for this program," I promised. "First we need people to work together."

Brian drew himself up beside Erica. Smiling, he slipped his arm around her waist. "We been together for six months now."

"Working," Erica corrected him. "He said working together."

He squeezed her suit beneath her breast. "You think it hasn't been work?"

Laughing, Erica slapped at his hand. She tucked down, and came up clutching her juice carton. "Hey," she said, "good luck!"

Nine Brahma bulls were locked into the pens behind the arena. Under their horns they gazed through the slats. Dark oval eyes revealed no urgent meanness, simply an on-going contemplation, as each bull pondered how to shatter the boards that fenced it in and the bones of the first man it met on the other side.

I brought another lemonade for Father Ted. A stillness settled in. A good crowd, it gave its approval to hard work, laughed at luck, good or bad, but hushed if anyone was hurt. Or likely to be. So the stands were silent for much of the bull riding.

The event was almost finished when a bull flung a rider from Fort Collins. He landed underfoot; we saw the horns plunge. The cowboy's knees jerked up, sank. Clowns tumbled into the arena, one wearing baggy pants, the other green shorts over red long-johns. They wagged their arms and legs, taunting the bull to attack them. A pickup man galloped in on a roan and reined up, shielding the body on the ground. Behind them the paramedics rushed in and lifted the body between them. Brian and Erica carried off the cowboy half-covered by an orange blanket over the stretcher. Now a pickup woman trotted her horse beside the bull while the clowns teased it toward the gate to an empty chute. Suddenly the Brahma charged. The clowns leaped apart and the bull drove through the open gate. They swung it shut, then clambered up the fence in mock fright and for a moment we all gave way to nervous laughter. A minute later the ambulance pulled away, red lights over the cab whirling, the siren screaming.

"Folks, this next is a neck-twister," the announcer said. "But these ladies are worth the effort." The race would start at the far end of the straightaway, out of sight of the grandstand, and its finish was further along the stretch. We wouldn't see Linda and Blueboy until the whole pack came pounding up the track.

"Keep your eyes on the north end," said the p.a. "Once you see 'em, they'll fly by before you can blink." I put down my cup and Father Ted did the same. A last look at the program: seven of the nine riders were from Crags Landing. Only Marcella and Linda had come down from Lake Elaine. "Five furlongs for the ladies," the p.a. readied us: "First time ever at this distance. No winners in the start; no losers at the finish."

A bell clanged.

The horses stormed into view. A dust cloud trailed the pack; the next moment it swirled over the slower ones as they dropped back. Her braid flying, Sarah Hack leaned forward on Thrifty in a furious drive. Her high-strung grey had the best start. A length behind came Marcella Costa, white jockey's cap snugged over her black hair, her whip flailing Fair Weather. From a slow start Linda, her red hair bobbing, brought Blueboy charging into fourth place. Here, before the grandstand, the track broadened and the pack splayed out across the wider surface.

Linda urged Blueboy into third and challenged the horse just ahead, a stocky chestnut who lost interest and in the last furlong fell back to the pack. Blueboy tore by him and ran close on the rear of Thrifty. Fair Weather wanted to drift out like the others, losing ground as Marcella struggled to hold him in. But the added furlong put the finish line further down where the track narrowed once more. Thrifty romped under the wire. Fair Weather had gone wide; when Marcella tried to veer him in he bolted back too far and Linda was there ahead of her. Marcella sagged in her saddle, reining in to avoid bumping, and her horse plodded across the finish line behind Blueboy.

We were on our feet cheering as the horses trotted back. Linda greeted a smiling Sarah Hack; they touched hands, cantered away. Marcella kept Fair Weather down the track, cooling out. Sarah circled Thrifty in front of the reviewing stand; there was no one to present her award. Leonard Mix sat by the podium, the flag flapping overhead, while Angelo Costa ran down to confront a race judge at the finish line.

Father Ted pointed out Pearl Costa, a small woman in a polka-dot dress hurrying down from the box seats. In high heels she picked her way along the track, hopping bird-like among clumps of dirt. "Whatever is Angie's problem," he said, "his wife will keep him from making an ass of himself. She's had plenty of practice." The two men were locked in an argument, Angie's wide hat wagging. They parted as Pearl pressed between them, waving her hands. Arm in arm, Angie and Pearl left the arena, looking grim.

The judge approached the reviewing stand where he spoke to Leonard Mix. He walked over to Old Hannah's seat and she followed him back. He climbed the reviewing stand and she waited on the track where Sarah kept Thrifty in hand as he rippled with impatience. Linda trotted Blueboy back to join her. Clearly, Angie wouldn't return to award the prize ribbons. Now the judge handed them down to Old Hannah. Sarah dismounted to receive her blue ribbon as the p.a. crackled across the arena:

"Winner of the Ladies Saddle Horse Race is Sarah Hack. Her daddy's our Chief Park Ranger, so you know she comes from good stock. Name of that swift horse is Thrifty." The crowd clapped approval. I'd snapped a picture of Linda congratulating Sarah; I caught Linda beside Blueboy for another shot. "Runner-up is Linda Pell down here from Lake Elaine. That big fella is Blueboy." We whooped and clapped as Old Hannah handed the red ribbon to Linda. "Third place to Marcella Costa—you saw her riding Fair Weather—she's another of those gals from Lake Elaine."

We met Linda walking Blueboy out to the corral. Her hair was tousled and it was dark with sweat where it stuck to her forehead. Her cheeks were blooming and she looked happy, dusty. "Are you all right?" I said. "Are you as fine as you look?"

"I feel fantastic."

"You were wonderful." I put my arm around her. We kissed.

Careful of his neck, Father Ted removed his cowboy hat. "This belongs to you." He placed it on Linda's head, pressing down her damp curls. "You're the one who can ride a horse!"

It was a good fit. She kissed his cheek. "Thank you!"

Linda asked him to join us for dinner but he declined. He'd arranged a ride into town with Old Hannah and Mac Landis. "It's an early night for me. I say Mass at ten tomorrow."

"You're in prime time," she said.

"I'll make the most of it."

Linda hooted. "I'm sure you will!"

With stiff-necked haste he walked back to the stands. Linda turned to me, handing over Blueboy's reins. "Darling," she said, "one of us smells like a horse. I'm going to take a shower. Will you wait? Then we can eat."

When Linda returned from the locker room she wore the bandanna knotted loosely around her neck. "This did bring me luck."

"You almost won."

"Sarah was splendid." Linda shook her head, holding her new hat in place. "Thrifty had the speed. Sarah put it out there. They deserved to win."

"What was Angie sore about?"

"He claims I cut off Marcella."

"She let her horse run wide."

"The judge told him that. Marcella wasn't going to beat Sarah anyway. Not today." She took the reins and Blueboy fell in behind her. "Angie refused to award our ribbons. Old Hannah told me: 'Here you are, honey. If this was money you could bank it or drink it.' I told her Daddy will hang it in his study."

Just then we heard Marcella come up behind us, walking Fair Weather. Her black hair had slipped from under her cap and it framed a pale complexion. Her lustrous eyes glared at Linda. "Too many horses out there to suit you?"

Linda stiffened. "What are you saying?"

Marcella braced her hands on her hips. "Your horse lugged in on mine. You knew I couldn't get by."

"Is that what your father thinks?"

"Ask him."

Driving a large pink sedan, Angelo Costa had backed a horse trailer into the space reserved for the ambulance, and he joined Pearl coming up the path. "That horse is a menace," he told Linda. "And so are you."

"Marcella rode herself out of the race," Linda said.

Angie stood his ground with his brown-and-white boots planted in the turf beside the path. "You wouldn't let her in," he said.

"This can't help anyone," I said. "I'll tell you what will. Pull that trailer out before there's another injury in the arena. That's an ambulance space. You might think before you risk—"

"You're fine people to talk about risks. I saw what you did to Marcella." Pearl's dress was a swarm of sunny dots as she swung open the car door. "I've known your mother for years, Linda. You're not much like her, are you? But you're the image of your father." She climbed in, slammed the door, rolled down the window. "You Pells think you can do anything you please. And get away with it!"

"Angie changed the rules." Linda held fast to Blueboy's reins. "That's what made the difference."

"Christ, it's over!" Marcella pulled off her cap, shaking out her hair. The anger had ebbed from her eyes but they were alive as ever. "Let's forget about it." She led Fair Weather to the trailer behind the pink car but he balked at being headed in.

"She *forced* you out!" her father insisted. "You could've broken a leg. This horse, too." With his broad hat he gave the horse's rump a swat but it produced no movement. His boots dug into the turf. Clenching both hands, he delivered a solid shove like a two-fisted punch. Fair Weather's hindquarters quivered. The horse shuddered backward, dropped a hefty shit, then ambled into the trailer. Angie glared at his brown boots. "Don't just sit there, Pearl! Bring a rag, for God's sake!"

When A.J. had unsaddled Thrifty he sauntered over. "You rode a terrific race," he told Linda. "You did your best."

"I'm happy with it."

"You pushed Blueboy perfect. All the way to the wire."

"Thrifty had too much speed."

"Sorry," said A.J. "Where can we get together?"

"Some place close by," Linda urged. "Traffic will be awful." We agreed to meet later in that bar with the neon bronco. Then A.J. asked to see Linda's ribbon. He knew she cherished it and when he returned the ribbon he laid it carefully across her hand. "I'll take Blueboy back," he said. "I'll ask Sarah too."

"Yes, do!" Linda said.

He walked Blueboy through tall grass to his trailer in a meadow beyond the lot. It was spring grass still, full and green before the summer drought, and it parted to make a brief dark path as they walked through the meadow. He turned once to wave.

"See you in The Chute," he called.

13

In the Chute

Sarah Hack was with Akira in a booth in The Chute as Linda and I wedged through the crowd around the bar. It was a huge old bar and all dark oak. Stained glass panels on each side flanked shelves of liquor backed by a gigantic mirror. In the panels were scenes of a snow-capped Lassen Peak, the pine forest, a steamboat in the Sacramento River (one of those sternwheel passenger boats Grandpa Darwin provisioned at our dock), and an early view of Crags Landing: the old church and the gallows. Against one wall was a small dance floor. With a pitcher of beer and some chilled glasses we slipped around the couples dancing and joined A.J. and Sarah at their booth.

"I offered to take Sarah someplace nice for supper," said A.J. "To celebrate."

"But we ate here instead," said Sarah, and we laughed.

I sat with Linda and poured us a beer. The music from a rainbow jukebox was old-time country and western: sad vocals sung to a joyous banjo, fiddle, guitar, bass. The dance floor filled for "Your Cheatin' Heart," "San Antonio Rose," and "Red River Valley." When we danced Linda leaned into me but her exhilaration from the race had worn off and she was quiet.

"Would you rather sit this out?"

"No," she said. "I'm just sorry Daddy didn't come to see me."

"It's his loss." I held her close.

"I won't dwell on it. Not tonight."

"Darling, you don't need to."

"Talk to me," she said. "Tell me I'm pretty. Say any fool thing. Tell me you'll take me away with you."

"I will, you know. The minute you're ready to leave." Then I understood. This *was* her escape. All of it. Leaving me. Leaving her work—or her father's work, as she'd come to see it. Finally—hardest for her—leaving her family too. "I don't mean to make this more difficult for you," I said.

"You do love easily. Though I'm glad you don't take it lightly."

"What are you saying?"

"Dick, you'd hardly met me and you were in love with me. You *do* fall in love easily. But once you do, you can't let go."

"Does that frighten you?"

"Yes—it does."

"Do you want me to let go?"

"I wouldn't be here if I did."

"We're different now. When we're together."

"Yes—you're nearer to me now."

She said it simply, directly. And I almost missed it. I held Linda warm in my arms as we moved in a small circle among the crowd. Boots sliding over the floor; laughter from the bar. "I want you near me," I said. "Like this."

"Why?"

"Linda, you're the best thing that's happened to me."

"Poor you," she said.

"I don't think so."

People pushed past the jukebox, bands of light painting their faces as they edged by. We laughed at being crowded together; the room smelled of beer, tobacco, leather, perfume. Once while we danced we were brushed apart; came back. "I almost lost you," I said.

Here, give me your hand.

I'm here, yes, let's stay close.

Linda loosened the green bandanna. We stood there being bumped about as she wrapped it like a hatband and slipped it around the crown of her hat. "Now I can't be lost in the crowd," she said, as she put on her hat, and we danced.

Laughter turned us toward the bar. Danny LeFevre had his arm around the waist of a Saddle Tramp, her spangled blouse gleaming in the lights of the bar. When his hand slid onto her pink hot-pants she whispered something and he laughed in a loud and challenging way.

Back at the booth Akira Jagao had put on a clean cotton shirt, the long sleeves buttoned at the wrist though the room was warm. Sarah had undone her braid and her hair flowed over her shoulders. "You two had fun," she said as we settled in.

"It was fine," I said.

"I don't dance much," A.J. admitted, turning to Sarah, and pushing his hair back from his forehead. "Do you?"

Sarah smiled. "I like to try."

Before A.J. could take her up on her invitation LeFevre's voice boomed across our booth.

"Swell night!" He wore a western shirt with pearl-like buttons and he'd rolled the sleeves above his biceps. Folding his arms, he planted one of his alligator boots on the bench beside A.J. but he looked only at Sarah: "Hi, beautiful."

She flushed, paled, said nothing.

"You're a big winner today."

"It was a close race, really." Sarah shot a stricken look at Linda. "Linda almost caught me."

"I didn't see it. Anyway, you won. Didn't you?" He favored Sarah with a smile but his pale eyes were charged with a brash energy. "How about it, sweetheart? Want to dance?"

Sarah slid a glance at A.J., his dark eyes absolutely still; she must have sensed how uncomfortable he was. "We're resting," she said. "It's been a very active day."

"Might be a sweet night." LeFevre's boyish smile was bright enough to light the booth. "If you find the right man."

"We're together here," I said. "The four of us."

"Right, I'll wait." His glance flickered over A.J. "But not for long."

Turning, LeFevre shouldered into the crowd. He cut in on a couple, selecting a trim woman with dark brown hair. She wore a silk shirt, tight jeans, boots, and he danced her by our booth, their arms around each other. Her nails were crimson like her shirt. He put her on display for a moment; then moved her out among the others weaving through a haze of light and smoke that extended to the back of the room where a pair of pool tables basked under cones of yellow light.

"Who is she?" I asked.

"Cindy Klinger hosts a radio show," said Sarah. "Music and interviews. Promos for local events like the rodeo."

"Shouldn't be hard to interview LeFevre," I said.

Linda patted my hand. "Let's not be nasty."

We sat out the next tune while A.J. and Sarah went off to the bar. When the music halted and the floor cleared, through a curtain of smoke I saw Old Hannah at the bar. Listening to someone, she looked patient, comfortable in her black suit, her face crinkled in a smile. Next to her sat a squat, slope-shouldered man, his orange cap pulled down as if the light was too bright for him. Beside him wearing a fringed vest sat a middle-aged woman with small bald spots on a head of frizzy brown hair. "Hap and Harriet Mitchell," Linda said. "He owns the slaughterhouse. She manages the meat lockers. They'll be at the house tomorrow—friends of Father Ted."

"Anyone else I ought to know?"

"You've met Marcella."

"She's coming?"

"Mother invited her family. Because of Pearl. My guess is only Marcella shows up. You keep away from her."

"I'll swim across the lake. Back and forth."

"Underwater."

"All night." I put my hand on my heart and Linda laughed.

"Marcella *is* beautiful. And she knows it. I suppose I've always been jealous."

"No need for that." I put my arm around her.

A.J. and Sarah returned with a pitcher of beer, her finger hooked into one of his belt loops as they walked back together.

He filled our glasses as the music returned: two up-tempo banjos frolicking through "Roll in My Sweet Baby's Arms".

Sarah took Akira's hand. "Let's dance." They slipped from the booth as she let him lead her onto the floor.

"Akira doesn't know what he's in for," Linda whispered.

"Can he dance to that?"

"Sarah will help him."

She did. Boots scudding over the floor, they whirled in time with the others; A.J. awkward, enthusiastic, leading her, he thought—or did he know it was her doing?—his arm extended, twirling her out. Sarah, smiling, came skipping back to him.

The two banjos twanged and thrummed. As the crowd swung around the floor the smoke drifted upward and spread across the ceiling and obscured the glass panels above the bar.

We couldn't hear what Danny LeFevre said when he cut in to dance with Sarah. Akira's reply sounded sharp, LeFevre smirked, they glared at each other, and the tune ripped along with that manic strumming. LeFevre said something else and Akira's hand grasped his shirt, pulling it tight beneath his chest. LeFevre clamped a large hand over A.J.'s wrist and squeezed. I was out of the booth, starting across the floor. If a fight broke out, A.J. had spirit and a wiry strength, but LeFevre had height and thirty pounds on him, and most of that weight was muscle. He and I at least were closer to the same size. For an instant I wondered if A.J. had his knife with him. Had he pulled it? No. One fist was clenched at his side. I looked for the blade but there wasn't one. LeFevre, grinning, held the other wrist in a crushing grip. A.J. stood wide-eyed in mute pain, his mouth gaping. Then, just as I reached them, LeFevre let go.

A.J. wouldn't rub his wrist; wouldn't give LeFevre the satisfaction of seeing him do that. But it had to be burning. His face flushed with fury and shame, his fists clenched at his sides, he made a tight little bow toward Sarah, taking his leave. He strode to the bar and stood with his back to the dance floor.

Back at our booth Linda patted the bench beside her. "Dick, sit down." Her voice was thin with fear. "They won't fight?"

"No—not now."

"Don't fight Danny," she pleaded. "He's brutal."

"I believe it."

"And you mustn't let Akira fight him." She was trembling. "Please."

"I'll do what I can," I said. "But A.J. has to be careful. He won't back down. And LeFevre would love to tear him apart."

The music stopped and Sarah stomped over to us. A.J. arrived a step behind her.

Smiling, he slumped down. He pushed back his hair and flung his arms out on the table in that easy manner that had annoyed me when I first met him. And infuriated Linda's father. I'm sure he was still sore that LeFevre had danced with Sarah, but I think he was embarrassed, too, because he'd lost his temper, he'd been impolite, and Sarah saw it. Heard it.

"Akira, I'm sorry," she said. Nervously she turned her glass. The candle shook its quavering light across our table.

"No problem." He rocked his glass in his hands.

I went to the bar for another round. Old Hannah had left. Hap Mitchell was hunkered down on a stool between his wife Harriet and a blond-haired woman squashing a cigarette into an ashtray. "Listen to this—" he said.

"Hap!" said Harriet. "Don't tell that dumb dog joke."

"Why not?" Hap's orange cap now was perched on the back of his head. "What's wrong with it?"

"It's disgusting," said Harriet.

Hap whirled on his stool and winked at the blonde. "So?"

The blonde responded with a big-toothed smile. "Let's hear it, honey," she said.

"It's dumb and it's disgusting," said Harriet.

"Aw, it's okay," said Hap. He turned to the woman with the waiting smile. "See what *you* think," he said. "This man carries his dog into a bar. See, this dog hasn't any legs. None. So he carries him in. Bartender asks him, 'What happened to that poor dog? Was it an accident?"

"'Nope," says the man. "Born like this."

"Really?" the bartender says. "How old is he?"

"Nine years this summer."

"Nine years old! And no legs! Fucking amazing! I don't see how a dog survives for nine years without any legs to walk around on. That's one hell of a dog. What's his name?"

"No name," the man says.

"Aw, come *on*! You keep a dog with no legs for nine years and you never give him a name?"

"He don't need a name," the man says.

"He don't?"

"No," says the man. "Why's he need a name. He can't ever come when I call him."

Hap grinned at the woman beside him. She patted her hair. Then she laughed loudly, showing her teeth.

"Honestly," Harriet said. "Isn't that the scummiest joke you ever heard?"

"Just about," I said.

Harriet leaned over to the blond woman: "That's what I always say about Hap," she giggled. "He can't ever come when I call him."

Her hand on Hap's leg, the woman flashed a toothy smile.

"Honey," she told Harriet, "you better work on your call."

Hap winked at me and grinned.

"Bitch," said Harriet.

The woman laughed again and she didn't remove her hand.

"You got a good chance with Hap," said Harriet. "He likes blondes—they get dirty quicker."

I brought our beer to the booth. A.J.'s fingers drummed the table, tapping out the rhythm to "Foggy Mountain Breakdown." Sarah tried on Linda's hat. We said she looked fine. "No, it looks better on you." She handed it back. That last song cleared the floor but a slow tune, "Sweet Dreams," brought back the crowd. Then the pace picked up and the floor trembled. I danced with Linda again, holding her close, enjoying the scent of her hair, with my hand under the hat hanging down her back. We danced to a haunting number: "I Can't Help It if I'm Still in Love with You." True. We stopped beside the pool tables to watch the others dancing in the whirl of smoke revolving through the room.

A few men had stripped off their shirts. They were sitting with some women they'd just met, around a table up front, then one pair hurried onto the dance floor. The man was thick-set with dark red hair on his shoulders and chest. The woman wore a cowgirl's blouse with shiny button-snaps on her breast pockets. She wore jeans with the name Mary Lou stitched in white letters on the back of her belt. When they joined the others dancing, he held her hand in the air, one arm around her waist. Then he put both arms around her and Mary Lou reached behind him, tucking her hands beneath his belt. They swayed together. Another couple from their table rushed onto the floor, the man shirtless and the woman in a checkered top and denim skirt. Their laughter was louder than the music; they suddenly became the center of attention. That's when I saw Danny LeFevre unbutton his shirt, lay it over a stool, and draw Cindy Klinger onto the floor. They danced, her nails deep red on his blond back like spots of blood.

Now A.J. was up, peeling off his shirt, coaxing Sarah out of the booth. With his jaunty walk he started toward the dance floor. By the time they arrived Mary Lou had her blouse off, the hand of the ruddy-haired man was on the clasp of her bra, working it loose, and Cindy had shucked her crimson shirt so it hung draped around her waist and she was unhooking her bra.

People were yelling and laughing and I couldn't hear the music—the melody or lyrics—but I could *feel* a hard drumbeat: the insistent undercurrent of the bass, throbbing, as the crowd surged over the floor between the bar and the dim booths. The cloud of smoke dipped and drifted. Linda's hand gripped mine.

"Take me home?"

"You won't dance topless?"

Linda grinned. "Not here."

We looked around to wave goodbye but Akira's back was turned, his hair glistening in the smoky light, Sarah's hand on his spine as they danced. A.J. had loved her once, and now, with her encouragement, he might again. I remembered his swimming at Lake Elaine, wanting to impress Linda's father. Is that what he was doing tonight, for Sarah's benefit? Maybe sending a message to Linda as well: *Sarah sees what I'm worth. You missed it.*

Whatever was on Akira's mind, it was obvious Sarah Hack was interested now that she knew how he'd felt about her. She liked him at once, and I never doubted that her affection was genuine. Sarah was soft-spoken, thoughtful, good-humored in her quiet way, almost pretty, absolutely honest. Dancing with him, she looked fresh-faced, content to rest her chin on his bare chest. Her eyes smiled at us over his shoulder and she wagged her hand. When they turned we lost them in the crowd. Outside the noise from The Chute spilled onto the busy sidewalk lit by that big neon bronco, which added an electric hissing to the din. Car lights glared as Station Road was choked with traffic that coughed, sputtered, fumed, started up, halted, and gradually crept out of the darkness, illuminating the narrow street with a nervous, jittery iridescence.

14

The Blind

At eight o'clock a florist's van pulled into the driveway. A woman in a pink jumpsuit brought out armfuls of roses, lilacs, and sprigs of cherry blossoms. She carried the flowers across the lawn, and Annette and Linda saw to placing them throughout the house. Doctor Pell had selected a dozen of his irises and he'd reserved three tall vases for them.

I helped the woman close the van. Then Linda came out in a lemon-yellow dress with a crushed silk jacket and white gloves. Our greeting was a brief kiss; we were on our way to Mass with her mother. Her hair flamed in the sunlight and I thought of how she'd felt in my arms last night. When I'd brought her home from The Chute we found Annette in a housedress, asleep at the kitchen table, her head on her arms. With Linda's help before the rodeo, and a hand from Teresa, she'd spent the day cooking a ham and a turkey, baking rolls, rinsing lettuce, scrubbing carrots, jicama, green peppers, while Doctor Pell prepared the porch, the pier, the lawn, the flowerbeds. "We mustn't leave her here," Linda whispered. "Can you carry her?"

Cradling her in my arms, I lifted Annette from her chair. She snored softly, then was still. I felt her warmth and the weight of her sleep as her head rested on my shoulder. She'd worked herself to exhaustion and the smell of her sweat rose through the scent of her hair. Her loose-fitting dress sagged on her breasts and draped across my arms.

I followed Linda through the dark foyer to the living room and settled Annette on the sofa. She slept with her legs tucked up, childlike, as Linda covered her with a coat from the closet.

"What will your father do?"

"They'll find each other." Linda tucked the coat sleeves around her mother's shoulders. "If they want to."

We went quietly upstairs.

Linda switched on a desk lamp and dropped her hat there, in the lamp's yellow glow. Turning, she reached out, we embraced, she leaned her head on my shoulder and we pretended we were still dancing in The Chute. We circled and I saw the doll in the satin wedding-gown seated in the rocking chair, the small purse in its lap. "Just hold me?" Linda said as we stopped. I couldn't see her face but heard the anguish in her whisper: *What do you think of Sarah? Yes, I like her, too. But Akira: is he falling in love with her? No, I'm not disappointed. What a foolish thing to say! I'm not losing him; he wasn't mine anyway. That was all in his mind. You were jealous but you were mistaken. I'm glad. Yes, that I made you jealous. Or he did...You don't know how I've missed you. I'm sorry I didn't write. It was rotten of me. Yes. Dick, let's not be silly about it.* While Linda took off her blouse I unbuttoned my shirt. My hands cupped her breasts and I felt their warm weight in her bra. My lips brushed her hair, I kissed her ear, touched it with my tongue. She removed her bra and dropped it on the chair. I stroked her breasts and she whispered, "I like *that.*" We pulled off our boots and jeans.

It was six months since we'd been in bed together. At first it was too quick, we were so eager. Then I stroked her breasts, we rested, whispering. When we rolled over and made love again, Linda riding on top, my hips lifting with each thrust, we moved powerfully, quietly, except for the jouncing bed.

Half-dressed, carrying my boots, I went into the bathroom to shower and when I was in bed in the guest room I heard Linda in the shower. Then the house was still but the darkness was alive. From the screened window across the room I heard the pines creaking in the wind. Then the owl called again.

So regular were the hours of the Church of the Immaculate Heart that they were painted in fading black on an old white signboard beside the front steps:

Sunday Masses: 8, 10, 11:30 a.m.

Weekdays: 7:30 a.m., 6 p.m.

Confession: Saturday 3-5 p.m.

Just inside the red brick church stood a porcelain font for holy water, a small dish and dingy sponge resting in the bowl. By a stairway to one side a sign cautioned against overcrowding the choir loft: *By Order of the Fire Marshal,* and under this warning was a fire extinguisher, with instructions printed on the cylinder: *Hold upright. Pull pin. Push top lever.*

On a bright morning it was like entering a huge blazing heart—falling through stained glass windows a fiery light throbbed in the church, pulsing upon wooden pews and crimson carpet. Dark confessional booths flanked the walls. Crimson velvet covered two side altars lit by fluttering candles. Over one of these stood Mary wearing a blue robe, with a wide-eyed look of adoration or dread: *the fear of God.* Her palms were pressed in supplication; a heavy-beaded rosary was looped around her wrists as if she were a prisoner of her own prayers.

She stared at the wall above the main altar where a vast painted heart began to swell over the ceiling. From a wound in the lower portion three large drops of blood descended toward the altar. From the top of the heart a painted fountain of flame sprayed over the ceiling, over the heads of the parishioners who rose from kneeling and stood to hear the Gospel read. The main altar was built of tier upon tier of dark volcanic rock, but flowers and candles sprouted from its many niches. A scorched world had returned to bloom. Down in front of that glowing rock Father Ted turned pages of his missal, the lectern lighted by a small brass lamp.

With a hush of attention his parish awaited his first words to them in almost four months. I wondered whether he noticed that hush; did he prolong it for his own purpose? I'd come to believe he was capable of that much cunning.

"James I; 18," he said:

"'Wicked designs come from the deep recesses of the heart: fornication, theft, murder, adultery, greed, malice, deceit; our sensuality, envy, blasphemy, arrogance, hardness of heart—all these evils come from within us and render us impure.'

"This is the Gospel of the Lord," said Father Ted.

We sat down to hear his sermon.

"You know," he began, "I'm unfit to be your priest." His discomfort with his brace, as he repeatedly lifted his chin, was answered by shuffling among the pews.

"All these sins the Lord mentions in the Gospel this morning are in my heart. So I stand before you and I blush with shame because I'm your priest. But those desires boil in my heart, we carry the heat of our guilt, until a rush of blood betrays our shame. Many of you have travelled up the road to visit Lassen Peak. My brother, who understands this process better than I do, tells me about the activity under the volcano. All that heat and pressure building beneath the earth's surface, until the day it flings up the fire and vapor and rubble of an eruption, and it all comes to light. I mean this in much the same way our Gospel tells us those desires are in our hearts, until they surface, and we blush to see what we've done.

"If you'll bear with me this morning, I must speak first about my own shame. Then I'll speak about yours. Then I'll say something about God's."

At the mention of God's shame half a dozen parents ushered their children into the aisles and down the crimson carpet to the doors. They went on out and the doors gasped shut.

Father Ted looked across the lectern at his restless congregation with a smile of gratitude that we'd remained in our seats. "My friends," he said, "a holy man named Jules Beauregard, who lived much of his life in this part of the country, often asked himself: Why do we punish desire? Let's consider that curious question for a minute. Why do we restrict the most powerful impulses in our hearts? *His* answer was that our desires might lead us to love. And we're afraid of love. We fear its power to transform us. Change us. Once *that* happens, well, our self-control goes—" turning his shoulders, he glanced at the leaded panes shot through with scarlet light "—right out the window. So, yes, that can frighten us." The priest paused and I looked again at that large-eyed figure of Mary. "How does this happen to us?" he went on. "I think it happens when we begin to care more about somebody else than we do about ourselves. That holy man I mentioned? He learned this lesson because he loved a little child. My friends, don't worry too much about the love of God; that's only an idea. What matters is the everyday practice of caring about each other.

"But I didn't..."

It was going to be a warm day in the valley. Already the sun baked the brick church while we sweltered in the pews.

Father Ted's large hands touched the brace around his neck. "You may remember some months ago I was riding my motorcycle—a gift from you, good people; a gift which I abused—and an accident put me in the hospital. I encouraged a story about a pickup that ran me off the road. That truck, of course, was never identified. Because it didn't exist." He told us he'd grown tired of trail-climbing and stopped at a bar below Lake Elaine. He had a couple of beers—"I wasn't in uniform." he said, patting his vestments—the light was fading and he'd wanted to return to Crags Landing before dark. He wasn't drunk, but he'd been a little too relaxed as he came down the mountain road. His heavy shoulders swayed as he described his swerving, and the lectern swung in his hands, back and forth, until he snapped it to a stop. His missal slipped to the carpet. "I struck ice!" he said. The skid threw him into the rock face. "I did this to myself! As I wheeled down that road I didn't care about you or your troubles. Or the disgrace I might bring to my family. Or the problems I've caused my bishop. The truth is, I wasn't thinking about anybody else. I was enjoying myself. In a reckless way. It's that simple. So I ended up in the hospital. Then in a monastery. And here I am today."

There hadn't been a breath of air in the church. Now, back in the foyer, an usher switched on three ceiling fans. From the arch overhead they spun down gentle drafts. In response the candles on the altars snapped their tongues. Two more families left, the father and mother hushing their children down the center aisle in the pulsing light.

"Please forgive what I did," said Father Ted, "but never forget it." Candles twitched in the scarlet light. Pews creaked; people about to leave stayed to listen a little longer. "I left you because I was ashamed to see myself in your eyes...While I was in the monastery some of you prayed for my recovery. Others wrote to our bishop and asked him to dismiss me from this parish. You wanted to be relieved of the dark blot of my disgrace. I'd like to be rid of it as well. But how can we rid ourselves of our shadows? What will enlighten us? Well, you know, Jesus says, 'I am the light.' Then he goes down into hell, doesn't he? Under the earth. Down into all those sins and desires of today's Gospel. Think of the mountain as your heart; remember the magma is always remaking the material there. Until it pushes up into the world, breaks free, and pours out. Because whatever breaks your heart will break the mountain.

"In three days he emerges as the fire. Jesus once told us: 'Whoever is near to me is near the fire.' Do we blush to hear these words? The fire that burns us with our guilt is the fire of love, isn't it? Only if we care for each other can we know our guilt, feel shame, and hope to be forgiven.

"When you come to confession, though we can't see each other with the screen between us, yet you're mortified. You're shaken by your shame if you take the sacrament seriously. But many of you come too often. Don't come and tell the priest every piddling thing you did. I don't know if that's the sin of pride—*look what I did, God, look at me*—or is it just our infernal busyness? *I did it; it must mean something!* Well, don't bother with it if it doesn't break your heart. And don't send your children every week either. Little children, seven, eight years old, so scared they wet their pants; excuse me, but they do, the poor things. No, no, no. *You* come, not them. And only if you are shaken by your shame. As I am now.

"Now what about God? His guilt?"

Again people left their pews. Several parents herded their children out the doors. Father Ted's face glowed with warmth, his flesh ruddy over the white cervical collar.

"If God made us in his image, then he's like us, isn't he? He, too, feels shame. Remember how he ordered Abraham to slay his own son. *Horrible*; a fiendish story. But he stopped. He wouldn't make the man kill his son. He'd meant to—to test him with his own son, and he wouldn't hold back his hand. Jesus cried out on the cross, 'Why have you forsaken me?' God was so ashamed he couldn't answer. He hid himself and he's hiding still. Now we're told to slay our childish impulses. To strangle them with the strength of our will. And when you do this, and you destroy what you love, you turn to God for comfort. For approval." He lifted his broad hands, his palms toward us. "Silence," he said. "Darkness," he said. "Yours is the voice crying in the wilderness. You are naked and alone. Until you find each other in the warmth of your shame. Then you are blessed by that rush of blood like a fire that's been forming all this time in the mountain that is your heart.

"My friends, I'm unfit to be your priest. But you've helped me to feel my shame—that's what I've come back to tell you." In Father Ted's closing remarks was an announcement; his brown eyes were serious, his weighty face immobile, but his voice lifted, he couldn't conceal the pleasure it gave him to surprise us with it: "I won't be permitted to return to this parish. And I shouldn't be.

I won't ask the bishop for that favor. Still, perhaps we've changed each other for the better. It's like Jesus said, 'Whoever is near to me is near the fire.'

"God bless you now. And God bless the mountain. And God bless the fire in the mountain."

After Mass I thought Annette or Linda would want to talk with Father Ted but they didn't. We went straight to the car and drove up the road to the lake without a word. In the Pells' driveway I opened the door for Annette but she sat a moment, sniffling into a tiny handkerchief. "Well, he's done it—" She swung her legs into the sunlight, stood up, shaken. "He's finished here."

In the stillness we heard the engine ticking as it cooled. "He kept his word," I said. "He never mentioned Mercy House."

"He wouldn't dare." Linda peeled off one glove, then the other. "Once he leaves the monastery that's all he has left."

Doctor Pell carried a fence battery down to the pier and I brought a string of four paper lanterns. We loaded them into the boat, I untied the mooring and climbed aboard. The boat chugged away, bouncing once, twice, before settling into its steady *chop chop* through low waves.

We picked up speed bearing down on the blind, but he left the throttle open and overshot it. Swinging in a tight turn, throwing up a sheet of spray, he killed the engine and we rode back toward the brush-cluttered raft rocking in our wake. We cruised halfway around it just on momentum, the prow cutting quietly through the water. At the time I thought he'd made a mistake, approaching too fast. It was on our second approach that he cut the engine and we glided noiselessly around the raft. That's when I remembered the little radio-powered boat in the park in San Francisco: it had buzzed over the water, then suddenly went silent, but its momentum carried it further. That day Linda and I had brought Dorothy Geyer with us for a ride and a picnic afterwards. Less than a year ago; it seemed much longer when I thought of all that had happened since. Living with Linda and losing her. I began to see why the priest left me those pages from Jules Beauregard's manuscript: *Love changes me. It changes all of us,* he wrote. Will it? It better.

We tied in beside the raft. The blind was tobacco brush, manzanita, mule ear, aspen—the dry brush of last winter—woven through chicken wire joined to posts at the corners. We hung a lantern from each post. He brought two cups and a pint of Scotch from the boat. We sat with the battery between us, among the dry brush, while the sun blazed in a square of the sky,

"Your health," he said.

"Yours," I said.

We drank and he sat back with his weight on one elbow. "Do you ever shoot out here?"

"Just offshore," he said. "I like that 12-gauge."

"With the walnut stock?"

"That's the one."

"It's a handsome gun."

"It's my favorite. Do you shoot?"

"No," I said.

"It's an honorable sport, sir." In the stillness we heard the water lapping around us. "I wish Annette took an interest. She never has." The cup felt cool but the Scotch was warm in my throat. "I tried teaching her to shoot," he said. "She says she's too *small.* That's crazy."

I thought of Annette in one of her oversized dresses, her long hair drawn back, that shattered look in her eyes, and a shotgun at her shoulder. "She might not have the nerves for it."

"Certainly not now!" His laugh was scornful. "She's on her medicine again." The sun beat down on his sandy hair and his brow was bright pink. "I kept her clean for a day and she almost cracked up."

"She was hurting," I said.

"I hid it on the boat."

"That was Linda's guess."

"Smart girl." Sitting up, he took a swallow of his drink. "I had to give in on this. She has only so much energy. And this is a hell of a time to break down."

"Did she want help? A caterer?"

"Dick, we've always done things for ourselves. That's how our family is." Sitting back, his cup against his chest, he nudged the battery with his foot. He didn't have to explain. It was Annette who'd planned this party, wasn't it? He hadn't built their house to entertain anyone; it was a fortress for his family. If she wanted a houseful of guests, fine. Let them come. Once a year. And let her cook for them. I tilted my cup and tasted metal with the last of the whiskey. "I don't want strangers preparing our food. Serving our guests." Doctor Pell poured another round. "Annette understands."

"You're lucky Teresa can help."

"What a splendid girl." He sipped his drink. "She's bringing my brother." He laughed. "She's a splendid girl anyway."

"And A.J.?"

"I don't expect him until tonight." The blind rocked on the water. "Soon enough. Wouldn't you say?"

Had Linda told him about A.J. and Sarah Hack? I didn't think so. She hadn't been certain, herself, what was happening between them. "Last night," I said, "he was with us in The Chute."

Doctor Pell dismissed this with a wave of his cup.

"I've seen too much of that little prick."

"Listen," I said, "he's no threat to you."

"You two are pals now?"

"I didn't say that."

"He's been nothing but trouble to me." The brush around us quivered as the raft rose on a rill of water, then settled back into its nodding, sliding motion. "After tonight," said Doctor Pell, "I don't intend to worry about A.J. anymore."

Those were his exact words, spoken in a low decisive voice, but at the time I missed the point. "I'm happy to hear it." I swallowed the last of my whiskey. "When you're ready to discuss NEPA I'll arrange a meeting with Noah Geyer."

"Dick, I've thought about his project. It has merit. What do you need from me?"

"NEPA needs credibility. That's your job. And coordination. That's mine." I wanted Pacific Gas and Electric to lower the level of Lake Elaine before Lassen Peak might erupt, to avoid flooding. He understood a prompt response would be urgent: to evacuate homes, campsites, resorts. To call up a Search and Rescue unit. Alert hospitals in the valley. Protect a communication network: telephone, radio, television. I told him I'd meet next month with the Office of Emergency Services, in Sacramento. "You'll be getting about your business tomorrow," he said. "Who do you see in Crags Landing?"

"P.G. & E. The blood bank. Red Cross. Joe Sullivan."

"The sheriff?" The anxious light in his eyes reminded me of his wife. "What do you want with Sully?"

"His cooperation. He has to sit down with someone from the agency. It might as well be me. Until we do that we're just sheets of paper on his desk."

"You're right, of course." Doctor Pell leaned over, emptying the pint into his cup. "We'll make this work. You have my word. You can take it back to Noah Geyer when you leave."

"Before I leave," I said, "I want to be sure about Linda."

He downed his drink. "What about her?"

I'd seen him angry and worried about his family, but never quite as unsettled as this, his eyes swimming in a filmy blue light. "Our relationship," I said: "Hers and mine."

"Do your work and don't worry about that." A frown pinched his face, reddened by the sun. "Relationships are for people who can't cope with ideas."

I felt the Scotch and the sun now. My mind was muddled, so was his, and we weren't getting any brighter sitting here. I stood, offered my hand. He rose to his knees, his face enflamed. "Yes. Annette will be needing us," he said.

We wired the lights to the battery. "These won't take hold until dusk. After dark they'll give a bright glow," he said. He stooped to retrieve his bottle and I was surprised to hear him chuckle: "And they'll make LeFevre happy."

Across the lake a patrol boat droned like an angry hornet. A few sailboats, prim white moths, fluttered over the water. We chugged off and cruised back to the pier.

Doctor Pell knelt to pick some iris at the bottom of the lawn. Teresa Espinosa's dented white car sat in the driveway; so Father Ted had arrived. I went up the path. The door was open and I heard Teresa singing in that soulful voice from deep in her breast, the notes vibrant and clear like stones under water. She was so shy I was certain she'd stop if she heard me come in. Listening in the doorway, I looked back at the floating blind. Sunlight flashed across the water and you could hardly make out the lanterns. I went into the house. The perfume of fresh-cut flowers filled the air but the singing abruptly stopped.

15

Sunday Night

In the twilight the moon was an enormous eye above the brim of the lake. It cast its gaze across the water while a breeze rocked the lanterns strung over the pier. We'd set out a drinks table: wine decanters, a punch bowl, crystal cups, a silver ice bucket, tall glasses for gin and whiskey—a table of hors d'oeuvres: salmon pate, smoked oysters, tiny shrimp, dill-flavored dip, green peppers, mushrooms wrapped in bacon—another table would hold platters of ham, turkey, breads, cheeses. Later, desserts would appear in the dining room. The tables stood high on the lawn—between them you saw the iris beds—while a golden light from the windows and above the front door fell across the flowers, decanters, cups and glasses.

Marjorie Fennel, society columnist for *The Pioneer,* Crags Landing's weekly paper, arrived with her husband Bill; Annette hurried down the driveway to meet them. The band was tuning up on the porch, stray notes drifting over us as Cindy Klinger climbed from her red sports car and trotted up the stone path. She looked uncertainly at me, wondering if we'd met; beamed at Doctor Pell. "Hi there." She stroked her dark hair. "This is it, huh?"

His frown took in her gold-sequined mini dress, smoky nylons, a black belt to match her high heels. "Do I know you?" He sounded incredulous. "Does Linda?"

I introduced her. "I'm Danny LeFevre's date," she informed him, a hand on her hip. "He said you're having open house."

"We're having a party for our friends," said Doctor Pell. "This is *not* an open house."

"All I know is he told me to meet him here." She glanced at a gold watch on her wrist. "Guess he's still on duty."

We looked for LeFevre on the lake. The lanterns on the blind had begun to take hold in the oncoming dark. "I'm afraid so," said Doctor Pell.

"He'll be along," I said. "Want a drink?"

"I'll get it." A flip of her hair bared her shoulders. "Don't worry about me. I'll see how the band's doing."

Doctor Pell's eyes followed Cindy to the drinks table and over to the porch. "Who the hell is that?"

"LeFevre's friend."

"*New* friend." His voice heavy with resignation, he looked at the grass darkening at his feet. "LeFevre's the sort of man who only has new friends."

Sadly, I think he was right about that. And you could say the opposite about *him*. Outside his family his few friends were all of long-standing. But little acquaintance. That's the point, isn't it? The less they saw of him the longer their friendship endured. Kurowski for example. Old pals who hadn't met in years. A note, a phone call. Nothing more. Even in his family I imagined I saw the strain of living with Doctor Pell. Look at Annette hurrying down to greet the Fennels while her husband, reluctant, his mind on something else, pulled his gaze from the grass and marched down to join them. That tension in her eyes, in the fine lines around her mouth, it was never at rest. Always she looked ready for danger or disappointment. You wondered if his long absences—the Navy years; his field work since that time—might have helped their marriage more than the time they spent together. How else did she manage it? God knows, I tried to be his friend, too; for my own reasons. I'd told myself it was what Noah expected of me, for NEPA; but I wouldn't have been here except for Linda.

Leaving the house, she started down the path toward her parents. The gold light from the house burned in her red hair. She wore a bow at the waist of her peach-colored gown and when I stopped her she folded her hands across it. I put my hand under her arm. "You're beautiful."

Linda grinned. "No."

I kissed her, she bowed her head, and I kissed her neck. Her hair deepened as we walked out of the light. She stopped, she wanted me to admire her again. "Isn't it a lovely gown?"

"It's lovely."

"Teresa works wonders."

"You are a wonder."

"People are arriving." She placed her palm on my chest. "Let me introduce you."

Now that the driveway was filled the Pells' guests parked beside the road through the woods and walked under the pines and up the lawn to the house. The moon lifted itself over the lake to look down on a gathering of white dinner jackets, silk suits, soft-shaded gowns. Most of the people I met Annette had invited from Crags Landing. Others arrived by boat from across the lake, ringing the bell, treading the pier through pools of lantern light. A few were Doctor Pell's colleagues from the university, including his department head, Ike Wolfe, and his wife Judith. Several of Father Ted's friends from the Immaculate Heart parish came up the lawn together laughing, young men in jeans and jackets, one wearing a tie, one woman in a neon-blue jumpsuit. Wally and Winnie Hack walked up to meet us, Sarah wearing a rose-colored party dress. A little later Akira arrived alone, his eyes searching the crowd.

He wore a handsome blue suit that looked brand new. No, said Linda, it was a year old, he'd bought it for his brother's funeral.

We saw Marcella Costa at the bottom of the path and to Linda's surprise her parents were with her: Pearl in a mocha silk gown, Angie red-faced from two days in the sun at the rodeo, Marcella stunning, her dark hair in ringlets, her complexion pale, her gown as light as the moon. Annette greeted them, easing them into the gathering, and they were quick to climb the path to the busy tables. On the porch the four-piece combo was playing. A saxophone under the din of our voices; then a trumpet riding over it. "After yesterday this must be an effort for Angie. And Pearl," said Linda. "I'm glad they're here."

"Yes." Doctor Pell buttoned his dinner jacket, unbuttoned it, hardly aware of his hands. He seemed distracted. "Yes, let's have no hard feelings."

"Of course not!" Annette's hair, unpinned, reached down the back of her lavender gown. She looked chilled with her arms crossed and her hands covering her shoulders, as if for warmth. "I want everyone to have a good time tonight," she said. "Everyone."

"Mother, they will." Firmly Linda took her arm. "You'd better come inside with me."

Hap Mitchell was having a fine time. Doctor Pell had opened a bar in the foyer, we'd rolled up the rugs in the living room, people were dancing, and Hap took his drink down to the pier. The breeze had picked up and the moon rose, a big bright orb, its light breaking on serrated water. The lanterns were buffeted by the breeze, splashing their variegated light on the blind and the pier. Hap sat between the twin benches, dangling his legs over the water, and yanking the bell rope while he drank. *Clang!* The sound reverberated over the lake and bounded up the lawn. *Clang!*

"Who's banging that bell?" a voice asked.

"That's just Hap." Harriet Mitchell laughed. "Having a high old time."

Clang!

"Quiet him down!" a voice called.

"Kick his butt into the lake," Harriet replied, and the corsage on her bosom—all ribbons and tiny pink roses—waggled merrily. "That'll cool him off. See if it won't."

Mrs. Fennel headed toward me, a question in her eyes, until Harriet caught her wrist. "Margie! I've an item for you."

"For my column?"

"Look at this!" Harriet laughed, her hands cupping the flowers on her chest. "My boobs are blooming! First time in years!"

"Harriet!" Margie scolded. "Honestly, you're as bad as Hap!"

Clang!

"Doctor Darwin," Margie asked. "Should I know you?"

"I doubt it." I saw Linda drawing A.J. toward us. "I'm not a doctor. I'm not a professor either."

"You must be very bright about something if you're a friend of Doctor Pell's." Margie appeared permanently disappointed in me. "What are you, then?"

"I'm a government man," I acknowledged. "I don't know much about anything." A.J. thought that was hilarious. The joke was on me but he laughed so heartily I liked him in spite of myself.

Clang!

On the pier Hap rocked back and forth as the pealing resounded off the water. I saw Marcella in her white gown among Father Ted's friends by the boathouse. Their cluster opened to include Cindy Klinger. Someone—not Cindy; a man's voice—yelled: "Dunk the drunk!" Others took up the chant: "Dunk the drunk!"

Clang!

"Dick, do something about that bell," Linda urged.

I walked down toward the pier but the patrol boat was pulling in. That's all Hap needed. Seeing LeFevre tie in, he thought someone had called the police to quiet him. He scrambled to his feet and dropped his drink in the lake, glass and all.

LeFevre left his gun in the boat but his badge glimmered in the lantern light. On unsteady legs Hap hurried up the pier with the ranger striding behind him. We met on the path. "Jesus," Hap said, "they'll throw me in jail. Can't a fellow have a little fun?"

A.J. and Sarah danced barefoot in the grass. Marcella danced with MacArthur Landis. LeFevre with Cindy Klinger. I found Linda standing alone. We danced while the band played light rock, ballads, funky fox trots: music to keep people talking, moving. Toes tapped in the grass, fingers fiddled on sweating cocktail glasses, couples danced in the living room and across the lawn, inhaling the fragrance of the damp grass and the ink-black pines behind us. A whiff of pot drifted up from the boathouse. Now the woman who played guitar in the combo on the porch stood at the microphone and sang a jazzy "What I Did for Love".

Annette set candles in little red and yellow bowls on the tables. Their flames dipped and flickered like the lanterns swaying on the blind and above the pier.

"Mother's walking a high-wire," Linda worried.

"Her stamina is incredible," I said.

"It isn't stamina. It's her dope. It works until it snaps and she comes down hard."

"On your father."

"He's still sore at A.J."

"I saw A.J. dancing with Sarah."

"Daddy doesn't know about that. He won't believe it even if he sees it."

I left Linda looking after her mother and went to find her father in the kitchen. He'd draped his dinner jacket over a chair and set his platinum cufflinks on the table, beside the carving board. He was cleaving a sweet-smelling ham with a knife, dropping each thin slice so it overlapped another. Teresa came in with a meat platter. Her hair was piled high, secured by a mother-of-pearl comb. She arranged a new platter of ham, adding parsley sprigs and apple slices tinged with cinnamon. Then she left, passing with her platter under that moon-like circle above the door where the clock had been. Doctor Pell tapped the carving board with his knife. "Is LeFevre here?"

"Yes," I said. "I've seen him."

"A.J.?"

"Dancing with Sarah Hack."

"Enjoying themselves, are they?"

When I heard the controlled fury in that question I couldn't think what to answer.

"Anybody in the water?" he asked.

"One or two are wading by the boathouse."

"Swimming?"

"Not yet."

"It won't be long." He gestured at me with the knife. "Do you want to race A.J.?"

"No." I laughed at the suggestion. Then saw his face was serious. "The water's cold. The wind is up. It's not a good night for swimming."

"We'll see."

"I'll finish here," I offered. He should've been with his wife and their guests. "You can mingle with the others."

"I don't mingle, sir."

He was rinsing the knife when Annette walked in. "Oh, *here* you are!"

He smiled as if his face ached. "I wanted to be helpful." While I filled an ice bucket Annette slipped an arm around me. "Thank you, dear." Her eyes brimmed with worry. "It's a splendid night, isn't it?"

"And you *look* splendid."

"Do I?"

"You never need to ask."

Annette laughed softly. She was under control, or nearly so. She kissed my cheek and moved me toward the door. "Go dazzle some pretty thing."

"I'm trying to."

Annette laughed. "Must I call Linda to drag you out?"

"Yes!"

By ten o'clock the buffet platters were nearly bare but the drinks table had been replenished. Annette collected the candles while Teresa brought around desserts. We'd trooped into the dining room where we clasped our dessert plates like hard-won prizes. Couples were dancing in the living room and in the foyer too, the staircase rising like a graceful swan over the waves of energy rocking beneath it. Marcella Costa was left alone at the foot of the stairs but not for long.

"Hi, gorgeous." LeFevre's arm circled her waist. She smiled, turned away, but his broad voice overrode the din: "I don't mean to sound, you know, conceited. I just want to know how to turn you on. What's your secret? What do you like best about me?"

"I don't really know." Marcella looked up sharply. "It must be your modesty."

Give him a little credit, he knew better. His laughter boomed through the room. "I don't believe that—for sure!"

"Oh, good!" Marcella said. "We do have something in common."

She passed into the crowd and the next moment I saw her dancing with Mac Landis.

LeFevre wore a hurt look. I was about to ask if he wanted a drink when Cindy Klinger arrived with two glasses, one for him. "You didn't have to fall all over her," she complained.

"We talked. That's all." Ice clinked as he touched his glass to hers. "It was nothing serious."

"I know." Cindy sipped her drink. "You can't be serious when you're wearing that silly badge."

LeFevre gave me a knowing glance. "Don't let her fool you," he said. "Cindy loves a man in uniform."

Cindy smiled sweetly. "When he's *out* of his uniform." LeFevre laughed. "Won't take but a minute."

"I believe you mean it."

"You *better* believe it." His arm around her waist, they left the house. "Let's go down to the water," he said.

It was eleven o'clock when I walked to the boathouse with Wally Hack. He wanted to see the breakwater Doctor Pell had built years ago: how the boulders were set and if mortar was used (unlike Jules Beauregard's hut, it wasn't). By the time we finished the moon had climbed high above the woods and water. "It's late," he said. "For me."

"And chilly," I said. We started back.

"What do you know about Akira Jagao?"

"Only what Linda tells me." I understood his interest for Sarah's sake, but why ask me? "He has plenty of heart."

"I think Sarah's fond of him." Stopping, he sipped his drink. "She isn't taken by many men."

"Linda likes him too."

"Sarah's a sensible young woman. I trust her choices." Her father lifted his glass again; it touched his mustache, stopped there. "I don't think Doctor Pell likes him at all."

"No." I finished my drink. "I don't believe he does."

"You have any notion what that's about?"

"Father Ted says he tries too hard to control his family. I think that's true." No need to speak of A.J. supplying Annette with coke; Doctor Pell controlled that too, didn't he? "He's afraid of losing Linda." Wally tasted his drink, waiting for me to go on. "And his father died at Pearl Harbor. When he was nine," I said. "He can't see A.J. and not remember that."

"But his brother—"

"Was only two. It didn't leave the same scar."

Four young people at the edge of the woods shared a joint. They passed it around, took a hit on it, laughed softly.

"Akira runs those stables, doesn't he?"

"That's right." We tramped up the lawn to the house. "Linda says he works hard at it. He has to. And he does."

"I'm glad to hear that."

I saw Linda in the doorway; her trim silhouette, the lights of the house ablaze behind her. I waved and she lifted her hand.

While we sat at the end of the pier Linda put her head on my shoulder. My hand rested on her breast. "You're very tender."

"Not always." She leaned into me. "But I want to be."

By midnight the moon had passed behind the mountains. The wind was up and pushed toward shore; water slapped the pilings; the pier creaked as boats pulled their ropes taut. We heard laughter near the shore and Linda wondered who was there.

"Dick, what are they doing?"

A man and woman stood in shallow water, stooping, splashing each other, while another man watched. Linda's father came down the path with Akira and Sarah; we watched them pause, then leave the path and walk down to the water's edge.

LeFevre was shirtless and wore his pants rolled up as he waded out of the water with Cindy Klinger. She'd deposited her shoes and stockings in a little pile on top of her dress on the grass. Her legs were wet and there was a wet sheen to her bra and panties. She wore LeFevre's badge pinned to her panties.

"Welcome to the show." She laughed, shaking out her dress.

The man who'd been watching them was Hap Mitchell. He teetered on his heels, glass in hand, giggling. "Hell of a pahdy," he said. His voice was foggy; he was catching a cold. "It's always one hell of a pahdy."

Doctor Pell stood behind A.J. and Sarah, his eyes on LeFevre reaching for his shirt. "You young folks having fun?"

"Sure," said LeFevre. "Water's fine."

"It's *cold!*" Cindy slipped into her dress. Shook her hair.

"Too cold to swim? Dick tells me no one has nerve enough to swim tonight."

"Daddy," Linda pleaded.

"I don't buy that. A.J., what about you?"

"Sir?"

"Not too cold for you, is it? Friday it wasn't." Doctor Pell managed a smile. "You'll take on all comers, won't you?"

"A race?" A.J. glanced at Sarah. "Where to?"

"From the boathouse to the blind," Doctor Pell suggested: "Since we have those lights out there."

"I don't know." A.J. looked across the water to the lanterns swaying above the raft.

"What's to know?" LeFevre asked. "Nothing to it."

"Think so?" Doctor Pell waited.

"Any time." LeFevre, smiling, held his shirt in his hand as he put his arm around Cindy. "I'm ready any time."

"All right." A.J. bristled. "You're on."

LeFevre stifled a laugh. "You and me?"

"Why not?"

"Some of us have had a few drinks," I said.

"Not too many." As LeFevre stroked Cindy's neck his hand disappeared under her hair. "I've never had too many."

"You always say that." Laughing, she shook her hair again. "Don't you, Danny?"

"Well—anyone else?" Doctor Pell sounded relieved and positively mirthful. "This *is* a party, isn't it?"

"Hell of a pahdy." Hap Mitchell lurched himself around and toddled up to the house.

"I'll bring my boat," said Doctor Pell. "And pick you up at the blind."

LeFevre started down the shore with Cindy as the band wound up a swift piece which left the dancers laughing at themselves, applauding. I heard Linda say: "Daddy? I'll get some towels." She went striding up to the house.

"What's the point?" I asked A.J. "This is foolish."

"Only if I lose." His smile was brash but Sarah looked worried. She whispered something and A.J. frowned.

"The water's cold," I cautioned. "You'll cramp."

"I swam two days ago. You saw me." A blade of black hair flicked across his brow. "No cramps. No problem."

"It's a long way for you to swim."

"I can whip him, Mister Darwin."

"All right." I shook his hand. "Good luck."

Sarah smiled with guarded pride. Maybe she believed him but I didn't. I tried again. "You heard Cindy. The lake's cold. It's choppy."

"I'll be fine."

"Keep something in reserve. When you're tired change your stroke." I heard myself speaking like my first coach: "Breathe on both sides. You'll be more comfortable."

"I'll be fine. Really."

"Stay close behind him. Draft off him; swim in his wake. Let him do the work."

"Then he wins."

"All you want to do is swim to the blind."

"No—that isn't all."

"And climb into the boat."

"If you say so." He took Sarah's hand.

"You don't have to do this," I said.

"They're waiting," he said.

He sauntered down to the boathouse with Sarah.

LeFevre, stripped to his shorts, stood on the breakwater. Cindy sat on the grass above the shore where the woods almost reached the water. I didn't want to watch so I walked up the lawn to listen to the band. Father Ted approached in the dark; a turtle-like wobble of his limbs while the brace supported his neck. The flare of his match was like a flashbulb lighting his face. "Last one." He lit his cigar, his hand cupped to shield the flame from the wind. "No more after tonight."

"Teresa told me you're quitting."

"Those kids from my parish—are they smoking pot?"

"Over by the woods."

"I'll talk to them." He chuckled.

The four he meant had gone down to the shore. "They want to watch the race," I said. "But it's too dark."

When he drew on his cigar its small bulb of ash brightened. He expelled a stream of smoke into the night. "What race?"

"A.J. and LeFevre."

"You're joking." He lowered his cigar. "Are they high?"

"LeFevre, a little."

"This is crazy."

"It's your brother's idea."

"It's *no* contest."

"Tell A.J."

"Can't you stop him?"

I pointed out the woman in the pale dress by the boathouse. "Sarah Hack is with him. He wouldn't back down in front of her. Linda was there, too, when Bob brought it up. Though A.J. isn't in love with her. But I think he loves Sarah. And always has."

"Does Bob know that?"

"No."

He lifted his cigar; inhaled. The ash glowed. "Maybe you ought to tell him."

Why should I? Anyway, he was out in his boat, wasn't he? He was on his way. To pick up the swimmers at the blind.

"Oh, Christ!" I said.

I ran down to the lawn.

Couples by the shore moved toward the pier for a better view. I ran smack into a woman, striking her shoulder. She spun, fell, as her companion cursed me. Then the woman's voice: "Dumb bastard!" The boathouse loomed dark between the woods and water. I was clambering onto the boulders of the breakwater when I heard Cindy complaining, "Why don't we watch from the pier?" Then Sarah saw me. Shouted, "What's the matter?"

I was too late.

A.J. and LeFevre were gone. By the light of the moon we saw their arms flashing through the water.

I dropped my jacket and pulled off my shoes. Water sloshed the rounded stones, breaking against the larger ones. Out in the water one swimmer went splashing ahead of the other. Toward the lanterns of the blind rocking in the dark. I told myself to dive shallow and surface quickly. That part worked.

Pull and drive. My high school coach had taught that a long stroke produced power. But the wind made for high water and I gagged on a mouthful. It was hard to sustain any rhythm. And, Christ! it was cold. I thought I'd warm while I swam but I still felt the chill slap of the water.

In the tossing water I couldn't see if I was gaining on either swimmer so I sighted on the lanterns. Easy to pick out against the dark. That's where they were heading, wasn't it? To the blind. Yes, you dumb bastard. You helped him set this up.

I shook that thought from my head—his questions about swimming; about distances; his maneuvers with the boat this afternoon—and I tried to remember what I'd been taught about maintaining tempo. Long stroke, easy turn, drive and pull. Let the water lift you. That's what it's there for. Not to pull you down.

After that I tried to keep my head down. But it wasn't long until I was aware of someone splashing there ahead of me. Now I saw both of them but I couldn't catch LeFevre in front. A.J. was floundering just ahead. He was spent, but determined, pummeling the water with labored strokes.

He couldn't beat LeFevre; it didn't matter that I knew that. What mattered was that Doctor Pell knew it. He was counting on it.

LeFevre, reaching the raft, climbed onto the blind. His flesh red and yellow in the lantern glow. A.J. looked exhausted. He struggled, splashing, gaining little distance, still some forty feet short of the raft, when I heard the engine noise.

Where was the boat? We heard it but couldn't see it because it was hidden by the blind.

I told myself I could still catch A.J.

But swimming toward him, I heard the rasp of my breathing. And A.J.'s frantic splashing. No other sound. The engine was muffled. Just like this afternoon; the same maneuver.

Silently, the boat appeared.

Turning, it glided toward us.

I looked from LeFevre standing on the blind, grinning, a fist in the air in mock triumph, to A.J. thrashing in the water.

Behind A.J. the boat closed its arc, riding its momentum, soundless, bearing down on him. LeFevre saw this too. Now, from the edge of the blind he saw A.J. no longer flailing but writhing in the water, a drowning man, and in his eagerness to reach him he dove too deep. When LeFevre surfaced from his dive and came stroking toward us he was too late.

The boat loomed out of the night looking larger as it rode the water. At the last minute its beacon was switched on, flashing a beam of light over us, as if it was searching for us.

I swam toward A.J., lunging, letting the water lift me. I came down on his head and shoulders and my weight drove him underwater. He bobbed up and I grabbed for his hair; his shoulder. He slipped free. I groped for his head and held on, determined to drive him down, out of the path of the approaching prow. He fought me; fists and elbows. We were both fighting for air as we went down. *Down.* My lungs ached. Kick like hell, I thought. My throat burned. I was choking. Was I choking him? I let go.

We surfaced, gasping. Gulping air.

With a dizzy rush of relief I saw the blur of the lanterns.

The boat swept beyond us, its beacon raking the water. We rocked in its wake. I heard the engine revving now. Then A.J. was hacking, spitting up on my arm.

The boat returned. Its beam of light caught us in the roiling water. Then it fell too upon LeFevre lolling there. Blood on his blond head. One eye stared at the sky. At his torn shoulder shards of bone gleamed among the blood. Already his heart had pumped its last spurt into the lake. Where the gash through his neck cut the jugular vein blood bubbled in the water.

A.J. sat gasping for breath and I knelt over LeFevre as the boat plowed toward the lighted pier. We tied in where the water mirrored the glowing lanterns. Lifting LeFevre from the rocking boat, I felt sick. I was dizzy and afraid I'd stumble with him. It didn't help to see the colors skidding like oil on the water around us. I was standing in his blood as we lifted him from the boat and onto the pier. His neck had been ripped open; the head with its bristling crew cut and that wild-eyed stare lay on the torn shoulder; his face, shoulder, and chest were smeared with his blood. Under the lanterns the corpse was bathed in pools of light and our shifting shadows.

Sarah Hack ran onto the pier. Seeing LeFevre lying in his blood, she shrieked. A piercing cry. Then she ran to the house, clutching her dress as her feet flew up the path. Someone told the band to stop playing. We carried the body from the pier, my arm cradling his head, and laid it down by the bed of Japanese iris. When we stood up A.J. had caught his breath. "God damn you!" he shouted at Doctor Pell. "You tried to kill me!"

"This?" Doctor Pell bowed his head over the body at our feet. "This was an accident."

"You tried to kill me!"

"I'm sorry." Doctor Pell's voice was soft with shock. "I'm so sorry this happened."

"God damn you!"

Linda and Sarah ran down the lawn with their arms full of towels. Annette followed with the blue blanket from the porch.

I pulled A.J. away so Linda wouldn't hear him. The chill wind buffeted the lanterns above the pier. My clothes were soaked and drenched with blood. Shaking ourselves, we rubbed our arms, and Sarah brought over towels. "Are you hurt?" she asked A.J.

"I'm alive," he said.

"Your clothes," I said.

He shook his wet hair. "You saw what he did."

"Yes," I said. "I saw it."

He went down to the breakwater to get his clothes.

I walked back with Sarah; Annette and Linda had spread the blanket over the body. Guests emerged from the house: "What happened?" a voice asked.

"Is there a doctor?"

People fanned out in front of the flowers and the tables at the top of the lawn. Angelo Costa, quick for a stout man, hurried down the driveway, boots slipping on the gravel. Father Ted was close behind, his eyes dark with grief. "Dick, how could this happen?"

"Keep A.J. away from your brother!" I held his lapels in both fists. "Do you hear?"

The blanket spread its stain on the lawn. Cindy Klinger, Mac Landis, the Fennels, followed the priest to the flowerbed at the end of the driveway. Unable to bend his neck, Father Ted dropped to his knees beside the body and began to pray.

A voice said, "He's dead."

Someone screamed.

When Sarah Hack saw LeFevre lying on the pier she understood he was dead; she ran to the house and told her father. When I walked into the Pells' house, through the last of the guests followed by the band leaving, I found Wally Hack on the phone. He'd called for an ambulance, he'd called Sheriff Sullivan in Crags Landing, and now he was talking to one of the deputies.

I went outside. People looked ashamed, as if they shouldn't have been partying, drinking, dancing, if the possibility of death was among us. Were we all somehow responsible for this body under the blanket? An accident, wasn't it? The band crammed the instruments into their van. Whispering couples climbed into their cars, started up, turned in the narrow road, drove off. Cindy's sleek car followed the others into the dark.

Hap and Harriet Mitchell came down the stone path arm in arm. "Is it true?" asked Harriet. "Is he dead?"

"Yes," I said.

Her hair was frazzled; her face damp, ruddy. She'd been crying. Hap rocked on his heels. "Who is it?" Harriet inquired.

I told her.

"I hear he's naked," she said.

"He was swimming," I said.

"Hap's gonna be sick," she said. They went over to the woods, I heard him being sick, then they walked slowly to their car as the ambulance arrived.

Brian and Erica, the paramedics I'd met at the rodeo, confirmed that LeFevre was dead, replaced the blanket. Sheriff Sullivan drove up with his deputy, Billy Scott, with the red light revolving on the roof of his car. The paramedics peeled back the blanket for them and squatted in the grass watching.

Already LeFevre was somewhere else. I tried to remember the cruelty in his pale eyes; his booming voice; his aggressive posturing; everything I'd found obnoxious about him. Now I saw none of it. His bloodied head was turned away but it wasn't just that. His whole being had walked off into the woods, leaving us this muscular contorted corpse with its unlikely silence.

The paramedic eased the body onto a stretcher, fastening a white cover over it. Erica folded the blanket and laid it in Annette's arms. Then we lifted the stretcher into the ambulance.

Sullivan asked my name and Akira's. He already knew the Pells. "I know you, too," he said.

"Yes, I phoned your office. We talked."

"That's right." He asked about the blood on my clothes.

"We took him out of the water," I said. "And we lifted him out of the boat."

Sullivan questioned us, his hands in his pockets, while his deputy took notes. Where was LeFevre when the boat struck him? (Just this side of the blind.) Why was anyone in the water at this hour? (LeFevre and Akira were swimming a race. To the blind.) Was I in the race? (No.) Why was I in the water? (I thought Akira was in trouble.) Why? (He didn't swim very well.) Was the blind lighted as it is now? (Yes.) Was the boat lighted? (Doctor Pell said: Yes. I wasn't asked. Nor was Akira.) Well, the water *was* dark? (Yes. Yes. Yes.) Did Doctor Pell see the boat strike LeFevre? (No, he said, he saw no one in the water. He thought both men were waiting for him on the blind.) Did I see the boat strike LeFevre? (No.) Did Akira? (No.) Had LeFevre been drinking? (Yes.) A lot? (Yes.) Any dope? (Pot.) He inspected the boat and when he returned he said something to the priest in a low sorrowful voice. Then he said goodbye to Doctor Pell and touched the brim of his hat with a nod to Annette.

But it was Wally and Winnie Hack who left first, then A.J. in his ranch wagon with Sarah beside him, then Teresa took the wheel of her car and the priest eased into the passenger seat. Then the sheriff started the engine, the beacon swung through the darkness, and each of us was streaked with its red gleam before he led the ambulance down the road.

We were left alone on the lawn, unable to speak to each other. I was shaking, my clothes smelled of blood, but my mind was too numb to care. LeFevre's death left a distance between us, at first. Then it drew the Pells together in a way that didn't include me. Light from the windows flooded the flowerbeds as we looked across the empty tables at the desolate lawn. The wind flapped the corners of the tablecloths and rocked the lanterns. Doctor Pell walked down to disconnect the lanterns on the pier but he left them burning on the blind. When he climbed the path to the house his face was white with fatigue.

The house blazed with light. Over the floors bared for dancing—the rugs rolled aside; crumpled napkins, plates, glasses, ashtrays, flowers—over all of it a glaring silence. Linda sank into a chair, her head in her hands. Annette paced behind her, bright-eyed, brittle. Doctor Pell cracked ice cubes in the kitchen. *You aren't one of us,* he'd told me. He was right. Their grief and disgrace was mine too, but I had no place among them. I went up to the guest room and later I heard the others on the stairs.

I lay on the bed but couldn't sleep. The pines creaked in the wind. The owl called. Then in the quiet house I heard someone sobbing. I went quickly into the hall. Linda's deep-throated sobs shook the darkness. Her door was locked. I knocked but she didn't reply. I knocked again; no answer. I went back to bed and after a while all was silent. Sometime after three I fell asleep but before dawn I was awake, listening to the whirr of a plane overhead. I imagine Doctor Pell heard it too. A fly-over by that jet from NASA, its camera registering the heat in the hazard zones of the volcanic field. In the mountains and woods and all around the lake.

16

Necessary Questions

I didn't attend Danny LeFevre's funeral. For three days I was meeting with the chief of the Search and Rescue unit, PG&E, and a regional manager from Office of Emergency Services. OES was prepared to set up a field hospital if Lassen Peak or Mount Shasta erupted. An Energy Commission rep assured me PG&E was prepared for downed power lines, leaking gas pipes; repairs would be swift, power restored. The following week I drove from one small town to another among the mountain valleys, meeting with school board presidents, Red Cross reps, directors of county blood banks. Also bank executives who wanted assurance that loans would be available to landlords and home owners whose dwellings were damaged.

When I returned to Crags Landing I moved into the Riverside Hotel to await Doctor Pell's court date. Originally an inn on the stage coach route, it was half a mile from the old boat landing. My room, which looked across Station Road to the river beyond, was stifling hot.

I'd visited the Pells in the morning and now I had to phone Noah Geyer. I called him at home and Edna answered:

"When will we see you again?"

"I hope it's soon."

"We do too, dear. We miss your appetite at our table."

Hearing her dry voice I realized how much I missed the Geyers: their kindness, their quiet humor. I was afraid to ask about Dorothy "Is Noah there?"

He came on the line immediately. "Problems?"

I told him of the promises of cooperation we'd received in the past ten days. He was pleased but not fooled. "If the news is so good why didn't you call sooner?"

"It's Doctor Pell."

"You'd better explain."

He listened to my account of LeFevre's death. In the silence that followed I felt sweat on the back of my shirt as I thought of my visit to Lake Elaine: Linda reserved, doubting her father, ashamed of her doubts; Annette oddly aloof, her voice flat—was it fright?—her eyes always tracking her husband; Doctor Pell distraught but not the least preoccupied with his coming court appearance. Every spark of anger gone from his extinguished eyes. His sorrow and shame were about to overwhelm him. "It was no accident," I said. "Except that he killed the wrong man. In his view."

"Dick, are you certain?"

"Absolutely."

"Will he stand trial?"

"He has a preliminary hearing in two days."

"He's hired a lawyer?"

I told him Mac Landis would represent Doctor Pell.

"Will you testify?"

"That depends on the District Attorney."

"What's the charge?"

"Involuntary manslaughter," I replied. "Landis says his intent has nothing to do with it. The court has to prove that he recklessly caused LeFevre's death."

"Can that be proved?"

"I don't see how."

"The Pells must be devastated."

"I was with them this morning. The tension in the family is terrible. Linda's exhausted. Her mother's withdrawn. But I don't believe the hearing itself is what worries Doctor Pell."

"You don't think he'll be indicted?"

"Landis told him the charge was filed because the victim was a park ranger. The DA has to be seen supporting people in law enforcement. At every level. But this is mostly a formality. There's no way to prove LeFevre's death wasn't accidental. Or to demonstrate that Doctor Pell was reckless."

"But we abandon him." Noah sighed into the phone. "NEPA gives him up. As if he were guilty. Is that what you propose?"

"He leaves us no choice." I'd opened the window and the curtains, yellowing with age, trembled in the flame of a breeze. "He's no longer a viable figure. He's a liability."

I should have known Noah would want to think this over; I stood at the window. Light flashed from the tops of cars along the baking street. "Wait until he's had his day in court," Noah said finally. "Then write to him. It's the decent thing to do."

"Decent?"

"I want to be fair."

"What's fair to Danny LeFevre?"

"We can't do anything about that, can we?" His response had been reasonable, fair-minded; which wasn't what I wanted to hear. Across the street, beyond the shaded park, sunlight shattered on the river. "From all we know of Doctor Pell," said Noah, "you can't expect a confession."

"No."

"And the evidence is inconclusive?" Noah wondered, thinking aloud. "Without his confession the court won't indict him. Because they know they can't convict him."

"No," I said. "Nobody can do that."

Giant junipers shaded the old courthouse with dark green branches where jays jumped about, busy among the berries. My father told me itinerants who camped along the crags barely finished building the landing when they had to erect a gallows on the high ground above it. Here, where the center of town stands today, a huge valley oak provided wood for their purpose. They were river men (which he unfailingly mentioned first), luckless miners, traders, trappers. The next generation brought ideas of a settlement. Newcomers tied in at the log-sunk landing and climbed the crags as others arrived by wagon, more each year, whole families among them, and raised their cabins, stables, barns, pens, a store. Then a tavern, a bank, a church, a school. Their grown children, he said, pulled down the gallows and built in its place this courthouse of quarried stone as if to insist that law is firm and objective; more balanced and formal than the men and women who define it, enforce it, or violate it. They built it large enough to house the courtroom, cubbyhole offices, and committee chambers necessary to an ordinary life. But around its grey walls they planted these deep green trees to say we understand that law and nature are not the same.

My grandfather's generation added a gold-plated dome in imitation of the capitol down in Sacramento. Pillars towering over the foyer supported the dome and its surrounding skylight. Sunlight poured down, spilling over the tile floor. In the shadows stood vending machines stocked with cigarettes and candy, and a gumball dispenser placed by the Veterans of Foreign Wars. Cigar and cigarette smoke hung in the air but the foyer was mercifully cool. On one wall hung a slack fire hose like the skin of a dead snake. By the doors to the courtroom rose two vertical beams joined at the top by a crossbar; it was the upper portion of the oak gallows uprooted from this site. The wood was dark with age, thickly varnished, the crossbar studded with hooks for hats and coats.

In the courtroom spectators in shirtsleeves or bare-armed filled the seven rows of seats. I sat on the aisle beside Annette; Linda next to her in black dress, black pumps; then Father Ted. At the head of the aisle a low wooden gate swung on quick hinges; when people familiar with the room passed through—the two attorneys, the court reporter—they turned, keeping a hand on the gate to close it quietly. Doctor Pell had marched through paying it no attention and heads spun at the angry *crack!* as the gate smacked shut behind him.

He sat at the defense table between Mac Landis and Old Hannah; Leonard Mix sat at the people's table, briefcase open. It was this area Old Hannah called 'The Pit'. Though almost at eye-level with spectators, it appeared much lower because the judge's bench and the witness stand loomed above it with the tiers of the jury box rising to one side. No jurors were present for the preliminary hearing; above the empty seats in the walnut-paneled box sunlight falling through the boughs of a juniper streamed into the room. It was a room dominated by the dark wood of the judge's bench and the jury box, the walnut chairs upholstered in black leather, while the streaming light polished whatever metal could be found: the cylinder ashtrays, an aluminum drinking fountain, and the recording equipment where Janice Hohlmeier sat with her stenotype machine between her knees. From her tiny desk a microphone on a double-jointed arm reached over to the witness stand.

Sheriff Sullivan was the first witness and Leonard Mix dealt with him discreetly. Essentially, he suggested, they were on the same side: the DA wanted justice to be served; the sheriff was sworn to protect the community. Sully, as coroner, testified to the cause of LeFevre's death. As sheriff he related what he'd learned from questioning each of us. To Mac Landis he acknowledged there was no eye-witness to the boat striking LeFevre. To Mix he admitted there was no dispute that it *had* struck him.

At this point Landis rose to request a dismissal. A young man who'd shown woeful judgment and recklessness died of a terrible accident. What was the point in filing a charge against Doctor Pell? He knew the answer, Old Hannah had explained it to us; but he waited, his head bowed in the falling light, his hands clasped behind him. Let Leonard Mix explain his position; let Judge Bierman see how tenuous it was. Involuntary manslaughter (*Man II*, Mix called it, addressing the judge) was an open door: if no negligence was shown the defendant walked out a free man. But if intent to injure crept into the evidence, or if the victim's death was caused in the heat of passion, the door slammed shut and the DA re-filed the charge as a felony homicide (*Man I*). Unlikely on the evidence the sheriff offered. But should it happen, Old Hannah would direct Doctor Pell's defense. On the bench the Honorable Oliver Bierman listened, glasses glimmering. At each side of the bench a small lamp glowed. Light from one lamp fell on his notepad, light from the other on a shallow bowl of walnuts. Just now Judge Bierman's attention was focused on Leonard Mix.

Awaiting a decision, the DA returned to his table where he sat forward, elbows on knees. When Judge Bierman denied the motion to dismiss Mix had his way. He leaped to his feet, thanked the sheriff in a perfunctory tone, then dove into his briefcase for a clipboard of notes. Wavy hair glistening in the warm light, he called his next witness. His silk suit crimped his shoulders, hugged his chest, pinched his flat waist. While Akira Jagao was sworn in Mix waited, tense, tapered like a flame. He'd filed this charge against the defendant, he began, "Because activities preceding the death of Mr. LeFevre raise certain necessary questions." With the patience of the court, he said, he meant to pursue these questions now.

As Mix leaned toward A.J. I remembered when I'd seen him at the rodeo, impatient to mount the stairs to the judges' stand. In the courtroom that eagerness looked more menacing and I wondered if A.J., neat in his blue suit, felt its threat.

"Mr. Jagao, how did you happen to be swimming a race against Officer LeFevre, late at night, in the dark—" Mix sounded incredulous; hoping we'd feel the same. "Was this your idea?"

"Doctor Pell," said A.J. simply.

Mix, hands on hips: "Explain?"

"I was dancing with Sarah—" A.J. smiled at the memory "—we were dancing in the grass. By the house."

"Miss Sarah Hack."

"Yes, sir." His smile vanished. "Doctor Pell approached us. He stood in our way. We had to stop. He put a hand on my shoulder. A hand on hers. I thought he wanted to dance with her. It seemed silly—a man his age." Someone snickered. Scowling, Judge Bierman palmed a walnut from the bowl, passed it from one hand to the other. "That wasn't it at all," A.J. went on as Doctor Pell frowned. "He offered to take us out on his boat."

"And that appealed to you."

"Sarah said it might be fun."

"And you agreed."

"I didn't want to refuse."

"For the young lady's pleasure."

"Yes—" A.J. let fall a pause. Mix picked it up at once.

"And?"

"I felt it would be rude," he replied slowly, spacing each word. "To refuse him."

"You were being polite."

"Yes, sir."

"Because he was your host."

"No, sir—because he hated me."

"Why do you say that?" asked Mix, as Doctor Pell looked on.

"Objection!" Landis bolted to his feet. "Your Honor—"

"Sustained." Judge Bierman glowered at the stenographer. "Strike the question and the reply." He clenched the walnut in his fist.

"Mr. Jagao," Mix resumed, chastened, but only a little: "you are acquainted with the wife of Doctor Pell." District Attorney Mix examined a witness without phrasing his questions as questions. He made statements, sometimes with a rise in pitch on the final word; then waited for a response. Did he do this deliberately? I wondered. Because he knew the reply he expected to hear? I remembered the *Meditations* of Jules Beauregard; how the old hermit constantly questioned himself on the subject of his guilt and his love.

"You've known Annette Pell for some time. You may have performed services for her." Mix dropped his gaze to his clipboard as if reading his notes. He'd said just enough to let A.J. know the sheriff had staked out his house and stables. Only a threat? Or would he ask about dealing coke to Annette? Would Landis let him? "You're on good terms with Mrs. Pell?"

"Objection!" Landis called out. "Irrelevant."

"Sustained." Judge Bierman passed the walnut from hand to hand.

"I'll rephrase," said Mix. "You get along well with Doctor Pell's wife. And with his brother, I believe. However, it's your opinion that Doctor Pell disapproved of you."

"His daughter and I are friends," said A.J. softly.

"Is that why he disapproved of you?"

"Objection!" Landis again. "Calls for a conclusion."

"Sustained." Judge Bierman, patience strained, rapped the bench with the walnut; a sound of knuckles knocking against wood.

"Whatever his reasons might be—" Mix glanced at his clipboard then launched into a summary and I wondered how Landis or Old Hannah felt about this; he had a maddening facility for crowding past arguments and testimony into his next question, keeping his version of the case foremost in the mind of the court: "—whether it was your friendship with his wife, or his daughter, or for other reasons, you believed he hated you."

"I was surprised because he came up to us acting friendly. He wasn't usually like that. Not with me. I thought I should go along with him."

"But, as it turns out, you and Miss Hack didn't go for a ride in his boat."

"We started down the path to the pier. Where his boat was. Then we met Danny LeFevre."

"You'd met him previously."

"The night before." A.J. caught my eye. Then Linda's. "We were in The Chute."

"What was your impression of Officer LeFevre? At that time."

"I'm sorry to speak this way," said A.J. quietly. "But he was rude. Loud. Conceited. Anybody could see that. Mr. Darwin didn't like him either. Or Linda. He acted like a bully." He cupped his palms on his knees; forced himself to say the words: "He tried to come on to Sarah."

"The following night, when you were at the Pells' house, did he show a similar interest in Miss Hack?"

"No, sir." A.J. lifted his gaze; I glanced behind us to see Wally Hack, in uniform, listening intently.

"Still you were wary of him," said Mix. "You disliked him. Were you jealous of him?"

A.J.'s black hair flicked over his forehead. "Not really."

"Forgive my meddling in your personal feelings," said Mix. "I thank you for your candor." A.J. acknowledged this unexpected propriety by sitting upright as ever; alert. "Let's return to Officer LeFevre," Mix continued. "Why did you stop when you saw him, Mr. Jagao? What was he doing?"

"He was wading in the lake. With Cindy Klinger."

"Miss Cynthia Klinger," said Mix. "And you recognized Officer LeFevre there in the water with his friend."

"No, sir."

"How can that be?" Mix feigned indignation with his own witness. Or so it seemed to me. Clearly he was well prepared; I felt he knew the answer that each question would receive. "Officer LeFevre had been on duty that evening. Wasn't he the one man at the party wearing a uniform? And a badge?"

"He wasn't exactly in uniform." Hesitating, A.J. threw a glance at Wally Hack. "And he wasn't wearing his badge."

Mix leaned forward. "What do you mean to say?"

"He had no shirt on. His pants were rolled up. He was stooped over in the water. Splashing Cindy."

"But Doctor Pell knew who he was. He knew it was Officer LeFevre because he'd seen him wade into the water with Miss Klinger. Before he went up to find you. He knew who it was before his eyes could have told him, didn't he? Recall, if you will, what Doctor Pell said to you when the three of you stopped on the path."

"He said, 'There's Danny...LeFevre...' Something like that."

"Then he led you down to the water to see Officer LeFevre. And his friend. I wonder if you recall anything unusual about Miss Klinger," Mix prodded A.J. "Anything out of the ordinary."

In the silence that followed Judge Bierman glared at his gavel. And, once, tapped the walnut on the bench before him.

"She wasn't all dressed," said A.J. softly.

Mix leaned forward as if to hear better. He waited to hear more, tilting toward his witness. "It was dark," A.J. went on. "There were lanterns on the pier. And the blind. Lots of light up at the house. But there by the water it was dark. It looked like she was naked."

"Was she?"

"She was wearing a bra." A.J.'s voice fell. "And panties."

"Is that *all*?"

"She wore his badge."

"If she wore only those two items of underclothing—"

"It was pinned onto her panties."

"Objection!" Landis leaped to his feet. "Irrelevant. All of this."

"Sustained!" Judge Bierman frowned at Landis' interruption; and at A.J. for his indiscretion. Over his glasses he scowled at Leonard Mix. He lifted his gavel and with a wrist-snapping swing shattered the walnut under it, to an explosion of delight from the spectators. With his penknife he probed the demolished shell while Mix retreated to the people's table. He withdrew, but his gaze never turned from A.J. Leaving his clipboard on the table, he collected himself, then he began his return, a step closer with each question.

"And when you met Officer LeFevre and his friend," he said, "you challenged him to a race."

"No, sir." A.J. twisted on the witness chair. "Doctor Pell suggested we swim to the blind. He said he'd pick us up at the blind with his boat."

"You're certain that was Doctor Pell's idea?" I looked across Annette to Linda in her full-sleeved black dress, her hands clutching her gloves, her red hair subdued in the warm light. Did she guess where Mix was leading? Overhead fans stirred the air with a steady whirr. "Mr. Jagao," the DA went on, "you didn't challenge Officer LeFevre? Maybe showing off just a little. For your girlfriend. May the best man win—"

"No, sir."

"And he didn't challenge you? Here's his chance to whip you in a race and impress Miss Klinger."

"No, sir."

"Doctor Pell asked *you* to swim a race. Anyone else?"

"Whoever would do it."

"His object was to get you into the water, away from the shore, in the dark? He didn't care who your opponent might be."

"Objection! Unwarranted speculation." Landis slapped the table with his palm. "And it calls for a conclusion."

"Certainly does," said Judge Bierman. "Sustained."

This time Mix didn't back away; he leaned toward his witness as if he meant to charge up to the stand. "Did Doctor Pell say why he wanted you to swim a race that night?"

"He said it would be a good challenge. Fun to watch."

"In fact were many people down by the water watching? Can you say how many?"

"I saw only Sarah and Cindy."

Mix managed to look shocked, dark eyebrows arching up. "Just two," he said. "Where was everyone else?"

"I hear some others came over after we were in the water..." At the defense table Landis whispered a question to Old Hannah; she shook her head. "It was late. And cool," A.J. continued. "Most people, if they hadn't gone home, they were up at the house, drinking. Dancing."

"So the race wasn't very entertaining. Since so few people were on hand to see it. One might suspect it was staged late in the evening so there'd be few witnesses." Old Hannah's black-coated back shifted; Landis looked ready to leap up; Judge Bierman glowered. Mix rescued his argument by turning it into a question: "Did that thought cross your mind?"

"Not then."

"It *has* occurred to you since that night."

"Yes, sir."

"Mr. Jagao," Mix shifted quickly, "are you a good swimmer?"

"Not really."

"Had you ever swum that distance before?"

A.J. lifted his gaze. Though the ceiling fans whirred the old building baked in the heat. "Once," he said. "Two days before. I meant to swim to the blind but I turned back."

"You couldn't make it."

"No, sir."

"I don't suppose anyone saw you fail in that attempt."

"Doctor Pell," said A.J. "And Mr. Darwin."

In the sweltering courtroom I held Annette's hand, feeling how frail she was. Her gaze remained fixed on her husband seated between his lawyers, his spine so erect his coat didn't touch his chair. She'd put her hand in mine in her anguish for him. She wanted only that he should be free. Free of the worry and disgrace of this hearing; free of any guilt in LeFevre's death. Free to bring back to their home the ferocity of his will. I looked across to Linda who wasn't watching her father now. Listening intently, she'd bowed her head, her hands in the lap of her coal-black dress. A fitting shade, the Trappists might agree, for a world made of charcoal.

"You knew Officer LeFevre was a park ranger," Mix continued, his weight on the balls of his feet, his face thrust toward A.J. "Did you know he was assigned to boat patrol?"

"Sarah told me," said A.J. with a stiff dignity.

"Surely it occurred to you that he'd outswim you. Which he did. Easily."

A.J.'s pride was challenged; he bristled, his eyes brightened; then he lounged in the chair, feigning indifference. "It was no contest." He flashed a smile. "I tried. But he beat me."

In the suddenly quiet courtroom Leonard Mix, leaning closer, appeared to tremble before the witness stand. A.J. straightened, wary. "Mr. Jagao, you had no hope of victory. I wish I could understand why you agreed to this competition."

"To show Doctor Pell I could do it." A.J. snapped a glance at the defense table. Doctor Pell nodded knowingly.

"And?"

"I'm ashamed to say." He bowed his head. "I wanted Sarah to think well of me. I wanted to impress her." He went on without lifting his gaze. "And I wanted to make LeFevre look bad."

"You disliked him," Mix sympathized, "because of Miss Hack."

For the first time Doctor Pell's blue eyes looked baffled.

Judge Bierman was polishing his glasses with his handkerchief. He stopped; looked down at A.J.

"I'm sorry," said A.J.

Leonard Mix bridged the distance between them as he leaned now on the witness stand. "In front of Miss Hack you were urged to compete. To impress her, you accepted. Though the distance was beyond your capability. As you knew. And Doctor Pell knew."

"Yes, sir."

Judge Bierman wiped his brow with the handkerchief. Mix fired questions without pause and let A.J. choose which one to answer: "The night was cool. The water was cold? You could have cramped."

"Mr. Darwin warned me about that."

"Did he?" Mix ignored this reply. "At best an average swimmer, you were urged to compete against a man expected to beat you by a comfortable distance. Which he did. You couldn't decline because you wished to prove yourself to Doctor Pell. To Miss Hack. To Officer LeFevre. You had no choice but to accept this dangerous, unfair, foolhardy challenge?"

"Objection!" Landis leaped up. Furious, he slapped the table. Old Hannah in a show of support struggled to her feet.

"Sustained." All patience drained from his face, Judge Bierman eyed Leonard Mix with disdain. "You'll save your summaries for the appropriate time. I won't warn you again."

"Your Honor, I apologize." Turning from his witness, Mix seemed to notice for the first time the rows of spectators. With a smile of satisfaction he said, "No further questions."

Court was in recess as we gathered in the foyer but Landis and Doctor Pell hadn't joined us. Father Ted lit a cigar, Old Hannah offered to extinguish it with the fire hose, and we moved to a quiet corner, away from the drinking fountain and vending machines visited by spectators who filed out of the courtroom, stretched, yawned, drank, chewed, and trooped in again.

Just as antiquated but more spacious, with its tile floor, stone pillars and high ceiling, the foyer, even without fans, was cooler than the crowded courtroom. Still Linda looked wilted and Annette was white-faced, too tense to be tired. They must have understood from A.J.'s testimony that Doctor Pell had planned his death. And how that plan went wrong. But no case could be made against him. After the recess I'd be called to testify, Landis again would move for dismissal, this time he'd likely get it. An hour from now Doctor Pell would walk out with his wife and daughter and drive home to Lake Elaine, a free man.

A.J. and Wally Hack came out, saw us, and moved off to the drinking fountain.

Dust motes danced in the light streaming down from the dome. Old Hannah, hair white as snow, withdrew a pale hand from her pocket and touched Annette's arm. "You mustn't worry so," she said. "There's not a thing in the world you can do."

"I do regret that we've dragged you into this," Annette confided. "I'm so ashamed."

Old Hannah waved a hand before her face, dismissing the thought. "I'm sorry for you, dear. And for all of us."

Teresa Espinosa came over and took Linda's hand. "I'll pray for you, lady." Her large eyes brimmed with tears as she hurried out of the courthouse.

"You won't find a better friend," said Father Ted.

"If prayers *are* heard I want to be in hers. And yours."

The priest tapped ash from his cigar into his palm. "I'm afraid mine are very simple."

"How *do* you pray?" she asked.

"I ask for peace of mind."

"And not for a wish to be granted?" Linda's eyes found her mother standing with Old Hannah.

"I don't know what's best for people." Father Ted drew on his cigar and exhaled a plume of smoke. "I pray that whatever happens they're able to bear it."

"Is that what you ask for me?"

"It is."

She faced him with a dead-level look. "Thank you."

The door to the courtroom opened and Doctor Pell stepped into the foyer. At once he noticed Old Hannah. "There you are!" He spoke bitterly to her: "Mix hasn't asked anything about the accident. Isn't that why we're here?" His glance caught Wally Hack and A.J. by the fountain. "If I'd wanted to kill someone would I invite him to a party at my house? Would I ask my brother to witness it? A priest?" He stared at me as if he'd forgotten who I was. Maybe he had. "Would I invite a houseful of guests to watch me do it? And a park ranger? LeFevre carried a gun, for God's sake."

"Time," called Officer Scott, beckoning from the doorway.

Annette started toward her husband slowly, delicately, as if the earth might shift beneath her feet, the tiles break, the floor gape and swallow her. At his side she tottered; he held out his arm to support her. Before he could catch her she sank to the floor. Wrapping her arms around his legs, she hid her face, her long hair streaming down to his feet.

I was relieved that Linda wasn't in the courtroom when I took the witness stand; easier to testify without her listening. Across The Pit I saw A.J. and Wally among the spectators. And Marjorie Fennel, Harriet Mitchell, Pearl Costa, one or two others. I suppose business kept Angie away. However, it was Angie Costa who'd recommended Mac Landis to represent Doctor Pell, and the young attorney hadn't failed him.

But I was wretched under examination. The worst of what I knew couldn't be confirmed. Mix understood it; he grasped the outline of Doctor Pell's actions and knew he had no grounds for a successful prosecution. Old Hannah understood too; I think this knowledge was at the heart of her sympathy for Annette.

At the edge of The Pit sat Annette with a sad kindness in her eyes. Linda's seat was vacant—I assumed she was late returning—while Father Ted fidgeted in the heat of the courtroom, patting his chin with his handkerchief.

Leonard Mix's first question: Why hadn't I entered the race?

"I was asked. Before LeFevre," I said. "I declined."

"Because the conditions were unsafe."

"Because I don't compete anymore."

"Did Doctor Pell ask you to swim against all comers?"

"No," I said. "Just A.J."

"Interesting." Mix leaned forward, hands clasped. "Doctor Pell asked you to swim a race against Mr. Jagao. And no one else."

"Correct."

"You declined to compete." Down in The Pit he stepped toward me on the balls of his feet. "But you dove in, after the others were in the water, and tried to catch them."

"I tried to catch Mr. Jagao."

"You thought the water was too cold for him."

"Yes."

He leaned further: "You told him so."

"Yes." I testified that I'd given some tips about open water racing, but I didn't know if he used them.

"Mr. Darwin—" Mix glanced at his clipboard: "were lanterns visible on the blind before you dove into the water?"

"Yes."

"I don't suppose you could estimate the speed of Doctor Pell's boat as it approached you in the water."

"No. I could not."

Mix stalked the witness stand, pacing across the front of The Pit. He stopped. "Was its headlamp on?"

I looked at Linda's vacant chair. She wasn't late; she'd left. I was anxious to get down from the witness stand and find her. In the seat next to hers Father Ted dabbed his forehead. I remembered the boat turning in the dark, then a light flashing over us. "At one point it wasn't," I said. "Later, it was."

Landis rose, but Mix anticipated his question: "At the time of the accident the headlamp *was* on."

"Correct."

When the glint of antagonism left his eyes I knew he'd given up. All he had left was to repair the park ranger's reputation and I was happy to help him do it. "You did see Officer LeFevre reach the blind."

"I saw him standing on it."

"And Mr. Jagao was still in the water."

"He was floundering in the water."

"The ranger returned to the water and swam toward him."

"Yes." I volunteered, "I believe he thought Mr. Jagao was drowning. I don't think he saw me behind Mr. Jagao. I think he meant to rescue him."

Mix smiled as if he'd just met a new friend. He seemed to withdraw to the people's table without actually taking a backward step. At the defense table Landis again was on his feet.

"Mr. Darwin, you were as close to the scene as anyone—" Landis stepped forward: "Do you attribute the death of Officer LeFevre to unsafe lighting?"

I glanced at Doctor Pell slumped beside Old Hannah. "No."

"To excessive boat speed?"

"No."

"To any unsafe condition in the lake?"

"No."

Landis sat down at the defense table. Mix had no further questions and I was excused.

Doctor Pell's face, pinched in concentration, was blanched by strain; the effort to hold his world together. Why was he brought here? LeFevre had been killed; the town was talking about his death; the DA was an elected official. Yet he had no evidence of wrongdoing, no hope of a conviction. He'd sought a preliminary hearing to let the public see that fact. Had his neighbors heard someone was smoking pot at the Pells' party? A young man had provided coke for the hostess? The ranger who died had been swimming naked in the lake? Mix let people see that he knew what their whispering was about. But he'd be a damned fool if he'd prosecute in Superior Court a case built on nothing but questions and innuendo. Questions weren't reasons, and this hearing had revealed no compelling grounds to try Doctor Pell.

I was just stepping down from the witness stand when Old Hannah rose slowly, leaning forward, her fingers splayed on the table. Doctor Pell remained seated, pale with fatigue. Landis again requested the manslaughter charge be dismissed, stating, as cause: "Insufficient evidence of negligence. Or any criminal act. Or intent to do any sort of harm whatsoever."

Judge Bierman removed his glasses, polished each lens, and shutting his eyes, rubbed the lids with his knuckles.

Old Hannah cleared her throat to catch his attention. Glasses in place, Judge Bierman fixed his gaze on her, peering into The Pit. "Not to mention the impossibility," she offered. "that so little evidence could obtain a conviction in Superior Court."

A smile broke beneath Judge Bierman's sparkling glasses. "You're not going to mention that?" This was the opportunity he'd waited for to end the hearing, and his gentle sparring with Old Hannah signaled his appreciation. "The court understands counsel doesn't mean to be judge and jury. Nor does she wish to predict the future. Only to caution that a weak case prosecuted in Superior Court won't serve the interests of justice." He watched her white head nod. "I'm amazed how informative counsel can be," he mused, "on matters she claims not to mention."

Old Hannah politely maintained a poker-face. Landis allowed himself a sly grin.

"Motion granted," Judge Bierman ruled. "Doctor Pell, you are free to leave this court. The charge against you is dismissed for lack of sufficient cause."

I hurried out of the Pit and the gate cracked shut behind me like a rifle shot. I saw Father Ted, unable to lean across Linda's empty chair, reach over to pat Annette's hand. I looked in the foyer but I knew Linda wasn't there. Outside the steps blazed with light and the street was still. I waited for A.J. and Sarah to come down the courthouse steps and we went around the back to the parking lot. That's where the priest found us.

"Linda's gone," I said.

"Her parents' car is here," said Father Ted.

"Teresa isn't. And she'd take her anywhere."

"Yes," he said, "she would."

But where?

17

A Tourist's View of Hell

A.J. thought Linda would go to the stables. "She'll ride Blueboy into the foothills. Then, before sundown, she'll bring him back to his stall."

"I hope you're right," said Father Ted.

"I doubt it," I said. I was the one who believed this time she'd left for good. This time she wouldn't come back.

The priest rode along in my car, A.J. brought his station wagon, and we drove across the old iron bridge over the gleaming river and up to Sawyers' Stables.

Birds hopped across the roof of the house and glided over the grass. The pasture and riding arena stood empty; the horses were in their stalls. A.J. had left Sarah Hack to look after them while he was in court. Now, when she stepped from the house, her hand reached for the swing and its chain made a grating sound.

"Linda was here." Sarah wore jeans and a checkered blouse and her blond braid rested on her shoulder. "Teresa Espinosa brought her. She wanted to see Blueboy."

"What did she say?" I asked her.

"Very little."

"Tell me—please."

"She took her bridle from the tack room." Sarah fingered her braid in the bright sunlight. "I thought she wanted to ride her horse. But she just wanted to see him. And feed him."

"Feed him?" said A.J. "At this hour?"

"A bucket of grain. And water. I thought it couldn't hurt. And it's her horse."

Blueboy had munched much of his grain by the time we arrived. Puzzled by our interest, he flicked an ear; switched his tail. I looked into his stall. "I don't see the bridle."

"Took it with her," said Sarah.

"I don't imagine they drove into town," said Father Ted.

With a shake of her head Sarah's braid slipped from her shoulder. "They went up the road," she said. "To the lake?"

"Looks like Teresa took her home," the priest concluded.

Jays squawked at our approach to the house; then winged away to the woodpile. Father Ted followed Sarah into the kitchen for a glass of water.

"Mr. Darwin, I remember what you did that night." In the shade of the porch A.J. had folded his suitcoat over his arm. "Thank you," he said.

"He would have killed you."

"Sarah thanks you, too," He loosened his tie.

"I wish I'd been quicker. LeFevre would be alive today."

"I share the blame for that," he said. "I can't forget it."

"No," I said, and we shook hands. "I won't either."

Father Ted emerged from the doorway mopping his brow with his handkerchief. Sarah, drawn with worry, followed him out onto the porch. We left her there with A.J.—while they stood beside the swing she held his hand in hers—and we drove up to Lake Elaine.

The dented white car in the Pells' driveway was Teresa's. She sat behind the wheel, crying.

"Linda—" Teresa began, but she broke down and couldn't speak. Then she was out of her car, plucking a tissue from her purse as Father Ted put an arm around her. "She's so unhappy," she managed, as he comforted her.

"You brought her here?" I asked.

She nodded into her tissue; looked for another.

"Why did she leave?" she asked the priest.

"She's ashamed of her father," he said. "And frightened."

"I'm frightened for her," said Teresa.

"Linda has been leaving for a long time," he said. He'd been as close to her as either of her parents—perhaps he understood her better than they did—so I shouldn't have been surprised that he'd seen this too. He took out his house key but the door was open. I heard the phone ringing. Was Linda calling? Were her parents calling her from the courthouse? The phone in her father's study was closer than the one in the kitchen. But when I stepped into the study it stopped ringing.

I switched on the lamp. What was different?

The lamp threw light on the NASA photo of the volcanic park. On the gun-rack with the rifle and 12-gauge. The poster showing *Scenes of Deformation.* The twin bookcases holding Doctor Pell's rock samples. The model of the *Arizona.* His duck decoys. But the photo of Linda and Sarah stood alone, her trophies were missing. Gone too were her prize ribbons.

"Look what we have here." Father Ted found Linda's trophies in a wastebasket beside his brother's desk. Each one had been smashed against the side of the desk, scarring the wood. The trophy horses were crippled; the riders' heads were snapped back as if they'd been shot. "She wanted her father to find these."

Teresa waited at the front door. Some of her color had returned; it lifted her spirits to be able to help the priest.

"Where did Linda go?" he asked.

"I don't know. I don't know. I don't *know*!"

"What did she take with her?" I asked. "Besides the bridle?"

"An armful of clothes. Her ribbons." Teresa stifled a cry. She'd remembered something else: "*La novia.*"

"The bride?" asked Father Ted.

"*La muñeca,*" she said.

"Her doll?"

"And her boots."

I ran upstairs to Linda's room. Impossible to know which clothes she'd taken but the rocking chair was empty; the doll dressed in a wedding gown was gone. No message in sight. I went down to the music room. Her flute was missing.

Father Ted walked out to the driveway with Teresa. "I'll look in the park," I said. "We were there with her—A.J. and I—last week. She'd brought her flute. She might have gone back."

"I'll come with you," the priest offered.

"I'll need your help," I said.

Father Ted turned to Teresa. "You'll wait? Her parents are on their way. Someone ought to be here if Linda comes back."

"She isn't coming back," I said.

It was midweek and not many people were in the park. When I pulled into the lot by the Visitors Center there sat Linda's car. We looked for her among the small group viewing the exhibits but she wasn't there. We stopped by the ranger's office but Wally Hack hadn't returned from the hearing in Crags Landing.

We left my car in the lot at the base of Lassen Peak. A wisp of steam floated over the volcano and, beneath the steam, snow glowed around the peak. The upper slopes were glossy snow or bare talus. A scattering of white pine. Further down, mountain hemlock stood out among small brushy pines. A few hikers straggled down from the summit but Linda wasn't among them. Wherever she was she'd be alone.

We hiked into the hydrothermal area of steaming vents, bubbling mud pots. The smell of hydrogen sulphide gas permeated the air. From the magma chamber two miles beneath our feet clouds fumed up, steam fluttered from crevices between rocks. Sulphuric acid ate away the soil. Around us the earth steamed, trembled.

"God, what a sight!" said Father Ted.

"A tourist's view of hell," I said. "That's what your brother called it."

"Bob said that?"

"Linda told me."

"He's looking at all the hell he needs right now."

"It'll be worse," I said. "Without her."

"We'll find her."

"Before she hurts herself."

"She's too strong to do that."

"You saw what she did to her trophies," I argued. "And why did she bring the bridle? Why did she take that little doll?"

"God knows–I've no idea." The priest looked like he was going to be sick. Bending from the waist, he rested his hands on his knees. Then straightened; lifting his chin above the white brace, his face shining with sweat. "Let's go on."

We crossed a creek and hiked on through wild flowers and passed among the pines and came to Cold Boiling Lake. "We had a picnic," I said. "Not far from here. We talked about what we'd do if the volcano erupted. If you knew you were about to die."

"What was Linda's answer? You must remember."

"She said we should comfort each other."

"And if we can't?"

"Set an example for someone else."

"Oh, my God," he sighed.

But I'd begun to hope.

"You told me she's too strong to hurt herself."

He stared into the blue water with its fringe of bubbles breaking the surface. "Yes, she is."

"We keep looking," I said. "That's what she wants us to do."

The priest fumbled in his pocket for matches. But when he found them he didn't light his cigar. His hand closed around the matchbook and he dropped the cigar into his coat pocket.

"Where do you think she is?"

"I don't know," I admitted. "I hope she'll tell us."

Patches of snow glowed in the clearings among the pines and a breeze flowed across the water. We walked around the tiny lake, and beside a clump of pumice we found Linda's black leather pumps, the ones she'd worn in court this morning. She hadn't hidden them; she'd left them here in broad daylight to be found. "Teresa said she brought boots," said Father Ted.

"Yes," I said.

Now I thought I knew where to look. Across a long meadow we pushed through broken forest to another clearing; then a stand of hemlocks. We came out on a clear-running creek and the meadow, rich in wild flowers, where I'd listened to Linda' s flute and A.J.'s guitar. Two Oregon juncos buzzed the creek bed. Veering away, with a shrill *cheek-cheek,* the birds wove over the grass.

I meant to look for Linda in the grove behind this meadow. But along the creek we came first to a stand of ponderosa; as she knew we would. Four pines with the breeze brushing their boughs. Hung from the lowest bough was Linda's bridle. The reins secured it with a knot and it held a bundle that stirred in the breeze. She'd used the bridle like a basket to hold her doll and the slim black case for her flute. I laid them on the ground and her uncle knelt to examine them. Taking the purse from the doll's hands, I snapped it open. Linda's ribbons were wadded into it. Father Ted opened the black case and showed me her silver flute. I blinked back tears. The priest mopped sweat from his face and wiped his eyes. "She wanted you to find this," he said.

"At least she's alive," I said. I wrapped the reins around the bundle, put it under my arm, and we started back. The snow-capped volcano gleamed in the late sunlight. At the base of Lassen Peak I set Linda's things in the trunk of my car. We drove back to the Visitors Center but her car was gone. Where?

As we drove down the mountain road the pines thinned until the sun slanted across open meadows. We passed Sawyers' Stables, crossed the bridge into town, and I delivered the priest to the rectory. Teresa's car sat by the curb so Linda's parents must have arrived at Lake Elaine and sent her home. From the Riverside I phoned the Pells and told Annette what we'd found.

The next morning I drove to Lake Elaine. Thunderheads hung over the mountains; a grey light shivered on the lake. No word from Linda. In the quiet of their house her father looked tormented.

Annette told me he'd eaten nothing since they returned from the hearing. "And he can't sleep," she said.

The court had failed to indict him for killing LeFevre but that hardly mattered. *To go unjudged is not to go unpunished,* Jules Beauregard had written, and Doctor Pell was living proof of the old trapper's admonition. He shuffled through the silent rooms, his hands needlessly busy, adjusting the position of a chair, drawing the dining room drapes in the early afternoon. With a fresh Scotch he slumped into the sofa on the porch. I'd come to say goodbye. He looked at me with lifeless eyes.

"Where is my wife?" he asked.

I left him sitting in silence and went to find Annette. She had walked down to the pier and was seated on one of the twin benches. I sat across from her with the bell behind us. Her hair was bound in a tight bun; she wore no makeup, her only ornament was a necklace of earth-colored stones.

"I can't blame Linda for leaving." Annette's voice was as cool and level as the lake. An osprey swooped and its ghostly image skimmed past the pier. "I'm eternally sorry for my husband. But I don't want to be here either. I won't leave him. But how can we live here? How are we to live together?" Annette clasped her hands. "He's lost Linda. He knows he drove her away. The truth came out in court. Enough of it. He *did* try to kill Akira, didn't he? That's why Danny LeFevre died. Dick, we have to live with that. But Linda doesn't have to live with *him*. That will be no life at all."

I knew she spoke for herself as well. "I've brought her flute. Her ribbons. And her doll. Do you want them?"

Annette touched her stone necklace.

"What is it?" I said. "You're afraid."

"I don't dare let Bob see them. It might break him completely." Crossing her ankles, she tucked her feet beneath the bench. "Will you keep them for Linda? Please."

"What can I do for you?"

"For *me*? Nothing."

"For your family then."

She smiled sadly. Father Ted had overstayed his leave and needed transportation to The Gate of Heaven. I offered to take him there on my way to San Francisco. A wisp of hair had slipped free and her fingertips brushed it back.

"What you must think of our family," she said.

18

The Fire Watch

The sun was a blazing bowl that spilled its intense heat over the earth. Trees bent above their shadows, the blond grass rippled in an undercurrent of breeze and returned to implacable stillness. From cornfields crows struggled upward through the heat as if rising from the bottom of a river and beating toward the surface for air. Slowly they circled, settled. They hung like black flags in the somber trees as we drove by.

"What'll you do?"

"I've asked to be released from my parish. The bishop may be reading my letter this minute."

"And smiling?"

"He'll be happy to oblige me." Father Ted seemed embarrassed; his laugh was like a nervous cough. "I'll stay in the monastery until I can return to Mercy House. That's where my heart is." He pulled a cigar from his pocket. "But I can't operate Mercy House under the auspices of the church. And I'm unworthy of the priesthood; it's time I faced that fact."

We passed a brief oasis that floated up in the dry grassland. Two horses grazed in a freshly watered pasture. "Most people must be unsuited for it," I said.

"That's true." Smoke from his cigar swirled through the car then drifted off. In the orchards the air was still. The fruit stand beside the road sagged under the sun, its window boarded shut. "By the way, there'll be a cot for you in the guest house. Father Stanley says stay as long as you like."

"I'll sleep there tonight." I thanked him for asking the abbot for the cot.

"I'll drive to the city tomorrow."

"You're dead tired, Dick."

"I have to find Linda."

Late in the day we bumped down the dirt road to the parking lot outside The Gate of Heaven.

Brother Adam handed a huge key ring to Father Ted. Also a flashlight. With an insistent look in his long face he reached for our luggage. Lifting the wings of his eyebrows, he examined the priest for an argument. The two exchanged signs and Brother Adam loped off to the guest house with our bags.

"The abbot wants me to take the fire watch." Father Ted gave me his briefcase as we started up the road. "It's already late for the others," he said. "He may as well let them go to bed."

"Is he testing you?"

"He wants to see if I'm a willing worker. He needn't worry; it's my favorite chore. You're left alone to walk anywhere within these walls. Most of the men are asleep. And the peace of this place eases into your blood."

"Admit you like it and he won't let you do it again."

The priest laughed and the keys clinked at his side.

Where the orchards left off we could see beyond the stone wall across the grassland to the edge of the valley. Twilight had settled on the foothills, the canyons were filled with shadows.

The crest of the mountains cut into the sky for a few more minutes. Then dusk obscured that sharp outline and the mountains themselves disappeared in the dark.

"Time to start," said Father Ted.

We searched the barns and stables for a whiff of smoke, a cigarette smoldering in straw. In the tractor shed we swung the light around oil drums and gas cans and looked for clumps of rags.

As we moved among the sheds night deepened and The Gate of Heaven sank beneath it. No tractors worked the fields. No trucks coughed in the dusty road; no power saws ripped the air. Steeped in silence, the monastery returned to what it was when Jules Beauregard built his hut behind the blacksmith's shop.

Behind the hermit's hut we unlocked the smith's shop and examined the outlets and a tin of coals. Near the carpenter's bench I held the light while Father Ted sifted a handful of wood shavings. In the ceramics shed a potter, his cigarette on the table's edge, sat drawing a design. Father Ted wagged his finger; the monk took a final puff and rubbed the butt into the floor. He signed that the kilns were cold, he was just making some sketches. As we went out the priest patted his coat. "I'd like a smoke myself."

The wooden church and the sacristy stood empty. In the paneled library two monks were reading by candlelight at separate tables. A swivel fan threw its breeze between them. One man rose when he heard us. Shielding his flame with his palm, he nodded that he was on his way to bed. The other glanced from the fan to his candle to show us he'd be careful with it.

In the laundry room a steam iron sat upright on the board. It was recently used; I felt its warmth. I unplugged the cord and Father Ted set the iron on a metal plate.

We passed quietly through the two floors of the dormitory. "Dick, you have to keep a sharp eye. These men work hard and they sleep like babies." In the stillness I heard harsh breathing; a soft snore. Windows were open and a breeze rippled through the dark quarters. Asleep in their cubicles men stirred on their straw pallets as we walked by.

We stepped outside and went up the road. Father Ted knocked on the door of the bakery. The knob began to turn from inside but slipped. A half turn; it slipped again. He gave me a quizzical look and knocked once more. Now the knob was jiggled from inside but wouldn't turn. Out of patience, the priest seized the doorknob. He shoved; the door thumped open, bumping a stunned Brother Smudge. His hands were caked with flour. I saw patches of it on his chin and nose; a red patch on his forehead where the door had bumped him. He seized a cloth and wiped flour from the doorknob he'd been trying to turn. Father Ted glanced around the room and we left. "Nothing can go seriously wrong in there," he said. "He'll outlive all of us."

Finally we entered the refectory. The dining hall was quickly done but in the kitchen we checked old stoves, the broiler, both ovens; electric outlets; the bent plug behind the freezer; the frayed cords from the refrigerators.

We came into the road outside the guest house. Crickets strummed in the dark. Growing up I had watched the Sacramento River rippling below my window before I fell asleep, comforted by the living night. A breeze in the shore trees. Night birds calling. The current murmuring in its bed. Just past our dock stars flickered on the water like candles carried in an endless procession. Here too the night lived, stirred. Not only behind a few bright windows in the blackness of the monastery, but in the sighs of sleepers in their cubicles, the rustle of orchard leaves, insects restless in the fields. Careful to awaken no one, we went quietly up the steps to the guest house.

I knew at once it was Jules Beauregard.

Stepping into the dark house, Father Ted had switched on the light and we stood before the death mask of the old trapper mounted in a glass case in the entranceway.

"Who made this?" I asked.

"Two monks. Immediately after his death."

Working quickly with beeswax, they'd formed an incredible likeness. The priest caught my curious look. "Yes, beeswax," he said. It had provided the hermit with mortar when he built his hut. A decade later the monks used it to take his death mask.

Beauregard's face had been formed by the land he'd lived in. Taut, dry, cracked by the baking sun on the valley and the winter chill of the canyons. But it wasn't the work of weather alone. Around his eyes and mouth and underlining his jut-boned jaw were ridges so deep they could have been carved by a hunting knife; it was a face formed as well by his conscience. His daily indictment of his innocence; his unsparing search for his motives however dishonorable they might be. What surprised me wasn't the ferocity of the hermit's face—his story prepared you for that—but the compassion in his eyes. He'd looked inward for so long to examine the extent of his guilt that his outward gaze came to register, on others, an astonishing sad kindness.

In the days after the eruption of Mount St. Helens—while rescue teams brought out the injured and dead—many of us wore a kerchief or a sanitary mask hiding half the face. But here, bathed in light, a mask *revealed* a face. For forty years the hermit had looked on those corpses in the cave of his heart. His eyes were benign but at their corners and around the closed mouth were lines engraved by years of torment when he couldn't confess his shame to those who survived the slaughter. "You can see the pressure of his conscience," said Father Ted. "The pain it caused him."

"Until it killed him," I said. Brother Adam had left our luggage on the floor. I pushed the bags aside. We stepped back "Why is it kept in this house? Away from everyone else?"

"The monks want to share his spirit with any guest who visits here. After all, Beauregard first entered this monastery as a guest. And perhaps that's what he always was."

I thought, too, that the hermit's mask must have tested the cheerful benevolence of the monks. His kindness, intensified by misery, opened his solitary face to the suffering of others, with an expansive sorrow. It wasn't a face we'd seen among the monks I'd met: clearly not Abbot Stanley; not Brother Raymond or Brother Adam. Not the glib guest master, Brother Bert. Not even, God help us, Brother Smudge. Still it seemed this community of souls included the hermit as well. It was then I realized this face also was familiar to Father Ted; he'd been living in these rooms before I'd brought him to Lake Elaine. But he hadn't told me about the death mask because he wanted it to surprise me. It did. Its unspoken pain made me think of that boy in Chinatown; his mouth open, too proud to cry. Then I saw LeFevre's wild stare as his blood gurgled in the water. "I have to tell you something," I said.

The priest put his briefcase on the bureau. In his large hands he carried a crystal ashtray with a scalloped rim like a translucent flower. It must have been given to the monastery; too costly for the monks to have purchased it, too glamorous for their use, it remained in the guest house. Seated on the edge of the bed, the ashtray beside him, he gave his cigar a measured look. "No more after this." He struck a match; held it burning between his thumb and finger. "I mean it."

"Listen," I said.

He lit his cigar. "What is it?"

"Call it a confession—

"You aren't Catholic."

"I have to tell you this. Though you don't want to hear it."

"I'm sure I don't." His cigar tapped the ashtray." But tell me."

"I was with your brother that Sunday afternoon. Before the party. We took his boat to hang lanterns on the blind. He made the same maneuver around the raft. He cut the engines to kill the sound."

"A practice run?"

I sat on the cot. He understood well enough. The smoke of his cigar drifted through the room.

"I knew he hated A.J. You knew it, too."

"I told him so," said the priest. "He denied it."

"But it was true."

He smoked quietly, considering. "Yes."

"Noah asked me to work with him. I had to prove I could do it. I wanted Linda. It was my fault she left me. I was willing to overlook anything to be with her."

Though his gaze fell the cervical collar held his head upright. His solid face looked heavy with fatigue. "Dick, you couldn't have guessed what he was planning. No one did."

"I knew how your father died. Bob despised A.J. and I saw what he did with the boat. We both knew A.J. couldn't reach that raft. But I shut my eyes." Listening, Father Ted examined his smoldering cigar. Its ash fell onto his black pants. His hands opened in a gesture of helplessness. "When I did see what was happening," I said, "I never thought of warning LeFevre."

"Akira told me what you did for him."

"Danny tried to help, too."

"I know," he said. "I'm sorry."

"That's not much comfort."

"I don't want to give you comfort." He exhaled a long breath of smoke. "What comfort can we give LeFevre's parents? What comfort is there for Annette? Or Linda?"

"I have to find her."

"I hope you will." The priest stubbed out his cigar in the crystal flower. "Saint Paul, you know, tells us that love never ends."

"Paul said that?"

"*Corinthians*, unless I'm mistaken." Rising carefully, he walked in his deliberate way into the bathroom. I heard water running. Then he was back, standing by his bed, still thinking about his niece. "We like to promise love lasts forever," he sighed. "The terrible truth is, it *does*."

19

October in the Park

Before daybreak men were singing. Later when I got up, Father Ted already was out of the house. I washed and shaved and walked over to the refectory, entering by the kitchen door. The monk seated at the carving table lifted his eyes in recognition. I didn't know him from the others but he remembered having seen me when I was here before. He shuffled to the counter and poured a cup of coffee. I went out and sat on the doorstep and drank the strong black coffee, then walked back to the guest house.

The buildings made a white island among the fields. All around, emerging from the night, trees shook down their shadows and stood shining in the early light. Beyond the orchards and shade trees dew glimmered on the grass. I brought my bag out the gate to the car and drove the dirt road to the freeway.

In the fresh light trucks rolled along lugging produce from the farms. Others were packed with cattle or black-faced sheep from the ranches. A bridge lifted over the river. Down the valley the river widened where its banks gave way; it uprooted brush and carried off trees in its current. Silently it moved like memory, purposeful, relentless, unforgiving. I didn't want to think of Doctor Pell's treachery; I didn't want to remember why LeFevre had died, because I was part of that too. I only wanted to find Linda.

Down from the bridge the road led through fields where birds stirred in thick warmth. All morning the sky flamed above barns and silos until the valley receded behind brown hills, billboards, roadside diners, gas stations. Across the Bay Bridge the freeway, swollen with traffic, poured into the busy city.

I spent the late afternoon in my flat looking through mail, mostly bills, and that evening I went to have a drink with Noah and Edna Geyer, and to show Dorothy the photos from the Crags Landing rodeo. But Dorothy was in Children's Hospital for observation. "For the past week," Edna said. She rarely drank; but as we sat at the kitchen table she was halfway through her second Scotch and soda.

Noah brought the Scotch to the table and freshened our drinks. "We'll bring her home tomorrow," he said.

"These are for her." I showed them the photos of Linda, Father Ted, A.J., and Blueboy; Sarah, A.J., and Thrifty; and the Rodeo Queen seated on her sorrel, resplendent in white hat and jacket glittering with rhinestones.

"Dorothy will be delighted." Her father beamed over the snapshots. Her mother thanked me for taking the trouble. "It was no trouble. I wish she'd been there."

Edna brought a pitcher of ice water from the refrigerator "What are you doing?" Noah asked as she topped off first his drink and then mine. Then her own.

"Watering the flowers," she said.

His eyebrows lifted. "You were drinking soda."

"I don't feel like opening another bottle." She sat down.

"I'll open it for you."

"I'm fine." She laid her large hand on his wrist. "Let's just talk."

I told them how the hearing had ended. How Linda slipped out of the courthouse. "When she saw what her father had done she had to get away."

Edna glared at her glass. "You have no idea where she is?"

"None."

"I feel sorry for that whole family," she said.

"I'll wait to write her father," Noah said. "NEPA will do without him. But we don't have to tell him so, just now."

"You're right; he's in terrible shape. He has only Annette and he hardly knows she's there. I'll phone you if I find Linda."

"Please do." Edna brushed back a strand of hair. With a warm look she asked, "Are you tired, dear?"

I suddenly was. "God, yes."

She kissed my cheek. "Go home. Now."

I pushed up from my chair and felt the fatigue in my legs. I said goodnight. "Give my love to Dorothy."

"Dick, go easy for a few days." Noah followed me to the door. "You don't need to be in the office tomorrow."

"I'd like to meet with Kurowski," I said. "To see if Linda has come by the lab. If she's asked him about her job."

Nothing about Doctor Pell's death surprised me except the timing of it. I learned the news the next morning in a Post Street coffee shop where I'd stopped for breakfast before driving down to USGS headquarters. It rated a half-column in the *Chronicle* because he'd been a recipient of the National Medal of Science, known for his work at Mount St. Helens and Lassen Volcanic National Park. During a search initiated at his wife's request, his body was discovered by Deputy Sheriff William Scott, in a boathouse on the

Pells' property at Lake Elaine. Distraught over "personal problems", he'd died of a massive self-inflicted head wound from a 12-gauge shotgun, of which he was the owner, according to Joseph Sullivan, Sheriff and Coroner of Caliente County. "He is survived by his wife Annette, daughter Linda, and brother Theodore. Funeral plans have not been announced by the family," the piece concluded...Sometime during that night when I walked the fire watch with his brother in the monastery, Doctor Pell took from his gun rack the shotgun with its handsome walnut stock and went out to the privacy of the boathouse and blew his head off,

I used the pay phone back by the restrooms to call Noah. He'd read the paper and Edna had heard the news on National Public Radio. I told him I'd talk to Kurowski anyway. I wanted to be busy. I'd be at work tomorrow morning.

"Whatever's best," he said glumly.

I drove down the Bayshore Freeway in a fierce wind that buffeted the traffic. In Menlo Park I turned off for the USGS Headquarters, a big beige complex. Building 5 was designated for "Earthquakes, Volcanoes, & Engineering". I was early for my meeting with Doctor Kurowski but he waved me into his office. He settled behind a metal desk; all around us were metal shelves holding books, binders, a scale, a tape deck; the chairs were perched on rollers. The room looked comfortable for Kurowski and heavily used, though it suffered from being freshly painted in white and a sunny yellow. "Nice and light, isn't it?" He sank deeper in his chair. "I can't say I like it much." I wheeled a chair up to his desk. He'd read the paper too. "What a terrible shame—" he said. Doctor K was a thick-set man with a full head of white hair brushed straight back. Sitting behind his desk, he plowed his fingers through his hair. "It's awful, isn't it? It's just dreadful about Bob."

"You were old friends."

He looked up, said nothing, folded his hands. His face was weighed with sorrow.

"He spoke fondly of you," I said.

"Bob Pell?" He looked surprised. "It isn't a great shock that Bob would take his life. But the manner of his death. Isn't it bad enough? Why give out all those details?" Pushing back his chair, he planted his feet firmly. His hefty frame shivered. "You read that and it's hard to shake off. My wife caught it on the morning news. His poor daughter. What an awful thing for her.'

"You've heard from Linda?"

"Not one word since she left here."

"She hasn't applied for her job in the lab?"

"If she walks through that door I'll hire her again. We were pleased with her work. But puzzled. I'd want to know why she left." His solid body swiveled in his chair. He glanced around the bright room. "Maybe this is a poor time to ask."

"Yes, it is."

I shook his hand at the door and went out into the gleaming wind. I drove up to San Francisco, leaving the freeway, pressing into city traffic, impatient to get home. From a florist's shop downtown I sent a sympathy card to Annette with a note of support. Back in my flat I wrote to Linda at her parents' address; surely she'd come home for the funeral. I wrote to Father Ted at The Gate of Heaven.

And then, nothing.

No word from Linda, Annette, Father Ted.

Each day I returned from the NEPA offices hoping to hear from them. I couldn't call Annette and add to her pain. With Father Ted in the monastery I couldn't call him either. Then I thought of the one person I could speak to who'd certainly have attended Doctor Pell's funeral. Who'd attend the funeral of anyone in that family to express by her silent presence her respect and grief. She'd probably been to LeFevre's as well. An operator gave me the number of the only Espinosa family listed in Crags Landing and I dialed. A full-throated voice, warm, intimate, answered the phone.

"Teresa?"

"Yes."

I introduced myself. "I'm sorry to trouble you."

"I am not troubled."

I'd reached her on the evening after the funeral. She'd driven to The Gate of Heaven to bring Father Ted to Crags Landing and she drove him back to the monastery afterwards. There were relatives she didn't know. Wally and Winnie Hack were there. Mac Landis had brought Old Hannah. A few professors. Geologists. Most of the day, Teresa said, she was with Annette.

"And Linda?"

"She came. And left."

Did Teresa know where Linda went?

"Forgive me," she said. "No."

"Thank you," I said.

"I am sorry," she said.

The rest of the summer I read reports on Lassen Peak, on the degree of volcanic activity in the park surrounding it. On the preparation, or lack of it, in public services. I read the morning paper and watched TV news every evening, for the story of a missing young woman found in the city. Or out in the valley. Or in the mountains. Until you lose someone you don't realize how many hundreds of others are lost, all around us.

Often I followed Linda into a store or turned to see her leaving an office building. I rushed up only to catch a wary look from an unfamiliar face. One Saturday night in September her favorite flutist, Jean-Pierre Rampal, was performing at Herbst Hall. I thought if Linda was in the city his concert would bring her to the theatre. I arrived early to catch sight of her but the hall soon filled. Then the lights dimmed; impossible to pick out anyone in the audience. Rampal was splendid. At the end of his program he obliged a raucous audience with one encore after another. On the final burst of applause I bolted for the exit, turning to meet other faces as the house lights came up.

This search was senseless. I had no idea if Linda was in the city, and I'd almost decided to stop looking for her. But on a Sunday morning in October I awoke wondering if she might attend Mass. I drove over to St. Mary's in time for the ten o'clock service. Bright light spilled through narrow windows, illuminating the entire cathedral adorned with fall foliage. I sat at the rear and when the Mass ended I remained, watching the young women in fresh autumn dresses walking up the aisle to the doorway. I went out among the families chatting, stooping into cars.

While I ate lunch in the Japan Center a couple walked by, pushing their little boy in a stroller. He was mushing an ice cream cone into his chin, dribbling it onto his shirt, grinning. Later in the day the fog rolled in. I caught a bus downtown, then walked to my flat. From the landing I heard the phone ringing. Fumbling to unlock the door, I flung it open and hurried in.

"Just in time," Edna said. "I was about to hang up."

"Oh, hello," I said. "It's you."

"I'm quite aware of that," she said.

"I thought you were someone else."

"Obviously." I heard her dry laugh. "Dear, can you come to dinner? It's Noah's stew so there's plenty. And I'll toss a salad."

I told her I'd bring a bottle of wine.

"Seven o'clock," she said.

When I arrived with a bottle of zinfandel the aroma of the stew warmed the house. I opened the wine. Edna wanted a fire but Noah stood fussing at the stove. I asked Dorothy to bring newspapers; sitting in front of the fireplace, we laid down kindling, set two logs on top. When the blaze flared up she whooped with pleasure.

It was two weeks since I'd seen Dorothy. Now her shirt hung on her shoulders and arms; her cheekbones caught the candlelight but her sunken cheeks held shadows. I'd expected to see her hair draped to her shoulders; instead, it was fastened with a blue comb in a small bun at the back. Loose strands slipped over her temples. While we sat at supper in the candlelight her green eyes were aglow with the fire that consumed her strength. Once after she'd been riding with Linda I'd thought this vivid look was caused by exertion. Maybe it was. Now her flushed pallor looked lovely, natural, but hurried. As if her body must assert itself early and all at once; it couldn't wait for a later opportunity. Suddenly she slumped in her chair, too tired to eat. "Sorry."

"I don't mind," her father said.

"I do." Dorothy stared at her unfinished meal. "I used to have a monster appetite," she confided to me. "I could eat the whole pot."

"I'll save your carrot cake," said Edna. "Want to watch TV?"

"Thanks." Dorothy left the room. We heard the set click on.

Edna served the cake and the three of us sipped coffee, then cleared the table. In the living room we found Dorothy asleep on the sofa, the fire fluttering behind its screen. Her chin rested on her shoulder. Falling asleep, she'd tried to block the light from the television with her thin arm flung across her face. I was shocked to see how easily Noah lifted his daughter from the sofa; how light she was. She seemed to weigh little more than a large doll, like that one of Linda's.

Months ago I'd worried about Noah; I thought he'd break down under too much strain. Now that seemed unlikely though Dorothy was failing. Holding her limp body, he looked more able than ever. Maybe he was right; he'd grown too soft or sensitive to function in the world. But in this house he and Edna had made a world in which each could live. After all, it wasn't love that died, but the people who teach us what it is. When he carried Dorothy to her room I turned to see Edna watching him, too.

"Thank you, dear."

"For what?" I asked.

She looked down over her glasses. "For not asking."

She knew the question was on my mind.

"If only she'll be with us for another year. That's what we've said these past two years. Now we ask for this month. And next month. At this stage her remissions are brief. Every day's a blessing," she said. "You can see she's lost weight. Can't you? And she tires quickly."

"You know how I hope—"

"I try not to hope," Edna broke in. "My hope isn't important. Her being here is all that matters." She bent over, plumped pillows in the corners of the sofa, stood up. She gazed at the wavering fire and it danced on her lenses. "I know she's slipping. But we can't hold onto her too hard or she'll feel our fear. It frightens her and she blames herself for it." Edna turned to face me. "You saw the sadness in her eyes at dinner. She isn't sorry for her life. She's sorry for us. I can't bear to do that to her. I have to love her and let her be. Be thankful for every day that we have her with us."

Noah came back. "I put a blanket over her feet."

"I'll undress her," said Edna. "Or she'll wake up in her clothes in the middle of the night."

In the kitchen Noah poured a Scotch for both of us. We brought our drinks back to the fire. He used the poker to nudge the glowing logs; they crumbled into fresh flames snapping at the screen as we settled on the sofa. On the coffee table were tile coasters for our drinks and a pile of snapshots.

"You noticed Dorothy's hair?" Noah sipped his Scotch. "It's coming out in clumps."

"Her medication does that?"

"That means it's working. Sort of," he said. "Next week we'll shop for a wig."

I put down my glass. "What do her doctors say?"

"Her last bone marrow count was nine percent. Down from twenty-nine. That's a significant decline. If it lasts."

"I'm sure she feels better being at home. This has to be good for her."

"It's good for *me*," he said. "But it's no wonder the poor girl's tired. We went to the park today. Took these pictures." Sitting up, he set his drink on a coaster. Shoved it aside. "She loved the ones you brought her from the rodeo. After supper she was going to show you these." He began leafing through the photos: A jogger in a clown costume who stopped to flash a red-lipped smile at the camera. A rock formation in a patch of sunlight. Flowerbeds. A small waterfall. The riding stables. "Dorothy can't ride anymore," said Noah. "But she wants to see the horses. To be around them again. One of those gals found a quiet pony she could sit."

The photo showed Dorothy on the pony, her face brightened by her gleeful grin. Edna held a rope halter in both hands. Behind them, almost lost in shade, stood the instructor in jeans and a plaid shirt, a green bandanna around the crown of her hat. Noah pointed her out. "She picked out the pony for Dorothy. She wouldn't pose with us but she let Edna hold the halter." But Linda *was* posing, wasn't she? Knowing she was in the camera's range, though just barely, she hadn't turned away or walked off but waited there, a tense figure watching from the shadows.

I phoned the Geyers the next night.

"I'm going to the park on Saturday. To the stables. Would Dorothy like to come with me? We'll be very careful."

"I'm sure you will," said Edna. "Suppose you call Saturday morning to see if she can go. I know she'd love to."

That night, unable to sleep, I lay in bed watching the lights of the traffic flashing through the room. Each day I went to work impatient with myself and with every report I was to evaluate. At night I returned to my flat, ate supper, listened to music, went to bed; refused to read a newspaper or watch TV. Saturday I was up early, made coffee, paced through the flat, and finally phoned. Noah sounded uncommonly grumpy. "Oh. You," he said. "We asked Dorothy last night."

"What did she say?" I asked. "Is she up to this?"

"Oh, yes. She can hardly wait."

"When can I pick her up?"

"Dick? Do you know it's seven-fifteen?"

"Sorry–I suppose I woke you."

Noah snorted into the phone. I heard Edna's sleepy voice beside him in bed attempting to pacify him. We agreed I'd come by at noon. "We'll give Dorothy some hot chocolate," he said.

"I'll pack our lunch. I'll bring a warm blanket, too," I said. "And I'll keep an eye on her."

"I know you will."

I filled a picnic basket with sandwiches, bananas, oranges. I put in a thermos of coffee; cups. Paper napkins. I brought the basket and blanket down to the car.

When I climbed the wooden steps to the Geyers' house Edna was waiting at the door. I greeted her with a hug and she gave her glasses a nudge on her nose. "Dick, let her pet the horses. And she can sit on a quiet pony. One of the girls will hold the reins." She grasped my hand. "But she's not to ride by herself. Nothing more than a pony walk and keep it brief."

"I'll see to it."

Noah in his slippers and a rumpled robe shuffled into the living room with Dorothy. A grin puffed out his cheeks. "Enjoy your outing, you two."

"We will!" Dorothy wore boots with her jeans but her mother reminded her she wasn't to ride. She tugged at her sweater, eager to be off; Noah handed her a jacket for later in the day. "Ready?" I asked.

"You bet."

Driving to the park, I wondered if her parents had told her why I was going to the riding stables. "Your father looked awfully happy," I said. "Downright cheerful."

"He ate a monster breakfast."

I decided not to ask. If she was acting innocent it was for my benefit. I parked the car on the street. We walked to the traffic light and crossed into the park. Once we'd passed the little lake and the inner road we could smell the hay and dung of the stables and the mud of the corral in the deep shade. A few riders trotted down a trail among the trees.

At the stables men and women and two teenage girls had gathered around the rental office. A man barked orders for their horses to be brought over. Two women in jeans and sweaters and Linda in a plaid work shirt, wearing her cowboy hat with the bandanna, fetched the mounts from the stables. They saddled them in the clearing while Dorothy watched intently. Then Linda, leading a grey pony, marched across the damp ground, shoulders back, shifting in her skirt, her trim buttocks switching as she walked.

I called her name and Linda swung around.

"Hello, darling." She met my eyes with a cool gaze. From her hat a thatch of red curls had crept out. "I heard you were looking for me."

"I had to find you."

The pony shied but she held the halter. "Did you?"

"I have to talk with you."

"I work until two."

"I'll wait."

"I brought Shady for Dorothy." Linda brushed the pony's mane. "Same one she was on last week. She's quite gentle."

"You knew we were coming," I said.

"I saw you cross the road."

"I left my car outside the park."

"You thought if I saw it I might run off."

"Yes," I said.

"Well, I haven't run," she said. "I haven't been hiding from you." Her small chin tightened. "Edna and Noah saw me last week. I was sure they'd tell you I was here. I wanted them to. If you were interested."

Dorothy, squinting, stood at the edge of the clearing in a splash of sunlight. "Dorothy knew you were here?"

Linda nodded gravely. "Until I talked with her parents I wasn't aware you were looking for me. I hoped you were. But I didn't want anyone else to see me. I was so ashamed."

"Of your father."

"Now I'm just sorry for him." Her blue eyes welled up; she'd begun to cry quietly. I took her hand. "Dick, do you see? Whatever I do he's with me every day. He's with me even now." She stopped abruptly. Her face was wet with tears. She took off her hat, removed the bandanna, wiped her face with it. "Both of them," she said. "They'll always be with us."

LeFevre forever lying on the lawn with that wild-eyed look as she brought her father's blanket to cover the bloodied body. Her father on the boathouse floor with his skull shattered by a blast from his shotgun.

I put my arm around Linda and she buried her face in my chest. I felt her hand on the back of my neck and when she looked up I kissed her. "What do you want?"

"This," she said. "This is what I need."

"It's all we have."

"It's enough," she said. "For now."

The pony, Shady, waited with her head bowed. Linda gave the halter a tug and we walked on. "I phoned Teresa about your father's funeral," I said. "I was a day late."

"I hoped I wouldn't see you there." Linda laid her hand on my arm. "It was too hard for me. I let Teresa help me more than I should. She took care of Mother most of the day. I had no right to do that."

Dorothy stepped further into the sunlight; pallor more noticeable, her cheeks cups of shadow. As she reached to stroke the bridge of Shady's nose I saw her needle wounds from feedings and transfusions, dark blotches on her hand and arm. Linda took sugar cubes from her pocket, the pony bowed to nuzzle them from her hand; with a swing of her legs Dorothy landed astride Shady's back. She rested her cheek in the grey mane. Linda placed her hat on Dorothy's head. She sat up, feeling the hat with both hands, and beaming. "I'll be the Rodeo Queen."

"You're the best one I've seen," said Linda.

For a while Dorothy was content to pat Shady's flank and stroke her mane. Then Linda led the pony in a walk to the corral and back. Dorothy slid into my arms and I set her down. Linda led Shady back to the stable, went to wash up, and shortly after two o'clock she met us by the park road.

"I brought sandwiches," I said.

"I'd like to sit by the water."

We crossed the road to the little lake. Ducks wandered into the grass and Dorothy ran over to watch them. We set the picnic basket on the bench beside the water. "I was worried about you," I said. "I found that bundle you left us."

"Mother told me at the funeral." Linda raked her hand through her hair. "I suppose I was out of my mind. I felt I was saying goodbye to both of them. But I couldn't speak. I took those things I loved and left them there."

An ocean wind arrived and with it the first streamers of fog seeped through the trees.

"Where will your mother go? She doesn't want to live at the lake any longer."

"She's put the house up for sale. She moved into the Riverside last month."

"Will you keep this job?" I asked. "I saw Kurowski."

"I'll call him one day, I'm sure. But I like this well enough for now." Linda glanced back at the stables. The wind pushed the fog through the trees. Her hair lifted along her neck, her shirt tugged at her breasts. A couple with a small boy and girl crossed behind us, ducks darting past. "The parents are nice, most of them. The kids are a joy! Some have never seen an animal they could touch except a cat or dog. The delight this gives them! I love to see that. To be a part of it."

Dorothy returned and we spread the blanket on the grass. "Hungry?" Linda asked. "I'll bet you are."

"Mm," said Dorothy. "I am."

I brought the basket and Dorothy's jacket. As fog flowed through the park the air dimmed and cooled. We drank coffee and Dorothy sipped hot chocolate. She pulled her jacket on and we huddled over our sandwiches. Dorothy finished half of hers. After we'd eaten she walked beside the water, ducks trailing behind her. When she turned they stopped, as if she were leading them in a drill and they awaited her next command. When they saw she had nothing to feed them they waddled into the water.

"Does she know her condition? How acute it is?"

"She's been told."

"But she's so brave," Linda said.

We watched the ducks struggle upwind on the lake. The wind raked the surface of the water; it glinted like shattered glass. Linda began to cry quietly. Sucking in her breath, she dried her face with the bandanna. "I don't always cry like this."

"It's all right, dear."

"I'm happy you're here."

"Yes," I said.

Wearing Linda's hat pushed down over her hair, Dorothy watched with a solemn expression as the ducks maneuvered on the water and the fog approached. I walked over; her arms hung limp. "The queen wants a carry," she said.

I stooped and she climbed up. Her legs rested lightly on my arm and her head on my shoulder. I brought her to Linda waiting on the blanket. Fog wallowed in the flowerbeds; tumbled over the grass. I set Dorothy down. "I don't want to leave," I said. "But it's time I took her home."

"Dorothy," Linda said. "Give my love to your father and mother."

"Come *with* us." With one hand Dorothy held onto her hat; with the other she gathered wrappings into our basket: "Please."

"I'd love to." Linda sat back on her heels, smiling. "If your friend doesn't mind the company of another young lady."

Puzzlement dimmed Dorothy's eyes but a moment later the veil lifted. "Am I a lady too?"

"The queen is always a lady," Linda told her

Dorothy scrambled up from the blanket. "I can walk to the car."

Fog surged through the trees. It whirled over the grass and glooming water, pitching the late afternoon into dusk. We hurried down to the street and stopped at the traffic light. Cars rolled by, families heading home for supper. I reached for Linda's hand. Then in the chill my arm went around her. Tired, Dorothy turned from the traffic and flung herself into us. With that fierce fatigue of children she clung to both of us. Linda stroked the girl's back, soothing her, shielding her from the cold. The darkness increased, and with it the chill in the air, as we pressed together keeping warm. We made a close circle, the three of us, while we waited for the light.

About the Author

George Keithley has published fiction in TriQuarterly, Sewanee Review, North American Review, Colorado Review, Brilliant Corners, and other publications, earning a Raymond Carver Short Story Award and Pushcart Prize nominations. His award-winning epic The Donner Party, a Book-of the-Month Club selection, has been adapted as a stage play and an opera. Poetry and essays, appearing in the New York Times, Harper's, Agni, and American Poetry Review, have earned the di Castagnola Award and the Pushcart Prize.

He's been a visiting writer in Russia and traced the Emigrant Trail from Illinois to California. He lives in Chico, California with his wife Carol.

CPSIA information can be obtained
at www.ICGtesting.com
Printed in the USA
FSOW02n0834101214
3810FS